When All is Said

Anne Griffin is the winner of the John McGahern Award for Literature. Shortlisted for the Hennessy New Irish Writing Award and *The Sunday Business Post* Short Story Competition, Anne's work has been featured in, amongst others, *The Irish Times* and *The Stinging Fly*. She's worked in Waterstones branches in both Dublin and London, and for various charities.

Born in Dublin, Anne now lives in Mullingar, Ireland, with her husband and son. *When All is Said* is her debut novel.

Anne Griffin

When All is Said

SCEPTRE

First published in Great Britain in 2019 by Sceptre
An Imprint of Hodder & Stoughton
An Hachette UK company

4

A CIP catalogue record for this title is available from the British Library

Hardback ISBN 978 1 473 68299 3
Trade Paperback ISBN 978 1 473 68300 6
eBook ISBN 978 1 473 68301 3

Typeset in Sabon MT 13/16.5 pt by Palimpsest Book Production Limited,
Falkirk, Stirlingshire

Printed and bound in Great Britain by Clays Ltd, Elcograf S.p.A.

Hodder & Stoughton policy is to use papers that are natural,
renewable and recyclable products and made from wood grown in sustainable
forests. The logging and manufacturing processes are expected to conform
to the environmental regulations of the country of origin.

Hodder & Stoughton Ltd
Carmelite House
50 Victoria Embankment
London EC4Y 0DZ

www.sceptrebooks.co.uk

For James and Adam

WANTED:

Edward VIII Gold Sovereign Coin, 1936.
Willing to pay top price. Any condition considered.
Write giving amount desired to Thomas Dollard,
3 Fennel Way, London.

*From the Classified Advertisements section of
the International Coin Enthusiast Magazine,
May–June, 1977, issue 51.*

Chapter One

6.25 p.m.
Saturday, 7th of June 2014
The bar of the Rainsford House Hotel
Rainsford, Co. Meath, Ireland

Is it me or are the barstools in this place getting lower? Perhaps it's the shrinking. Eighty-four years can do that to a man, that and hairy ears.

What time is it over in the States now, son? One, two? I suppose you're stuck to that laptop, tapping away in your air-conditioned office. 'Course, you might be home on the porch, in the recliner with the wonky arm, reading your latest article in that paper you work for, what's it . . . ? Jesus, can't think of it now. But I can see you with those worry lines, concentrating, while Adam and Caitríona run riot trying to get your attention.

It's quiet here. Not a sinner. Just me on my lonesome, talking to myself, drumming the life out of the bar in anticipation of the first sip. If I could get my hands on it, that is. Did I ever tell you, Kevin, that my father was a great finger tapper? Would tap away at the table, my shoulder, anything he could lay his index finger on, to force home his point and get the attention he deserved. My own

3

knobbly one seems less talented. Can get the attention of no one. Not that there's anyone to get the attention of, except your one out at reception. She knows I'm here alright, doing a great job ignoring me. A man could die of thirst round these parts.

They're up to ninety getting ready for the County Sports Awards, of course. It was some coup for the likes of Rainsford wrestling that hoolie out of Duncashel with its two hotels. That was Emily, the manager, or owner, I should say, a woman well capable of sweet-talking anyone into the delights of this place. Not that I've experienced much of those myself over the years.

But here I sit nonetheless. I have my reasons, son, I have my reasons.

You should get a load of the enormous mirror in front of me. Massive yoke. Runs the length of the bar, up above the row of spirits. Not sure if it's from the original house. Ten men, it must've taken to get that up. Shows off the couches and chairs behind me all eager for the bottoms that are at this minute squeezing into their fancy outfits. And there's me now in the corner, like the feckin' eejit who wouldn't get his head out of shot. And what a head it is. It's not often I look in the mirror these days. When your mother was alive I suppose I made a bit of an effort but sure what difference does it make now? I find it hard to look at myself. Can't bear to see it – that edge, you know the one I mean – haven't you been on the receiving end of it enough over the years.

Still. Clean white shirt, crisp collar, navy tie, not a gravy stain in sight. Jumper, the green one your mother bought me the Christmas before she died, suit and my shoes polished to a shine. Do people polish their shoes any more or is it just me who practises the art? Sadie'd be proud alright. A well-turned-out specimen of a man. Eighty-four and I can still boast a head of hair and a chin of stubble. Rough it feels, though – rough. I don't know why I bother shaving every morning when by lunchtime it's like a wire brush.

I know I wasn't what you might call good-looking in my day, but anything I had going for me seems to have long since scarpered. My skin looks like it's in some kind of race southward. But do you know what? I've still got the voice.

'Maurice,' your grandmother used to say, 'you could melt icebergs with that voice of yours.'

To this day it's like a cello – deep and smooth. Makes people pay attention. One holler to herself pretending to be busy out there at reception and she'd be in filling my glass quick smart. But I'd better not cause any more trouble than I need to. There's a job to do later and a long night ahead.

There's that smell again. I wish you were here, to get it: Mr Sheen. Remember that? Every Saturday, our whole house smelt of it. Your mother's day for the dusting. The sickliness of it used to hit my nose as soon as I came through the back door. I'd be sneezing from here to kingdom come for the rest of the night. Fridays now, Fridays were floor-polishing days. The waft of wax, homemade chips and smoked cod, warming my heart and making me smile. Industry and sustenance – a winning combination. You don't hear of people polishing floors much any more either. What's that all about, I wonder.

At last, a body appears from the door behind the bar to put me out of my thirst-ridden misery.

'There you are, now,' I say to Emily, a picture of beauty and efficiency. 'Here to save me the embarrassment of getting the drink myself? I was even contemplating going to ask Miss Helpful out there.'

'I got here just in time, so, Mr Hannigan,' she says, with a hint of a smile, laying down a pile of papers on the counter, checking her phone perched on top, 'we don't want you upsetting the staff with that charm of yours.' Her head lifts to look at me and her eyes sparkle for a second before settling on her screen again.

'That's just lovely. A man comes in for a quiet drink and this is what he gets.'

'Svetlana will be in now. We were just having a quick meeting about tonight.'

'Well, aren't you very Michael O'Leary.'

'I see you're in fine spirits,' she says, coming to stand in front of me, giving me her full attention now. 'I didn't know you were coming in. To what do we owe the pleasure?'

'I don't always ring ahead.'

'No, but it might be a good idea. I could put the staff on red alert.'

There it is – that smile, curling up, as delicious as a big dollop of cream on a slice of warm apple tart. And those eyes, twinkling with the curiosity.

'A Bushmills?' she asks, reaching for a tumbler.

'Make it a bottle of stout, to start me off. Not from the fridge mind.'

'To start you off?'

I ignore the worry that's crept into her voice.

'Would you join me for one later?' I ask, instead.

She stops and gives me a good long stare.

6

'Is everything alright?'

'A drink, Emily, that's all.'

'You do know I've landed the County Awards?' she says, hand on hip, 'not to mention a mysterious VIP who's decided to book in. Everything has to be perfect. I've worked too hard for this to—'

'Emily, Emily. There'll be no surprises tonight. I'd just like to sit and have a drink with you. No confessions this time, I promise.'

I slide a hand across the counter, my offering of re-assurance. Can't blame the distrust, given the history. I watch it steal away her smile. I've never fully explained all that business with the Dollards to you and your mother, have I? I suppose in part that's what tonight is all about.

'I doubt there'll be a lull,' she says, standing in front of me now, still giving me the suspicious eye, 'I'll try to get back up to you, though.'

She bends slightly and takes a bottle of the good stuff with her expert hand from the fully stocked shelf below – one can't but admire the neat order of the bottles, their harped labels all turned proudly outwards. Emily's handi-work. She runs a well-ordered show.

A slip of a young thing arrives through the door to join her.

'Great,' Emily says to her. 'The place is all yours. Here, give this to Mr Hannigan there before he passes out. And you,' she continues, pointing one of her lovely long nails at me, 'be nice. Svetlana's new.' With that warning she picks up her load and disappears.

Svetlana takes the bottle, locates the opener under the bar with a little assistance from my pointing finger, lays the drink and a glass before me then scurries to the far corner. I pour a bit until the creamy head hits the top of the tilted edge and then I let it settle. I look around and consider this day of mine, this year, these two years in fact, without your mother and I feel tired and, if I'm honest, afraid. My hand passes over the stubble on my chin again as I watch the cream float up. Then I cough and grunt my worries out of me, there's no going back now, son. No going back.

To my left, through the long windows that reach the floor, I watch the cars go by. I recognise one or two: Audi A8, that would be Brennan from Duncashel, owns the cement factory; Skoda Octavia with the missing left hub will be Mick Moran. There's Lavin's jalopy parked right outside his newsagents. An ancient red Ford Fiesta. Gives me the greatest pleasure to park in that spot whenever I find it vacant.

'You can't be parking there, Hannigan,' he'd shout, hanging out his driver's window once he'd arrived back from wherever he'd been. 'I can't be expected to be lugging the deliveries up and down the town now, can I?' His head'd be bobbing madly with that mop of wild hair, his car double parked, holding up the town. 'Do you not see the sign? No parking, day or night.'

'Course, I'd be leaning against his wall, reading the paper.

'Hold on to your tights there, Lavin,' I'd say, giving the paper a good rustling, 'it was an emergency.'

'Is getting the morning paper considered an emergency now?'

'I can always bring my business elsewhere.'

'Oh, that you would, Hannigan. Oh, that you would.'

'The newsagents in Duncashel has a coffee machine now, I hear.'

'You can move your feckin' Jeep on your way over so.'

'Not one for the coffee me,' I say, clicking open my door before getting in and sticking her into reverse.

It's the simple things, son, the simple things.

It's the end of the shopper's shift it seems. Hands wave, horns beep. Driver windows are down with elbows sticking out, having the final chat before heading home with full boots to a night in front of the telly. Some of them might be back out later, of course, transformed into shiny things. Eager to show off the new outfits and hairdos.

I raise the glass and pour again until it's full, ready for its final rest. My fingers, with their dark, crust-filled crevices, tap the side, to encourage it on. I take one last look in the mirror, raise my drink to himself there and swallow down the blessed first sip.

You can't beat the creamy depth of a glass of stout. Giving sustenance to the body and massaging the vocal cords on its way down. That's another thing about my voice, it makes me come across as younger. Oh, yes, if I'm on the blower it doesn't let on that I host a hundred haggard wrinkles, or dentures that have a mind of their own. It pretends I'm a fine thing, distinguished and handsome. A man to be reckoned with. On that, it's not wrong. Don't know where I got it from – the only one in the family blessed with the gift. It was how I drew them in, those out-of-town estate agents; not that they needed much convincing, what with our farm being on the royal side of the Meath–Dublin border, the envy of all around.

But those boys with their swanky ties and shiny shoes couldn't get enough of the place when I told them how far and wide she ran; nodding their heads, like those dogs in the back of people's cars. Rest assured, I put them through their paces. Let no man try to take my money without earning every brass farthing. Walked the length and breadth of my land until they couldn't see the colour of their shoes. All of them as eager as the next to get the business. No flies on them cowsheds, as my father would have said. I chose one in the end to sell my little empire to the highest bidder, Anthony Farrell. Had to be him – not because he impressed me with his patter, one was no different from the other in that respect. Nor was it the canny curve of his lip; it was simply that he shared your Uncle Tony's name. Seventy years dead and I still idolise the man. Young Anthony proved me right in my choice, not stopping 'til he'd the house and business sold for a hefty sum. I closed her up last night, the house.

I've been packing up each room over the last year. A bit every day. I named each box so you'll know what's what: Maurice, Sadie, Kevin, Noreen, Molly – hers was the smallest. All that loading and lugging nearly killed me, though. Only for the young lads Anthony sent over, I'd never have managed. Their names won't come to me now, Derek or Des, or . . . sure what does it matter? Mostly, I pretended to help; more the director of operations. They were well capable; you don't expect that of youngsters too often these days.

I kept the essentials out 'til this morning when Anthony took the last box in his car. It felt strange, Kevin, letting it all go. The smallness of that final box sitting in his passenger seat caught me. Not that there was anything precious in it, just the kettle, the radio, my few bits of clothes, shaving gear, you get the picture. I threw out what was left in the skip I hired. The *Meath Chronicles* were the last to get chucked. Never without the *Meath Chronicle* for the local mart news and the GAA results, even though I'd have watched the games on the Sunday. It was the local and county matches that interested me most. I must've had six months' worth of the thing piled up beside me on the sofa, in one big cascading mess by the end. Of course, when Sadie was around I'd have never gotten away with that. But, if I positioned them right, you see, they kept my tea at the perfect height. No sudden movements mind, not that there was any fear of that, I'm not as nimble getting off the couch these days.

Anthony is to store the boxes some place off near his office. Our lives in Dublin now – hard to believe. The important leftovers I have with me. In my inner breast pocket there's my wallet, a pen and some paper for the few notes, given my increasing forgetfulness. In the outer ones I have the hotel room key, weighty and solid; my father's brown and black pipe, never smoked by me but worn shiny and smooth from my thumb's persistent rubbing; a couple of pictures; a handful of receipts; my glasses; your mother's purse for her hairpins; my phone; and a couple of rubber bands, paper clips and safety pins – well, you never know when you might need them. And of course there's your whiskey, out of sight, wrapped up in the Dunnes Stores bag at my feet.

You'll be wondering about Gearstick, the dog. Bess, the cleaner, took him. Adam and Caitríona might be a bit upset by that. I know they loved playing with him on the trips home. Them with their leashes and him never been near one before in his life. Still he took it gracefully and walked under their guidance for the week or so you'd be around. A gentler soul, you wouldn't find anywhere.

Do you remember your mother when I got him first? But sure you were long gone by then. She was all: 'You can't be calling the poor wee thing Gearstick,' and him after chewing the gearstick in the car all the way home.

And I said:

'Sure what does he care?'

That was the first and only time he was ever in the house. Of recent months I've left the back door open, trying to coax him in. He'd reluctantly step over the threshold into the back hall, poking his head around the kitchen door but only to let me know he was there. Panting, he'd wait in expectation of some outing or other. No amount of cajoling with a bit of Carroll's sliced ham or even the fat of a rasher could bring him any further. I'd have been happy for him to sit with me as I watched the telly or even to just lie under the table when I was having dinner. But there was no budging him. I suppose I've not been afraid to raise a stick to him over the years so he wasn't going to risk it. In the end, he just lay down and slept on the muddied mat, drifting off listening to the muffled sounds of my life.

The day Bess came for him, she brought the whole family, husband and three children. All stood around smiling at each other, me doing my best impression of one, nodding and pretending we knew what the other was saying. They're from the Philippines; at least I think so, somewhere out foreign anyhow. The children bounded up and down the yard with Gearstick for a bit. He obliged, jumping and skitting alongside.

'What he eat?' Bess asked.

'Anything you have leftover.'

'Leftover?'

'The dinner.'

'You feed him dinner?'

'What's left, you know. A bit of bread soaked in milk, even.'

She looked at me, her brow contorting like I'd just farted. I could feel the will seep out of me.

'Anything, sure. Feed him anything.' I'd had enough. I stroked Gearstick's ear and watched his head tilt and his eyes close one last time.

'Good man. Go on now,' I said, pushing him towards her but he wouldn't budge. I patted his silky head then held my hand under his chin as he looked up, panting and eager, his tongue hanging out the side of his mouth. Everyone flashed before me in that moment: you, Adam, Caitríona, Sadie. Tiny snippets of the memories you'd spent with him. And I saw me too – him at my heel as we walked my fields over these past years. And I nearly said no. Nearly told Bess to turn her car around and leave us be. My eyes pleaded with Gearstick not to make this any harder but every time I inched away, he followed. What did I expect of that loyal soul, that he would just abandon me, like I was doing to him? My treason was a lump caught in my throat, refusing to be swallowed or grunted away. In the end, I could do nothing more than walk into the house and close the door. I leaned with my back against it, knowing that Gearstick was on the other side, looking up, watching and waiting for the handle to turn. I made myself move on through to the kitchen, refusing the temptation to look out the window as I heard the commotion of them trying to get him into their hatchback. Instead I kept on moving, mumbling away, trying to block out the weight of another ending, another loss in this worn-out life of mine.

I never asked where they live. Up in the city is all I know. In a walled back garden possibly, or worse, an apartment. I'm not sure Bess knows quite what she's letting herself in for with a working dog like that. It was her or the pound; maybe that would've been kinder. I know I could've given him to any of the boys around here. They'd have been glad of a dog as good as him, but then they'd have known, wouldn't they, that something was up. When Bess eventually drove away, I sat in the sitting room and closed my eyes, listening to the engine recede into the distance, imagining Gearstick's confusion. I ran a hand over my face, my mouth opening wide, warning away the burn in my eyes.

'Course, this is the first you're hearing of it all – the sale of the house, the land, the lot. I just, well . . . I just couldn't run the risk of you stopping me. I couldn't let that happen, son.

Svetlana's inspecting the bar. Looking at the bottles one by one, checking the fridges, her finger touching labels as her hand passes over each brand. Her head nods and her lips read silently, memorising. Every now and again her eyes land on mine as she looks out at the room. She gives me a tight-lipped smile and I raise my glass a notch in her direction. Out she goes from behind the bar with a cloth to each table and dusts it down again. Can she not smell the Mr Sheen? Through the mirror I can see her hands make circular movements shining the already shined. She moves stools centimetres one way then back again. A real worker-bee, this one.

After Anthony left this morning I headed for Robert Timoney's office. I've always said he's a solicitor a man can trust. Not one for sitting at the bar spreading rumours. Every inch his father. Robert Senior knew a man's business was no one's but his own. Not that I've let him in on everything. Anthony sorted a solicitor in Dublin so I wouldn't have to use Robert this time, didn't want him getting suspicious over the house sale and lifting the phone to you. Up to now, all I've asked him to do is to sort the hotel room.

'Is he around?' I asked his receptionist when I arrived into his offices earlier. She's a Heaney. You know her; you used to pal with the brother, Donal.

'He shouldn't be too long. You can take a seat there.'

I looked at the row of four black-cushioned seats, sitting right in the window, overlooking main street.

'And have the world know my business? I'll be in his office.' I was already mounting the stairs.

'That's a private area, Mr Hannigan!' she said, following me, her step echoing mine. Narrow stairs, no room for overtaking, I kept a steady, calm pace.

'It's locked,' she added, at the top, all smug like.

'No bother.' My hand reached up over the door frame, finding the key and showing her. 'All sorted,' I said. Her indignant face disappeared from view as I shut the door and gave her my biggest smile.

'That's breaking and entering, you know. I'm calling the guards,' she shouted through the door.

'Super,' I replied, from Robert's chair, 'I've a bit of business with Higgins, we can kill two birds with one stone.'

When she added nothing further, I tilted my head back

and fell into a welcome doze as I listened to her thudding down the stairs.

'Glad to see you're making yourself at home, Maurice,' Robert said, coming through the door not five minutes later, smirking, reaching for my hand. ''Course it'll take me all day to pacify Linda.'

I'm sure, young Linda's at home right now telling the same story to her father over the dinner. Him loving the roasting she'll be giving me.

'Robert, good to see you.'

I rose and began to round the table to the not so comfy chair.

'No, sit, sit,' he replied, taking the cheaper model. 'True to your word, what? Not a day late. I've the key, here.'

He laid his briefcase down on the table, opened it and handed over a good old-fashioned weighty key that I put in my pocket.

'Do they know it's me that wants the room?'

'A VIP, I said – "he'll take nothing less than the honeymoon suite",' he laughed. 'Emily tried everything to get it out of me.'

'Good, that's good. Listen, Robert,' I said, a little more hesitantly than is my usual style, 'I, eh, I'm moving into a nursing home over Kilboy way. I've sold the place and the farm to cover the costs. Kevin's helped me. Found a buyer over in the States.'

You'll forgive me, son, for including you in my deception.

'What?' he asked, his voice hitting a pitch that I'm sure only dogs could hear. 'And when did all this happen?'

'Kevin talked to me about it when he was over last. I thought nothing of it, thought he might forget the whole thing, if I'm being honest, but then out of the blue, about six months ago he calls me saying he's found a buyer. Some Yank who wants a taste of home. And here I am now, the bank account bulging and my bags packed. I'm surprised he's not called you. He said he would; mind you, he's been up to his eyes with the newspaper, something to do with Obamacare. He will though.'

'Well, now,' Robert answered, looking at me a little put out that we never used him. 'None of my business, I suppose, once all's legal and above board and no one's going to scam you.'

'No. It's all signed, sealed and delivered.'

'I'd never have taken you for a nursing home man, Maurice,' he said, not letting me off the hook that quickly.

'I'm not. Just couldn't take Kevin's nagging any more. An easy life, that's all I want now. It's hard enough with Sadie gone.' Tug at the heartstrings, son, works every time.

'Of course, of course. It can't be easy, Maurice. How long is she eh . . . gone, now?'

'Two years to the day.'

'Is that right?' he said, looking genuinely concerned. 'It doesn't seem that long.'

'It feels like a lifetime to me.'

His eyes moved away from mine as he started up his laptop.

''Course, I'm all for nursing homes,' he said. 'Book me in, I told Yvonne. Frankly, I can't wait to be pampered.'

A man can say that at forty years of age, having the comfort of a wife and two kids at home.

'So the honeymoon suite is your final farewell to Rainsford. Is that what the hotel and the room is all about?'

'You could say that,' I replied, taking a good look at the hotel, sitting across the road in all its sunbathed glory.

You know, I first came to work here in 1940 before there was any talk of it being a hotel. It was still the Dollard family home then. It was odd looking, they say, for what was a Big House in the country. The front door opening right on to the main street of the village, like you might see in a square in Dublin. The original owners must have liked the idea of having a village there to serve them, literally, right on their doorstep. No big gate, no long driveway – that was all to the back. Rows of trees, like stage curtains, ran out to the sides of the front of the house, marking the border of their land that stretched long and wide far out to the rear. Most of those trees are gone now, and the main street has extended to run round the hotel on the right, with a row of shops on the left. Any of the land not bought by the council for the town's expansion is still there, but it's not theirs any more, as we well know.

I was just a boy of ten, when I started to work as a farm labourer on the estate. Our land, my father's land, I should say, what little of it there was then, backed on to theirs. My time under their employment wasn't the happiest. So bad, that six years later when I left, I vowed never to darken their door again and wouldn't have, had you and Rosaleen not been set on having your wedding here. Never understood your obsession, or Sadie's for that matter. She was worse, going on and on about how magnificent it was and how luxurious the rooms were. Had me driven demented, with her gushing over the honeymoon suite. I thought the woman was going to have an attack of some description the day of the wedding fair. Of course, it could all have been an act, compensation for my lack of enthusiasm. I'm not one for pretending.

'The original owner's master bedroom, Amelia and Hugh Dollard, before the conversion,' the function manager said, beaming away like this was somehow astounding.

That's when I left you to it, heading straight for the bar. Sat at this exact spot and downed a whiskey, a toast to its demise. Don't know who served me back then, not this young one, that's for sure – in she wobbles now with a pile of glasses, God knows where she'll put them, they're stacked high already under the counters. I was never so engrossed in a drink in all my life that day. My head thought my neck was broken as I refused to look up, to acknowledge the place, or any of them for that matter, should they have been about. There were photos on every wall, in the corridors and rooms, taunting this hulk of a man with their history.

When you all eventually joined me, I bought the round, or should I say rounds, and listened to you rave about the chandelier in the banquet room and the view from the honey-moon suite.

'You mean the view of *my* land?' I said.

By then I pretty much owned every field surrounding the hotel.

'And isn't that why this place is just perfect? Looking out over the splendour of our farm. Your gorgeous rolling green hills, Maurice,' Sadie said, placing a hand on mine. I'd swear she was a bit tipsy.

The review went on for what felt like hours. And all the time, I swirled my drink and tried to drown you out. Rosaleen's family arrived then and off you all went on the tour again. That was enough for me. I left. Drunk as a fool, I drove home to sit in the dark.

To my utter surprise, though, I enjoyed your wedding, when it finally arrived. I suppose it was seeing you so happy, and Sadie too. I felt proud watching you take to the floor with Rosaleen for the first dance. And when we all joined you, me with Rosaleen's mother and Sadie with the father, I caught your mother's smile and laugh as she floated past. Later in the night, she even convinced me to have another look at that honeymoon suite.

'Isn't it just magnificent, Maurice? What I wouldn't have given for this when we were married. Couldn't you just see us now, Lord and Lady Muck?'

I danced her around the bedroom, nearly crashing into the dressing table, falling on to the bed. The drink had gotten the better of us. But my kiss was one of honest sobriety. Full of the love she had unleashed in me and gone on unleashing for all our years together. Not that we were the perfect couple. But we were good, you know. Solid and steady. At least that's how it felt for me. I never asked her, mind.

'I'll book us in. Someday, I promise, we'll have the honeymoon suite just for us,' I said, lying on the bed, looking at her. I fully believed my words. I wonder did she? And here I am now, two years too fecking late.

She died in her sleep. She always said that when it was her turn to go, she'd like it to be that way. Just like her sister before her, there had been no sign of any illness, no complaint. She'd pecked me on the cheek the previous night, before turning over with her halo of curlers tied up in my old handkerchief. The woman had dead straight hair that she wound to within an inch of its life every night. All that bother, I used to think, as I watched her from the bed and her at the dressing table – what was so wrong with those silky lengths that I only ever glimpsed for a second? But, do you know something? I'd give my last breath right now to see her at that mirror one more time. I'd watch each twist and turn of her hand with complete admiration, appreciating every stroke.

That morning, I was in the kitchen with the radio on and my shaving already done before I realised I hadn't heard the shuffle of her slippers or her usual humming. By the time I'd put the kettle on and still hadn't seen her, I knew something was up. And so I let the newsreader's voice trail after me as I made my way back down the corridor. Mick Wallace and his tax evasion. The image of that man's white, wispy hair and pink shirt froze in my brain when I stood at our door and realised she was still in the bed where I'd left her.

Mick fucking Wallace.

I touched her face and felt the coldness of her passing. My knees buckled instantly. Collapsed at the edge of our bed, I looked at her face only inches away. Contented, it was. Not a care. Still a red glow to her cheeks, or am I imagining that? My fingertips felt the softness of the lines around her eyes, then found her hand under the blankets. I held it between my own, trying to warm it. Holding it to my cheek, rubbing it. It's not that I thought I could bring her back to life or anything, it's just . . . I don't know, it's just what I did. I didn't want her to be cold, I suppose. She hated being cold. It's one of the only things I remember about her passing and the funeral – that quiet time with me and her alone, no one else. Don't ask me what happened after, who came or who said what, it's all a blur. I just sat in my chair in the sitting room, still holding her hand in my mind – my Sadie.

I phoned you, of course. At least that's what you told me when I admitted months after I couldn't remember. I should've been alright for you when you and Rosaleen and the children arrived to say your goodbyes. I remember seeing your arms rise to hug me as I stood at the front door and them falling back by your side when you saw my face. You offered me your hand, instead. You clasped mine tightly, and my eyes concentrated on the two of them locked together until you let go. You touched my shoulder then, as you moved past into the hall. I can feel it there still, the only signifier that you were more than just another acquaintance who'd come to pay his respects. The shame of it. I wish now I'd wrapped my arms around you and cried on your shoulder and given you the chance to do the same. But no, I didn't have the room for your grief as well as my own, it seemed.

What's more, I shouldn't have let you go home to New Jersey fretting about me. But I couldn't rise to it, could barely rise at all for that matter. If I managed to get out of the bed, it was just to make it to my chair in the front room. There I sat with Sadie, walking through our lives together, until a cup of tea appeared in front of me, wrenching me back to my unwanted widowerhood. And I know you wouldn't have returned to the States so soon after only for Robert convincing you that he'd look in on me and ring at the first sign of any problem.

You all came home again the following Christmas. We

were to go to your in-laws, Rosaleen's family, for the dinner. Good people, not that I made much of an effort with them over the years. I refused to go at the last minute.

'Too much to keep an eye on,' I said.

I knew they were only the half hour out the road but I couldn't leave Sadie, not the first Christmas, it didn't feel right. So you sent Rosaleen and the children on and stayed behind with me. Can't even remember what we ate. Soup from the press, maybe. They came back a couple of hours later with two black plastic bags full of the kids' presents and two tin-foil-covered plates of Christmas dinner.

Did I even manage to buy the children presents that year? That had always been your mother's department.

That was the start of it, the first of the talk about the home. Well, when I say that, I mean the first time it was ever discussed in my presence. I'm sure it had been the topic of many a conversation before it reached my ears. Sure I knew it would come. What poor widow or widower living alone out there hasn't dreaded its arrival?

'Would you feck off,' I told you out straight. 'Wouldn't I look the right eejit sitting in playing Telly Bingo with a load of old women in cardigans rather than out tending the cattle?'

In fairness, you laughed. That big, confident laugh – perhaps there's something of my vocal genius in you after all.

'Alright, Dad,' you said, laying a hand on my knee, 'we just thought you'd be safer there.'

'Safer? What do you mean *safer*?'

'Well, you just hear stories nowadays about people, you know, coming on to your property and—'

'Sure isn't that what this beauty's for?' I said, laying a hand on my faithful Winchester.

You looked bewildered. But I wasn't giving up my life until I was good and ready.

As hard as it might be to hear, in a way I'm glad you live as far away as you do. I couldn't stand the constant reminder that I must be a worry. I'd say your biggest fear is that I'd end up shooting some poor unsuspecting fool of a hill walker who might stumble on to the land.

Perhaps it's a small consolation but I hope when you're home you see that at least I'm clean. I manage perfectly on that score. I don't smell, not like some I could mention. Old age is no excuse for stinking to high heaven. Sparkling, that's what I am, having a good wash every morning with the face cloth and, of course, there's the bath once a week. I had one of those rail things put in about five years ago and now I can lower myself in and out as easy as lifting that first pint. I'm not one for showers, could never take to them. Whenever I look at one I feel cold, that's why I refused to have one installed despite your mother's protests.

My greatest discovery of late has to be the launderette over in Duncashel that collects my offerings and drops them back three days later. Not like the local one, you wouldn't find her doing anything as helpful as that. Every week *Pristine Pete's* gets my business, sending me back my shirts, crisper and cleaner than Sadie could ever have managed, however blasphemous that might sound.

And what's more there's Bess, cleaning the house. Twice a week, never fail. Polishing and scrubbing it back to perfection. I think your mother would've liked her.

'I'll take your best cleaner with no English,' I told the

agency in Dublin, 'I don't want anyone local. I want someone discreet who's not a gossip. I'll pay extra for her petrol if needs be.'

She cooks too. Leaves me a couple of stews for the week. Mind you, they taste nothing like Sadie's; in fact, I couldn't tell you what they are. It took me a while to get used to them. Garlic, lots of that, apparently. But I surprised myself when I started to look forward to them, especially the chicken one. All that time with Bess, keeping me going, Robert was killed telling me I could've gotten the Health Board to foot the bill for a cleaner and gotten Meals on Wheels into the bargain.

'Are you mad?' I said, 'I've never had a handout in my life and I'm certainly not starting now.'

Svetlana has sauntered over. Finished with her inspections and cleaning and glass stacking. She's been pacing the bar for the last few minutes, waiting for the hordes to arrive.

'You here for dinner later, yes?'

I like that name of hers. Svetlana. It's straight up, sharp yet still has a bit of beauty about it. I wonder how I look to her? Nuts, no doubt. Sitting here, lost in my thoughts, the odd mumble escaping every now and again. She leans forward on the counter, eager for something to happen, even a lame conversation with the auld lad at the bar will do, it seems.

'I'm not,' I say, and it's there I'd normally leave it. But tonight is no ordinary night. 'Is tonight your first night here?' I ask.

'Second. I work last night.'

I nod, swirl the last drop at the bottom of my glass, before downing it. Ready now to begin the first of five toasts: five toasts, five people, five memories. I push my empty bottle back across the bar to her. And as her hand takes it and turns away, happy to have something to do, I say under my breath.

'I'm here to remember – all that I have been and all that I will never be again.'

Chapter Two

7.05 p.m.
First Toast: to Tony
Bottle of stout

There's stirrings out in the foyer. Looks like the boys in all their finery are beginning to trickle in. I'll not have this place to myself for much longer.

'Another stout, there,' I say to Svetlana who looks like she's having an attack of first-night nerves. 'Keep that seat for me there. Don't be letting those lads take it. The best seat in the house.'

It's time for the little boy's room. One of the perks of being eighty-four, your legs get regular exercise from all the toilet trips.

'By the neck, yes?' she asks, as I'm heading off.

'Listen to you and the lingo,' I call back to her, not letting on my concern that I've left my trip a little too late, 'by the neck or the arse, I don't care, just make sure it's still in the bottle and from the shelf,' I say speeding up.

'One of these?' she says, halting my escape.

Can she not sense the danger?

'Aye,' I say, starting again.

'Glass?'

Heavens above.

'No, sure stick an auld straw in it and I'll be grand,' I call back to her.

'You joke right?'

I wave a hand as I disappear from view.

There were four children in my family. Four was relatively small, I suppose, for that time in Ireland. There were families of nine or ten or more all round us. We must have seemed odd. Two adults and four youngsters to a two-bedroom cottage. A luxury, almost. Tony was the oldest, then there was May and Jenny and me, the youngest. A year, maybe two, between the lot of us.

You never knew your Uncle Tony. He was long gone by the time you arrived. 'Big Man' – that's what he called me. I know that's what I became, six foot three and built like a house. But back when that nickname stuck, I was far from it. At four, I was the tiniest of things compared to the towering giant of him, or so he seemed to me. I imagine my little steps beside his on the road or round the farm. Always running to catch up, three of my little trots to his one stride. All the time him chatting to me, telling me about the hens we were feeding or the carrots we were planting in Mam's little garden or the ditches we were clearing. The man loved the land as much as my father. And I'd be looking up at him, trying not to trip while taking everything in, trying my best to remember, to show him I could do it too, relishing his praise.

'Now you have it,' he'd say, 'aren't you the great man.'

Despite my best efforts to keep pace, I'd inevitably fall or do myself some kind of injury trying to carry buckets that were far too big for me, just to be like him. He'd come back then and hunker beside me.

'You'll be better before you're twice married,' I imagine him saying, brushing me down, hugging me maybe, lightening my load then and slowing his pace for a while. You'd swear he was decades older than me, the way he used to mind me. But he was only five years my senior.

I'd have worked well into the evening with him, had I been let. But somewhere along the way my mother would come to fetch me.

'I'll be there in a minute,' he'd say to my protests, as she carried me back in. Me with my hands outstretched to him trying not to cry for fear he'd see what a baby I was. And would you look at me now, still at it, battling those tears.

I'd wait by the window in the kitchen for him then. Getting up and down on the bench, despite my mother's scolding, until he and my father finally finished their day.

I remember once when Father Molloy visited the house. Like all adults he was curious about what I wanted to be when I grew up. It seemed an odd type of question to me, I mean, the answer was so bloody obvious:

'Tony,' I said.

I couldn't fathom why he and my parents laughed so much at my reply. I walked out of the kitchen, leaving them there with the hilarity of it all and the good china.

The name 'Big Man' stuck from our school days. Tony had been walking the half-mile to the one-roomed school for a fair few years before I joined him. Rainsford National School – engraved in an arch over the front door – that's what Tony told me it read, as I proudly passed under it on my first day. Tony had me wound up the whole way there with the thoughts of how exciting it would be, what with all the children from around gathered in one place. I don't think I'd slept a wink the night before, either.

'Tony,' I whispered to him beside me in the bed, not wishing to wake Jenny and May, who slept behind the curtain that divided the room, 'does Patrick Stanley go to the school?'

'Of course he does.'

'And Mary and Joe Brady?'

'Sure, what other school would they go to?'

'And Jenny and May?'

'Would you stop your messing and go to sleep or we'll be going nowhere tomorrow,' he said, pucking me with his elbow.

I was up first the next day, asking the same stuff all over again. I walked in Tony's shoes, literally, that day. His hand-me-downs. I've no idea whose shoes he got. I strode through the school door, staring around in awe of the place that would make me as clever as my big brother.

'Well, now, and who do we have here?' a voice boomed as I entered. 'Another Hannigan is it? Get up here and let's have a good look at you.'

Master Duggan hauled me up, on to a desk at the front of the room.

'Would you look at the size of you, a big man, what? I hope we have a desk big enough to fit you and all those brains you're storing in that head of yours.'

I was 'Big Man' from that moment on.

I was beaming, proud of the welcome. I watched Tony laughing, elbowing his mates. I looked at the desks and the blackboard and the few books behind me on the master's table and felt a warmth for the place and the things that were a part of my world now. I was keen to get on with it, to prove the master correct. I shuffled my feet in anticipation and was down soon enough sitting at the very desk on which I'd stood.

Over the next couple of days the master drew all sorts on the board. We chanted our ABC's but I hadn't a clue that what we rhymed had anything to do with what he'd written up there with the white chalk. At first, I didn't mind too much that it felt out of my reach while the others, even Joe Brady who was three months younger than me, seemed to eventually get the hang of it.

The only thing I truly loved and kept me running up that road every morning was the football. At break time the master rolled up his sleeves and bent expectantly between the jumper goalposts. Or when nothing was coming his way, ran between them shouting:

'Would you kick the thing?'

'Mark him, mark him.'

'Pass it, man!'

The girls played with a skipping rope outside the back door, out of the way of the ball. Their laughter and scolding of those who weren't playing properly, reached me as I hurtled around the yard in a muck sweat of pure delight. I hadn't played much football before that. We had the hurls at home, but football was the master's game. I gave it all I had. A good man for a tackle. Thought nothing of diving in. And if Tony had the ball, well, I was stuck to him, all hands and legs, pulling out of whatever bit of him I could get a hold of.

'Stop, would you?' he'd laugh. He was like King Kong swatting away those planes. Put his hand on my forehead, the fecker. Holding me at arm's-length so I couldn't get near him. My arms flailing nevertheless. I fell, a hundred and one times. Blood and bruises. But it was of no consequence, it didn't dampen my enthusiasm.

'Good man, Hannigan. Up you get. That's the spirit,' the master called from the goal.

I couldn't get enough of his encouragement out there on our makeshift pitch. A welcome change from his silence and frustration at my efforts in the classroom. No amount of him reminding me which letter was 'b' and which one was 'd' helped me remember, let alone grabbed my interest. My enthusiasm for the books slipped down, away from me, like my fallen knee socks. In those moments all I wanted was to lay my head on the refuge of the rippled wooden desk, to feel its shiny surface from years of varnish and fingertips, and close my eyes.

His piling on the praise in the playground worked a treat. On I'd charge again, not giving a damn about any prospective injuries. But I was forever disappointed when he called time and took the ball and walked towards the back door. My stomach sinking at the thought of the darkness in that room, let alone the depression in my head.

I improved very little with my letters over the years despite everyone's efforts, especially Tony's. I spent most days with my head fuzzy, not able to catch up or understand the things on the board or on the page. Numbers weren't so bad. They made some sense. I could add and subtract and, in time, multiply. Tony saw my progress and pushed me on. All the way to school and all the way home, we'd practise. He'd make a game of it, making sure I knew my money and the time, so that Mam and Dad and Master Duggan might let me be. He tried with the words too:

'Think of a "b", like it's a stick man holding a *ball* in front of him. And a "d" is a *dumbo* hiding the ball behind him.'

I'd try to hold that in my head, 'ball, in front, dumbo behind'. And it worked, when the letters were on their own and not in the middle of words or at the end. That's when everything started to swim around on the blackboard or on the page and I couldn't order them or the sounds in the right place.

I punched Tony once on our way home when he wouldn't let up pushing me to get it right.

'Would you give over saying you're stupid, Big Man, you're as able as the next fella.'

'Go 'way,' I yelled, as he doubled over. 'I am so stupid,' I called back as I ran off into the bit of a forest that, back then, stood at the front of our house.

I'll admit that behind my tears, I was impressed that I'd managed to floor him. But as I ran, weaving my way through the trees, trampling on the fallen leaves and branches, the shame of it crept up on me. My exhausted body finally came to a stop at a clearing that faced west out across the Dollards' land. There, I screamed out my fury so loudly that I was sure its power reached over those fields, up the hills and down as far as Duncashel.

It was dark by the time I headed home that evening. My stomach told me it was about six o'clock when I walked through the door and heard the clatter of the tea things. My family's chat quietened as I slipped on to the end of the bench at the table. But my mother continued to fill the teacups like there was nothing untoward at all. I didn't dare lift my head, hoping they might all have the decency to ignore me. As I concentrated on my hands twisting in my lap, I heard my knife rattle against my plate. I looked up to find a slice of soda bread newly landed there. Tony. I didn't need to look to know, but still I raised my eyes to find his smile and wink.

Master Duggan wasn't the worst, I have to give him his due. When I hear the stories now of what kids endured back in those days, I'm lucky I wasn't beaten black and blue or worse. As the years went on it was like we came to an understanding, him and me, that he'd leave me alone when it came to asking questions, if I never made trouble. He never pushed or embarrassed me. Never stuck me in the corner or once called me lazy. I believe he simply didn't know what to do with me. We were together on that. Most of the time I asked if I could be excused to go to the toilet. Not that we had toilets, but it became our code, when he knew I needed a break. I roamed around the back of the school, over the wall in the fields, wandering up and down, looking out on the countryside below, seeing the neighbours at work. I'd go back after a good long stint out in the fresh Meath air, to listen and watch the others succeed and belong.

There was this one lunchtime, I must've been about seven, when I decided I'd had enough. Three years I'd been trying at that stage. By then, Tony had only a couple of months left in school. He was twelve and once June came he was leaving to work the land full-time with our father. The football had been particularly good that day. I had been brilliant. In my memory, I had scored every goal, made every deciding tackle, even getting the ball from Tony once or twice. I was a genius. And then the master called a halt to proceedings to get us back inside. I knew then, at that moment, that I couldn't. It felt like a weight had been planted on my head, not allowing me to move. I sat on the low wall that marked the school boundary, breathing heavily, watching the fallen-down socks and bruised legs of the others scurry and kick their way through the door. I could see the master looking at me. But he didn't move; instead he called Tony and whispered something in his ear. I watched them watching me, before the master headed on inside and Tony trotted over.

'Alright, Big Man? Come on, we have to go in.'

'I want to go home,' I said.

'You can't be doing that. Come on, the master will be waiting,' he said, heading on again.

I said nothing, not moving an inch.

'Listen,' he said, returning, his hand now between my shoulder blades, pushing me off the wall and ahead of him with some strength, 'the day's nearly over. We'll be out of here before you know it.'

I near fell in the door of the classroom, with the force of his pushes. I walked slowly by each table, my finger trailing along every one, to get to my seat, where I stayed for the long afternoon with a big sulky head on me.

'I hate it,' I repeated, over and over on our way home.

'It'll get better.'

'Yeah, right. Well how come I'm still as stupid as the day I started, then.'

I ran ahead of him, like it was his fault. Ran all the way back into the house. Flew in through the kitchen, ignoring my mother's gaping mouth and was down with the dust balls under the bed before she had time to stop me. Refused to come out. Lay there, picking at the threadbare rug that half-covered the cold concrete floor, listening to the muffled talk seeping through the slats of the latched wooden door.

'What happened, Tony?' Mam asked, when he eventually landed in.

'Nothing. Seriously. Nothing happened. I don't know what's got into him. I'll sort him.'

Tony sat down by the bed bringing me the glass of milk and buttered soda bread my mother always produced after the school day was over and before we headed off to find our father and the work he had lined up for us. Tony placed his plate beside mine. When there was no sign of me coming out he pushed mine in under a little further. I ignored the food for as long as my stomach let me, then I reached to take bits of the bread. Eventually I pushed them and myself back out and sat beside Tony. We said nothing. Just ate and looked at my sisters' bed opposite. Made to perfection, not a pillow or blanket out of place, the crochet-knitted cover, made by Jenny and May over the previous winter, that gave weight and warmth at night, spread smoothly on top.

'Do you think we should make one of them?' Tony said. 'One of those crochet covers?' I looked at him like he'd gone mad. 'Like I know women are good at all that kind of stuff but I don't see why we couldn't do it. It'd be fierce warm in the winter.'

'I'm not taking up knitting so people can laugh at me even more.'

'Hold on, Big Man, that's not what I meant.'

'Yes it is, you think all I'm good for is women's work.'

'Ah now, Maurice, that isn't what I was saying at all. And no one is laughing at you, either.'

'Oh yes they are. Joe Brady called me a dumbo yesterday when I got the spelling wrong.'

'So that's why you hit him,' he laughed, impressed. 'He's no feckin' genius anyway. He can't even tie his laces for feck sake. And have you seen the state of his ears? I mean no man with ears that stick out like that has a right to call anyone a dumbo.'

Despite myself, I smiled.

'Come on, Big Man. We'll figure this out, OK? Me and you, right. Me and you against the world, yeah?' He got me in the gentlest headlock and ruffled my hair. 'You'll be grand.'

But I wasn't. And every morning after, they had to pull me kicking and screaming from my bed. My father was pushed to limits that were not naturally him.

'Get out to blazes, ya pup.'

He pulled at me until there was nothing left in my grip of the leg of the bed and I gave way. I stood crying in my nightshirt. Screaming the odds, telling them I wouldn't go back. My mother had to dress me with me holding my body as stiff as I could. I refused to take a crumb of food and went to school defiant and starving.

Day after day, Tony walked by my side still trying to encourage me. While my parents had long given up coaxing and pushing me out the door, Tony never stopped telling me I was full of greatness. People didn't really do that back then, encourage and support. You were threatened into being who you were supposed to be. But it was because of Tony's words that I made that journey to school every day and suffered through the darkness, when my brain felt exhausted from not knowing the answers. I didn't want to let him down, you see. Couldn't let him know that I knew I was totally and utterly thick.

Even after he'd left school, Tony walked by my side every day to the door, enduring my silence. It was the only way I'd go. It had been his idea that for as long as our father could spare him the twenty minutes, he'd walk the road every morning. In the classroom I never raised my hand or heard the sound of my own voice. I would sink so low in my seat that I was sure if you were standing at the back of the room you'd think no one sat there at all.

It took three more years before the master decided to walk the road to our farm. It was after school and I was already home, busy with the chickens. When I saw him in the yard I hid behind the coop. My mother came out, wiping her hands in her apron, looking worried. They spoke briefly before she pointed towards the lower field to where my father and Tony were working and off he went. Tony came up not long after.

'What does he want?' I asked, coming out from behind the coop and running alongside him as he made a steady pace towards the back door of the house.

'I've no idea. I was told to go back up to the house for tea.'

'For tea? It's not that time. It's about me, isn't it?'

'I told you, Maurice, nobody told me anything. I'm starving. Listen, I'll be out in a minute. Go on you back to the coop.'

I did as I was told and returned to lean up against the wooden slats, to brood my way through all kinds of possibilities. The worst of which involved me being shipped off to some home for people who couldn't read one line of a book without breaking into a sweat. I walked in circles around and around the coop, kicking at the chickens whenever one ventured out and got in my way.

'Don't worry, Big Man, it'll all be OK,' Tony said, coming out after a bit, the remnants of my mother's soda bread still lingering around his mouth. But his eyes couldn't hide his concern, no matter how much he smiled.

'Whatever he says, Maurice, it'll be OK, you know that. We'll figure this all out together, right?'

I kicked at the straw, not able to raise my eyes to him.

'Big Man, come on now. What is it I always say to you?'

I kicked again, refusing to be shaken from my silence.

'You and me against the world. Isn't that it? Come on, say it, Big Man. Let me hear you.'

'You and me . . .' I mumbled, my head still down, the sole of my shoe scuffing the earth, not wanting to repeat his bloody refrain any more. Because the truth of it was, there was no 'him and me' in this war, it was just me and my stupidity.

'. . . AGAINST THE WORLD,' he chanted, 'that's it.' He gave me an encouraging puck to the shoulder.

We stayed in the coop until my father and the master came into view, walking slowly up the hill, deep in serious conversation. They stopped at the haggard wall to finish whatever it was occupied them. Then my father nodded, tipped his cap and watched him leave the yard. He looked over at Tony then, and beckoned him with the tilt of his head. He didn't look at me, but simply turned back down to the field with my fate in tow. Tony laid his hand on my shoulder and whispered:

'Remember what I said, me and you,' then fell in behind my father.

An hour later, the whole family sat around the long kitchen table for our tea, Tony showing no signs of distress at having to go through it all again.

'Master Duggan thinks you might be best working the land, Maurice,' my father announced, 'says you've grown grand and strong and that you'd make a fine farmer, like your big brother here. Well, what do you think? You're not one for the books anyway. Am I wrong?'

I let the seconds slip by, swallowing the bread in my mouth, imagining it slipping down my throat sinking into the pit of my stomach.

'No,' I mumbled in reply, not lifting my eyes from the plate. My head nearly stuck in it, I was hunched that low.

'Well, good, that's that then. Your mother will make enquiries at the Dollards' farm and see if they're in need of an extra pair of hands. No school tomorrow so. You'll work with us 'til something sorts itself out.'

My embarrassment hovered in the air between us, circling the teapot, the milk jug and the bowl of hardboiled eggs. I found it hard to swallow any further. Closing my eyes, I gulped at my tea, wolfing down my shame.

'Big Man,' Tony whispered later in bed, as we lay in the dark, 'this is a good thing. School's not for everyone. The land now, that's a whole different story. See those hands of yours, that's what they're made for.'

I lifted my hands to my eyes, trying to examine them in the pitch dark. I knew he was right this time, but still I'd wanted to be so much more, for him most of all.

*

People used to say the Dollard house was beautiful, not that my mother ever did, though. She worked there too, you see, in the kitchen. To a ten-year-old boy, on his first day at work it was nothing but creepy. My mother walked me over, she talked at me all the way. I was too distracted by the chestnuts that littered our path through the fields to take much notice. More specifically it was the conkers inside waiting to be cracked open. Huge, perfect beasts for thrashing Joe Brady's meagre offerings. I caught some of her words, though: 'manners' and 'respect'. But the reality of the life ahead didn't hit home until I was stuck under the watchful eye of the farm manager, Richard Berk. A stern man, a man well trusted by Hugh Dollard, the head of the house. Over my six years under his care, I often saw the two of them huddled together, heads almost touching, whispering. At ten, I had grown tall and was nearly as big as Mam, five foot two. I was broad and as strong as Tony. Berk hadn't hesitated in taking me.

My mother worked in the mornings, helping the cook with the baking. Ten loaves of bread a day, mainly for the staff. For the Dollards, she made apple tarts and scones and much fancier affairs when they had guests. On our way across the fields, my mother always sang a tune: *Goodnight Irene* was her favourite. I sang along with her. She loved to hear me sing, she said. A couple of years before, she'd signed me up for Father Molloy's choir. I was put standing on the altar with the other recruits, all girls. Not a note came out of my mouth. Petrified I was, at the very thought of any kind of public performance. I was sent home never to return. It didn't stop me from singing along with my mother whenever we were together, though.

I knew them all: *Boolavogue, I'll tell me Ma, McNamara's band*. In later years, I dazzled Sadie with my talent. I even sang you to sleep once or twice when she was at her wits' end. I'd stroke your forehead and off you'd go. Nowadays, I sing into the wind at the foot of her grave.

My mother was softly spoken. What words she said were to the point. Nothing wasted. Neither was she one for smiling. I remember her laughter because it was rare. Sweet and quiet, embarrassed for intruding almost. My uncle John, my mother's brother, brought home a banana from London on a visit, once. We'd never seen one before. He placed it on one of her willow plates, remember them? I think we still had some when you were little. Anyhow, there it was, placed right in the middle of the table like some precious jewel. My mother looked at it and laughed. Clear and melodious it was, like a song thrush. As each member of the family arrived to see the peculiar-looking fruit, my mother's laugh started up once more. I willed others to come so she wouldn't stop. I moved as close to her as I could, to taste and feel her happiness. I remember my head pushed in against the material of her apron, closing my eyes to hear her joy and feel her body vibrate. Irresistible. But, whatever chance I had of hearing her laugh at home there was no hope of it at work.

The Dollards were not kind to each other let alone to those who worked for them. My father was convinced it was their gradual demise in wealth and power over the previous fifty years that did it.

'It's the rent he misses. None of them can abide the fact we have our own land now.'

Their house hung heavy with the disappointment of the

small farmer winning the right to own holdings, however limited, under the Land Commission. Inside especially, from the bits I could see anyway. Red was about as colourful as it got and, even then, it seemed to be the darkest shade possible. But it was the family portraits that were the worst. Massive paintings of unhappy people, dressed in blacks and browns, with grey-black backgrounds that wouldn't have looked out of place in a funeral home. I worried for my mother being exposed to that six mornings a week.

'We need the money, Maurice,' was all she'd say on the matter.

I remember this one time, I must've been about twelve, no more than thirteen, I'd say, I was helping Pat Cullinane carry in logs for the fireplaces into the back hallway. I could hear a bit of lively banter going on in the kitchen.

'You want to make sure his Lordship doesn't catch you at that,' Pat called in.

'He's away off,' the cook replied, coming over to lean against the door frame.

'When the cat's away, is that it?'

'Well, it's not often we get the chance. Are you coming to join us?'

Pat had begun to wipe his feet on the mat when a fist pounded on the far door that led to the main part of the house, slamming it back against the wall.

'I don't pay you to laugh,' it said, loud and scary enough that I froze to the spot with a pile of logs in my arms.

It was Dollard himself, most definitely not away and most definitely blind drunk. Swaying in the doorway until his arm clutched the frame and propelled him into the room. Everyone was quiet, keeping their eyes on the floor.

Pat and me, hidden in the hallway, had a small chance of escape. But when Pat took a step backwards bumping into me, didn't I drop the bloody logs. Dollard turned our way. And like he was a fit young lad and not the old overweight mountain he appeared, he charged across the room. I caught the fear in my mother's eye as she tried to move but was halted by the cook's floured fingers gripping at her elbow. Dollard's slap stung hard and loud against my cheek, knocking me back on to the woodpile.

'Useless boy.'

Dazed though I was, it was the cook's white hands holding my mother back that I looked for. Through Dollard's swaying legs, I saw my mother's hand rise to her mouth. But thankfully, she didn't move. I lowered my head and rubbed where Dollard had struck, as his weight still loomed. And then from out behind the man's bulk, stepped a boy no older than me. I knew him to see, of course, he was the son and heir of the throne, Thomas Dollard, but this was my first ever interaction with him.

'Pick them up. Now!' he roared, pointing at the logs.

His spit fell on my hands and face as his words still shook inside my head. By now, I was one big petrified mess. I moved to stand, but the terror meant I fell forward on to his feet. He kicked away at me, one right in my ribs.

'You cretin. Move.'

I stood and steadied myself as best I could. I began to pull together the fallen logs, piling them with the others. I took my chances and glanced towards my mother and saw the cook turn her back to the sink.

'Next time I see you damage my father's property, you'll know all about it.'

'Thomas!' Dollard slurred, 'I'm master here. You run along and play with those dolls you like so much. *I'll* deal with this, thank you very much.'

'They're not dolls, Father. They're soldiers,' Thomas's voice shook, his eyes wide at the insult from his father.

'They look like dolls to me.'

Thomas blinked. Long, hurt, hypnotic blinks. I was so taken by them, that I hadn't realised he'd turned his attention back to me. His eyes, steady now, staring. I braced myself for another blow. But he simply turned and left, disappearing through the kitchen. Dollard senior, catching my relief, grabbed me by the neck and hoisted me high – my face now level with his, my legs dangling mid-air. I shut my eyes against his rank breath. But next thing, didn't the fecker drop me. I looked up to see him wobbling and shaking. One hand covering his eyes, the other reaching for the steadiness of the wall. Blinking rapidly, staring in at the kitchen then back at me, like he was unsure of his surroundings. Still on the ground, I looked away from his embarrassment. Seconds later, I heard him stumble across the kitchen, knocking some pots as he went. The door beyond banged shut. Everything was dead quiet for a second and then my mother was standing over me in a panic.

'Maurice, Maurice, would you look at me?' She was on the floor, my face in her hands, examining the damage.

'Stop Mam. I'm grand. Sure he barely got me,' I said, getting up.

But I was put on a chair in the kitchen and mollycoddled, nevertheless, until Pat had had enough:

'He's grand now. Come on, let's get this mess cleared up out here.'

After that, Thomas, the son, never left me alone. Beat the living daylights out of me. I took years of that shite from him. He taunted the other lads for sure, ordered them around like he was the man. Once, he made Mickie Dwyer move bales of hay from one side of the yard to the other and back again for the whole afternoon. Even Berk had enough of him that day and read him the riot act. But because I had witnessed his shaming at the hands of his father, I received special treatment. Being the youngest of the workers didn't help either. But to be truthful, I could've taken him with one blow, but I never fought him, never rose to his taunts. I let his fists fly unanswered, knowing not to risk our jobs or my mother's safety – it was her I worried most about.

It was of little consolation to me that Dollard senior beat him. We all knew it, everyone who moved in that place knew. I often passed a window and heard him going at it. I couldn't stand the sound of Thomas's pleas. That upset me more than his father's violence. Pitiful. A thing I was sure I'd never have done. Sometimes I'd hear Rachel, the little sister, trying to intervene and every now and again succeeding on his behalf.

'No, Daddy. Stop it!'

I imagined her swinging from Dollard's tree trunk of an arm as he swiped at Thomas. Sometimes but not often, as I recall, the mother, Amelia, even tried.

'Hugh! Please let him go. This isn't fair, and you know it,' she begged, on the day I got this scar, right here just below my eye. I was fifteen. I was passing alongside one of the open downstairs windows. As the lace curtains billowed out into the summer breeze, I caught a glimpse of Thomas's face. Red it was. Lips pulled back, his teeth jammed together. Dollard had a good tight hold of him in a headlock. The mother stood a little ways off, her hands twisting.

'Don't talk to me about fair, Amelia,' Dollard shouted at her, 'don't you dare lecture me about what's fair!'

I'd seen and heard enough to scarper. I might've managed it had Berk not blocked my escape, sending me to the milking sheds to muck out. I may as well've stood in the middle of the yard and called for Thomas to come get me. Quicker than I'd thought possible, Thomas was there at my back, a hunting crop in his hand. As I turned he struck me with it, the metal end slicing into my cheek. When I fell to the ground holding my face, he kicked my stomach again and again and again. Kicked like he'd never done before and with a strength that felt new. I endured every strike, every drop of his spit. Not a moan left my lips.

'Thomas, stop it!'

I heard Rachel's pleas as she stood at the shed door.

Curled up, I was, one hand on my face, the other trying to shield my body, not daring to look at him. I could hear his exhausted breaths heaving above me. His blood dripped on to my hand from the wounds inflicted by his father. I waited. She waited. But no further blow came. I watched his boots turn and walk back to the door, to his sister. His bloodied hand took hers. She looked at him like he was some stranger, a man she was not sure it was safe to go with. They left but not before she glanced back at me. After, I stretched my hand out to the straw and wiped what I could of his spit and blood away.

Berk administered the stitches. No anaesthetic, no disinfectant. Sat where I had fallen with a needle threading my face. He sent me home. A whole two hours off in compensation for having the shit kicked out of me and a scar: a memento of how lucky I was not to lose an eye. My mother bathed the wound, cleaning it as best she could. Later, as I lay on my bed in the lower room, I listened to the hushed voices of my parents in the kitchen, knowing they were talking about me. Tony stood at the foot of the bed, leaning against the closed door.

'He's nothing but a gobshite, Maurice,' he said, 'if I could get my hands on him I'd knock him into next week.'

'Ah, Tony, don't go doing anything now. There's the jobs to think of—'

'Feck the jobs, Maurice. No one has the right to do this to you.'

My father's knock came to the bedroom door. Tony stood away to let him through.

He stepped in and looked at us both. His face drawn and serious.

'There'll be enough of that kind of talk,' he said finally, his eyes firmly on Tony. All the while Tony's refused to lift from the ground, knowing full well that he could curse and threaten all he liked but nothing would change with the likes of the Dollards. And true to form, I got up the next morning with half my head bandaged and went across the fields as normal.

Months later, I was walking to the back paddock along by the house when I heard Dollard senior's shouts again. My heart sank, I can tell you. I walked on as quietly and quickly as possible. This time Thomas had his back to the opened window of an upstairs room. His hands were behind him, folded into fists. As I passed right under him, one of his hands opened, releasing something that landed right in front of me.

'But Father, I didn't take it. I didn't!' I heard him whine.

Without thinking, I reached down and grabbed the shiny thing from among the stones, putting it in my pocket and continuing on my way, smooth as you like. If I'd known back then how that decision of mine ruined the lives inside that house for generations to come, not least Thomas's, I wonder would I have walked on, stepping over its pull, its power. But all I knew then was revenge. If this small theft, I reasoned, of whatever it was I held in my pocket could inflict even a small moment of the pain Thomas had meted on me with his beatings and his disgust, then it was most definitely my due.

Despite the growing distance, I could still hear the yells and panicked replies of Thomas as something or someone hit the floor. I didn't look back. When I was safely clear, I ducked in behind a tree. And there, taking it out of my pocket, I saw it for the first time – a gold coin, with the face of a man I didn't recognise and writing I didn't even try to understand. Heavy and solid, quite impressive. I turned it over for as long as I dared. Throwing it up and down once or twice, before pocketing it again and smiling to myself.

Five hours later when I walked back the way along the same path, Pat joined me.

'Would you look at that bleeding eejit,' he said. We could see Thomas scrambling about under the same window from earlier. 'He's lost some coin or other of the father's. The old man's going mad, says he'll disinherit him if he doesn't give it back. Reckons he robbed it on purpose.'

Thomas caught my eye as we passed. I looked away like

I always did despite feeling an unfamiliar power. When out of sight, I smiled to myself as I caressed the metal lying snug and happy in my pocket with my thumb.

Oh, they looked under every bush and plant and in every pocket and bag, alright. That evening we were all lined up before we left for the day. But I was no fool. I'd it hidden in the nook of a tree that lay near our boundary wall. Even still, I was terrified when Berk approached me in the queue. He stood staring at my scar. My confession bubbled up behind my lips as his hands delved in my pockets and ran over my body. I held firm though, never gave away a thing. Disappointed, he passed on to Mickie Dwyer.

The next day mother and most of the kitchen staff were ordered to strip Thomas's room and the room in which the argument had happened; the labourers were ordered to search the yard below. The world stopped while we hunted on hands and knees over stones and clay and dirt and grass for something they would never find. Thomas ran between both groups.

'Have you not found it yet?' he moaned, standing above me, close to tears, pulling at his hair.

'What did it look like, sir?' I sat back on my hunkers and looked up at him.

'Gold, you dimwit, gold. Berk, what kind of imbeciles do you have working for you?'

He charged after the farm manager like he expected an answer to his question. I found a thruppence and ran up to him.

'Sir. Sir. I found it,' I said, with not one shred of guilt about me.

The relief on his face was something to behold. But it

was the misery that returned, as he looked at my copper offering, that was worth the wallop across the head from Berk. He ran from me, from Berk, off into the house.

Although we were questioned continuously over the coming days – the labourers by Berk and the housemaids by Dollard senior himself – it seemed without conviction. Everyone knew Dollard believed Thomas guilty. He'd washed his hands of him it seems. Sent him away within days and true to his word, disinherited him. At the time it struck me as odd that it was never reported to the police. As it turned out, they couldn't have, given how Dollard had come by it. But I wasn't to know that back then.

For weeks following, I was petrified they'd arrive at our door and ransack the place. But Tony had taken care of it for me, as he'd taken care of so many of my worries before. Assured me, they'd never find it under his pillow:

'Sure, who'll come near me when they find out I've got TB?'

Tony'd got consumption earlier that year. I hadn't a clue that cough of his was anything other than the usual hall-marks of winter: chills and runny noses and sore throats waylaying us like they always did. It went on for weeks, though. Not shifting, not stirring. Barked through the day and into the night. Sometimes it woke me but mostly he suffered on his own as I turned to the wall and dreamed my dreams. I was always a good sleeper back then. Dead to the world, oblivious to all about me until my body decided it was time to wake. I wonder now if I'd been a lighter sleeper, might I have caught Sadie, two years ago just before her last breath was taken, and pulled her back to me.

'Mam, is there nothing we can do about Tony's cough?'

May complained one day. 'It's keeping me awake. I'm making a hames of this bread, I'm that tired.'

But there had been no need to alert my mother to Tony's debility. I'd seen her watching him for days: as he crossed the yard slower than usual and coughed at the dinner table and slept in the armchair after the tea.

'You'll sleep in our room tonight, Tony,' she told him, the day he had lifted his hand to his chest.

'Mam, I'm grand, sure that honey drink you made me is working mighty.'

'No matter. You'll be in the upper room. We'll take yours. Maurice, you can take the chairs in the kitchen.'

What I didn't know until after he died was that my mother had watched her younger brother Jimmy die of the same thing. People didn't talk much of things like that in those days. Death and illness were sacred and silent, not to be stoked and stirred. But it seems for years she'd been on alert, watching us with our coughs and colds, ready to pounce. Ready to begin battle with the demon that had taken her favourite brother. With Tony, her time had finally come.

She washed the sheets and eiderdown from our bed that day. She and my father slept fully clothed under a blanket until they finally dried. Meanwhile I set up my chairs, one facing the other, in the kitchen. A blanket and my mother's winter coat around me. It was a while before I fell asleep that first night. I listened to Tony's cough, his constant call, as I tried to figure out what this change in sleeping arrangements meant.

The next day was a Sunday as I recall, and my father left in the trap when it was still dark and returned two hours later with Doctor Roche. I watched from the shed, as they went inside. I ran to Tony's window, to try to hear his fate. Jenny and May came out soon after. The three evictees stood in the blowing rain, waiting.

'It's got to be,' Jenny whispered to May, as we huddled under the dripping thatch, leaning into the frame of the window as far as we could.

'Don't say that, Jenny. Don't be wishing it on him.'

'I'm not doing that, for heaven's sake. I'm just saying, that's what young Wall died of and Kitty told me that's how it had started.'

'Quiet, Jenny, Tony might hear.'

Later, we went to Mass in Duncashel, not the usual local church, in order to drop the Doctor home. I felt sorry for the horse having to cart the lot of us that distance. Tony didn't come. We journeyed in silence. In the pew, I watched my parents pray in concentration. My mother's eyes shut tight, her wrinkles bunched up with the effort, as her busy lips tipped her folded hands.

After we got home, silence reigned. Jenny, May and me wandered about, waiting to be let in on the mystery. We never went near the shut door of the upper room where Tony slept. We moved between our bedroom and the kitchen, eventually deciding on the most sedate game of twenty-five I ever remember. After a while the girls rose to help Mother with the dinner while my father never lifted his head above his Sunday paper.

'Tony has consumption,' he said later, as we stared at our dinner plates. 'But you'll not say a word to anyone. Do you hear? As far as the world is concerned that boy has broken his leg from a fall in the field. Do you understand me now?'

The three siblings stole a glance at each other, then nodded our collusion.

'The Doctor won't say a word to anyone. He wants us to move Tony to the upper shed. He's afraid of it infecting the lot of us. But we'll tend him here. He'll not be put out . . .' My father broke off his words and balled up his fists and pushed them deep into his pockets. 'You girls will look after Tony in the mornings when Mam is working,' he continued after a bit, 'the Doctor has told her what to do. Rest is the best cure, he says. We'll not lose him. We'll not lose that boy.'

The word went out Tony had broken his leg. If people knew the truth, we'd have been done for. TB was as contagious as gossip. The Dollards would have let us go there and then. As it turned out, none of us picked it up, although I do believe it lingered with my mother and that's what hurried on her own death, years later. It was hard, keeping it a secret. People called. Well-wishers. Not often, mind, but the odd time, a neighbour would drop by. Jenny or May would run to meet them in the yard and make up all sorts before they got close to the house:

'He's not in great shape today. Sorry now, and you after coming over.'

'He's in a lot of pain. I'll let him know you called. It'll do him the world of good to know you're thinking of him.'

'He's up there now trying to do those exercises the Doctor gave him, but he's frustrated; you know how it is.'

I'm sure after a while people began to suspect. But no one ever asked us.

The only time Tony was left on his own was on a Sunday when the rest of us headed off to Mass. Despite being away from him for those couple of hours, that time was still all about him. I did some pleading for his salvation myself as I held the host in my mouth. To my left and right, I knew the others were doing the same.

The Doctor told us to feed him 'nutritious' food and give him stout every day, for the iron. Tony was thrilled at the prospect. But of course, it all cost money. Nutrition back then meant red meat and vegetables. We had the carrots, cabbage and potatoes growing out in the garden. Often that's all we had. White meat was not so much of a problem, what with the few chickens we had running 'round the yard. When one got too old to lay, well, then she ended up on our plates. The red stuff was more difficult. Every now and again though, a bit would be found from somewhere. We didn't begrudge him an ounce, that's not to say we didn't lick our lips as it roasted in the range. When I went up to him one evening, he told me to shut the door, all conspiratorial like.

'Here, Big Man, have this,' he said, as soon as the latch had lowered. There in his fist, in his handkerchief, he held a chunk of beef.

He must have had it there since dinnertime.

'Ah Tony, I can't be taking your food.'

'Jesus man, they were stuffing it into me. The size of it. It was like there was a whole cow sitting on the plate. Take it. I kept it for you.'

'They'll kill me.'

'I reckon they take little bites themselves. I could've sworn there was a hole in that piece when Jenny brought it in,' he said, smiling at me. 'For God's sake man, sure you're holding down two jobs now having to work with the auld lad when you get home from that place.'

All the doctors in Ireland would've been having heart attacks watching me take that from his spotted handkerchief, but I tell you now that morsel tasted like heaven. As cold and squashed as it was, it was pure tasty.

It felt wrong after all those days and years of Tony walking beside me to school, encouraging and supporting me, that I had to leave him in the bed every morning to go to the Dollards. I always left it till the last minute, hanging around chatting and messing with him when he was up to it, before my mother dragged me out the door. I went with a heavy heart, my boots feeling like they were filled with the weightiest of stones, slowing my path away from him. If I'd had my choice it would've been me waiting on him, bringing him his dinner, standing over him with a bowl when he was coughing his insides up, helping him up from the bed and getting him settled on the chamber pot so he could do his morning duty. The rest of the world could have mocked and jeered me all they liked but I would've done that and more for him if I'd been let.

I refused to allow the women to tend him all the time. I'd run all the way home from the job to grab his tea tray and bring it up before any of them had the chance. Gone, before Mam, long home from work by that stage, had time to protest. Although, I knew she approved as I caught her grin before I scarpered. Outside Tony's door, I'd hold the tray with one hand under it and knock with the other.

'Enter,' he'd call, like he was lord of the manor. 'Course, he knew it was me, 'cause I'd have given him my trademark rap on the bedroom window, five beats, as I flew in home earlier.

'Is that lazy fecker not up yet?' I'd say in the hallway as I hung up my cap, loud enough so he could hear.

I'd smile at his reply and lift the latch. But God forgive me, every time I saw his hollowed-out face, it was a shock. It was always, always, like I was seeing it for the first time. The laughter gone out of me, only the remains of an embarrassed smile that admitted how bad I was at keeping up the pretence that there was nothing wrong with the brother I adored and that he wasn't just one more cough away from leaving us.

'Big Man,' he'd say or splurt.

'Still codding us that you're sick, I see.'

I'd take my seat beside him on my mother's chair, the one her mother had bought her when she married. If Tony were strong enough, I'd put the tray on his lap and he'd feed himself. But as time went on he wasn't able to even pull himself up, and so I'd break up the bits of bread and feed it to him as he lay propped up slightly by a pillow. If he were in the eating humour, which wasn't often, I'd put the bread anywhere but near his mouth. It made us laugh. It wasn't that funny, I suppose, when I think of it now, but it was all we had.

Often, he was too weak to join in with my nightly updates on how my day had gone. I got used to the sound of my own voice, telling him what was going on over the boundary wall.

'What I find mad, Tony, is that our own fields can't be that different from theirs. But you should see the size of the stones I was pulling from those acres over there today. Boulders they were. Boulders. My back is near broken from them.'

Mostly he lay there listening. Not always able to reply.

'Dollard senior's getting worse, if that's possible. Since he sent Thomas packing he's like a briar. Apparently, the mother and daughter are no better. The cook says none of them are speaking now. I don't know, a disinheritance over one bloody coin!'

I felt no guilt that it was me and the coin lying under my brother's head that had caused Thomas's banishment. Tony was the only one I ever told about the extent of what Thomas had done to me. The beatings. The constant fear of them. I wore the scar for all to see but no one, not my mother or father or sisters, had ever asked how I was about it all. And do you know, neither would I have wanted them to, I would have felt like a right eejit telling them how much it still stung. But sometimes as Tony lay sleeping, his face wincing with pain, I went over it.

'Maurice,' he said once, spluttering away, giving me a fright 'cause I thought he was asleep, 'someday, achmm, achmm . . . someday that fecker'll get his comeuppance.'

'Take it easy, Tony. Here, take the water. Mam won't like me getting you riled up like that. You weren't supposed to hear all that anyway.'

He took the water and gripped my hand that held the cup. He held my eyes, his breath catching.

'Maurice . . . it'll come right, wait and see.'

When Tony slept with me beside him in the chair, his breath struggled to take in what it needed, growing more laboured with each day that passed. I'd sit watching the rise and fall of his sunken chest, willing it to cop on and right itself. The amount of prayers I said sitting in that chair, would have made my mother proud; decades upon decades of the rosary, my eyes squinting shut, asking God to get on with working a miracle. I'd stay like that 'til I fell asleep too and my father came to tap me on the shoulder and send me off down to the kitchen to get some tea myself before going out to do the jobs he couldn't do alone during the day. I'd rise and lay a hand on Tony's shoulder then, my parting words always the same.

'You and me, against the world, what? You and me.'

Every Sunday evening without fail, we crowded into his bedroom. The war of course had been raging away over beyond for years. And in 1946 the papers were all about the aftermath and how the world would change, and how the horrors in Germany would never happen again. The recriminations and rebuilding projects in Europe were in full swing and my father read it all to us from the paper he had bought after Sunday Mass. Squashed into Tony's room, with borrowed chairs from the kitchen, we listened to my father's voice read out stories of the world beyond us and beyond the secret of Tony's illness. After, we gave our own opinions and summations, disagreeing with the other or agreeing that de Valera had played the right card. Tony joined in when he could. But often I think he wanted to simply drift off to the sounds of our voices.

We knew we were losing him. It was like he was sinking into the bed, he had become so thin. Disappearing before our eyes. There was nothing to be done by us or the Doctor. His life ebbed away from our laughter and our care. I continued to sit with him, despite the awfulness and despite my tears that sometimes fell no matter how hard I tried to stop them.

'Ah Maurice, ya big girl,' he said, breathlessly one evening having woken to find me sitting beside him all red eyed. He nearly choked on the weak chuckle he managed. I laughed, a big hearty laugh. We were gone again then, laughing away the tragedy of it all.

I never saw my mother look so thin as in those last few weeks before he died. Up at the crack of dawn, even though she might have sat by Tony's side the whole night, catching snatches of sleep through his distress. We'd be gone over the fields then to earn the money to buy the rich food to save him. The only morning she asked to be excused was the day he died.

'I can't possibly do without you today, Hannah!' Amelia Dollard said, as she fiddled with the flowers in her hallway where my mother waylaid her, her eyes never once rising from the carpet. 'I've told you, Thomas is coming home and bringing the Lawrences. His school friend and his parents. They've been so good to him, through all of this, taking him on weekends and such, so we can't let him down. Poor Thomas – we don't often see him and what with Hugh away . . . well it's the only time he can get home. And we simply can't do without your apple tart. You've made enough, I hope.' Less of an enquiry than a demand, Amelia Dollard strode away, leaving my mother alone, looking at her hands, clasped on her aproned stomach.

I was tempted to call out to her. I heard it all, you see, through the open front doors. I'd been ordered to assist the gardener with the flowerboxes in the windows at the front of the house. Instead, I watched my mother turn, tilting her head back in an effort to reverse the flow of tears, and walk back to the kitchen. It was Jenny who arrived later, as my mother, with the mounds of baking complete, put on her coat to leave. She caught her at the back door, she told me that evening. I heard my mother's cry. Her wail rose above the rooftop, screeched over the tiles and down the walls to pound my head and shoulders as I trimmed the trees at the sides of the front door. I knew it was Tony. My legs weakened and I stretched a hand to a branch to hold me up. At that very moment a car pulled up to the house. I didn't turn my head, knowing who it was in an instant. I heard Thomas's boasts as he fussed with the car and hall door.

'1700s, maybe? Not exactly sure, but Father would know. Unfortunately, he's not around today. London, you know, bit of business. This way, this way.'

He never acknowledged me. Small mercy. If he'd as much as breathed in my direction, I might finally have landed him one. When the hall door shut, I spat on the ground after him, cursing them to hell. I was gone then. Half crazed, I ran the long way home at some speed, not wishing to pass my mother or sister. I burst through our front door, then into Tony's room.

'No, Maurice,' my father shouted, as he struggled to hold me back when I reached the bed. He held my arms, but like a man possessed I kept lurching forward. Eventually I wrangled free of him, firing my father back against the wall and fell on to Tony's frame. There was nothing but bone, no meat, no hefty muscle. Nothing. Every scrap, wasted away. I lay there, holding his skeletal arms, letting my anger go the way of his soul, up and up, until there was nothing left, just a pitiful murmur, that felt like it wasn't mine.

My father and May pulled me away when they heard my mother arrive. Her surviving children stood together, watching her enter. It's an awful thing, to witness your mother cry.

You cannot cure nor mend nor stick a plaster on. It is rotten. I wanted to tear out the pain of it. It took every ounce of restraint I had not to run from the room and charge through the fields damning those bastards, that bitch and her precious son, who had denied my mother her goodbye. My father stood above her with one hand on her shoulder and the other on her back. That weathered, veined hand moved up and down with the rhythm of her sorrow all afternoon, never once resting. His own grief in check. I wonder, as the years went on, when my father found himself alone, did the weight of Tony's loss stop him in the fields and lower him to his hunkers? Did he ever lay his hand on the earth to steady his body that heaved at the injustice of it all? But that evening it was my mother's cries that filled the house. On and on it went for what felt like hours, thrashing at her small frame, refusing to recede until the priest came. Even then, only quietening enough so she could hear the prayers.

That night was the longest I've ever known. Sleepless, save for snatches filled with furious dreams in which I was running, running from something or someone. I could feel the panic in my chest when I woke each time in a startle, unsure of where I was, pushing myself up out of my mother's chair where I'd fallen asleep by the range. Finally knowing I was at home, I'd settle back against the headrest and stare into the darkness, the emptiness of a life without Tony – my support, my rock.

I've no memory of getting ready the next day. How any of us turned ourselves out as smartly as we did I've no idea. The funeral was hushed and solemn, as you'd expect. Our tears fell on the wooden pews and our black clothes. Our grief not rising above a whisper until the prayers ended and we rose to bring Tony to his grave. As we men left our seats, my mother emitted a moan so despairing that I had to hold on to the back of the seat as it swept into me, causing my knees to buckle. She stood, supported by Jenny and May, linking her awkwardly, one behind and one in front, corralled between the seat and the kneeler, waiting to step out, to follow behind as we raised her son aloft and bore him down the aisle. As we carried the coffin from the church door, I heard wheels crunch on the gravelled drive.

The Dollards.

The car stopped at my rear. Father Molloy, to my horror, halted our procession as the footsteps approached. I watched him bow his head quickly in the direction of the newcomer.

'Father,' Amelia Dollard said.

The crunching continued until it stopped behind me. Bold as you like, wedging herself between mother and son, once again. She took my mother's limp hand and held it as if it mattered to her, my sisters told me later. But my mother didn't raise her head or squeeze her palm. Didn't move a muscle. For those seconds, as Dollard's voice mumbled to my rear, I thought of my father. I imagined his head leaning against my brother's coffin. Eyes closed against the insensitivity and embarrassment of this woman, wishing he could touch the fair hair of his boy one last time; arms aching and knotted hands reddening under the weight of death. I wanted to scream at her to get away, to stop her playacting, her hypocrisy. And then she was gone, just like that. The engine started and that was it. Father Molloy signalled, and we moved on.

I was sixteen when we buried Tony in the Meath heat. We listened to the prayers, joined in when required, mumbled the decade of the rosary and watched as the earth took him. Then, we walked away.

From that day on there was little left of my mother, of that gentle spirit that had once been hers. She never returned to the Dollards, neither did I. We coped without their money. I worked the land with my father. My mother stayed at home, hardly ever leaving. Our weddings were her one exception, May's, Jenny's and mine. Never uttered a word at them, though, never raised a smile. When I look back now at the photos, I see her weary, empty face and wish I could touch it, to soothe it. My father generally stood stoically by her side. His hand on the small of her back, I imagine, staring into the camera, demanding it to notice there was one guest missing. What conversations passed between husband and wife in the years following Tony's departure, I've often wondered? What might Sadie and I have said to one another had you died leaving us behind, forever caught in a loop of memories, inventing your future, lamenting all that you would never know? Or perhaps a silence might have descended – a delicate layer of protection holding us together, cocooning us away from the ugly awful truth of life and death, its gaping wounds, its noxious smells.

It's so hard to lose your best friend at any time, but to do so at such a young age was pure cruel. At sixteen I was heading into my life. Having travelled those precious years with Tony by my side, I now had to venture forth into the most significant of them alone. Without his guidance, his cajoling, his slagging. It didn't feel possible.

'He'll always be here, Maurice,' my father told me, the day we came home from the burial. We stood at Tony's door looking at the empty bed as he held his hand over his heart.

When he left to join the women in the kitchen, I too moved my hand to my heart. I pressed in hard as I could, trying to reach Tony, to turn on the switch that would tune him in.

'Big Man, ya gobshite.'

He came in, loud and clear.

And I laughed into my closed eyes, laughed down into my boots and into my fingers that had found him. And as true as I am sitting here holding this drink in these wrinkled, dried out hands of mine, he's never left me since.

After Tony died it was me who was set to inherit the land. One of the best things my father ever taught me as I worked with him was to embrace change. I watched him clear boundary walls before the war, turning it to tillage. After it was all over, he had it back ready for grazing, quick as you like. Dairy, that was his big thing then. He saw pound signs on the hide of every cow, and in every drop of milk they yielded. He had my heart broken with all the questions about how the Dollards had run their dairy when I had worked for them. I'd no desire to remember a thing about them, but he had me pestered until he knew everything I did. His sums done, before long we had the beginnings of our own herd.

'By the time the year 2000 hits we'll be the biggest dairy farmers in Leinster, feeding the hordes of Dublin. We'll keep their tea breaks flowing,' he told me. He thought he'd live forever. Sometimes I wondered might he make it myself. A horse of a man. But he never even smelt a whisper of the twenty-first century. He went in sixty-three. Collapsed in the fields one day, fencing. Mam, now she made it 'til seventy-five. Lived with us, right up until just after you were born. She needed the nursing home by then. She'd forgotten us all, except Tony. She'd constantly ask us when we visited her, if Tony was still down the fields and when he'd be back so she could get his tea ready. Over and over, she'd ask and we'd oblige:

'Soon, he'll be back soon.' She'd sit back contented then, but within two seconds would be back at it: 'And where's Tony?' It would have been kinder to have taken her sooner. But I wonder in those years after my father died, when she had her mind, how she dealt with his passing. I never asked her how she coped losing the person she knew best. The person who accepted her humanity and all the failings that came with it. The person who loved her unconditionally. The person whose hand was always there to hold. I wish now I had.

Rainsford lay on the border with the city. Transport costs were low so we could afford to be competitive with the big milk buyers. We were in demand. Even managed to land the Gormanstown Army Camp contract. That was a good one. The stability of that set us up rightly. Allowing us the security to keep edging on, borrowing and expanding more and more. Although there were years after my father died when the milk prices were rotten. I came through it though, buoyed along by selling some bits of land.

In the late fifties, you see, we had begun to buy up little plots wherever we could find them. Farmers with their bags packed ready to leave for England, desperate to take what might be offered. We borrowed, counting on the economic tide eventually turning in our favour. We handed over the criminally small payments to those boys heading off, asking was there anyone else around in the market. If we were given a tip, we went straight there, arriving at the next deal with cash in our pockets. Some slammed their door on our insult. But others took it, ready to trade in their farming life for that of barman or labourer or miner. I often wondered, did those hands that pocketed our cash ever ache for the touch of the soil as they held the smooth glass or the cold concrete or the dusty coal of their new lives? At night in their dreams, did they move with the rhythm of a scythe or reach to calm the hind of a cow before milking?

The canniest move I ever made, not that I knew it back then, was buying that strip of land on the outskirts of Dublin, not far from the airport. It was in the sixties, got it for buttons. Little did I know how high its value would reach as time went on. I sold it for a small fortune in the end. Prime zoned land. My intention was to keep it in pasture but when I realised what kind of gold my cows were standing on, I decided to dangle it out there, to see who'd bite.

'This is ridiculous, Maurice. Would you not call a halt to it?' Sadie complained at me one evening over the bidding war that had ensued. 'It's shameful, that amount of money being talked about. It's only a couple of fields. Kevin can't believe the madness. He says the country is heading for a crash, with this Celtic Tiger.'

Well, you can imagine how I took that.

'Is that what he says now? You can tell him the next time he calls from his ivory tower over there that I will in my arse call a halt to it.'

'Please don't curse in my house.'

'Listen, if those boys want to keep raising the stakes and battling it out, I'll not stop them. No matter what little Lord Fauntleroy has to say about it. And tell me, will you be objecting when the sale buys you that new kitchen you want?'

'You've enough money already to buy new kitchens for the whole of Rainsford. And don't be calling your son that, he deserves better from you.'

In the end I lied. Told her they'd offered €500,000 below what I actually got. Her heart and her conscience, nor yours for that matter, couldn't have taken the truth. But I'm sure my father and Tony danced a jig, the day the money finally landed in my bank account. Pure magic, son.

And as for all the Dollard land that lay over our boundary wall? I was twenty-one when the hearse drove Hugh Dollard to his chapel. I stood in line on Main Street with the town. They were all out, their heads bent in reverence to the man most of us had served at some stage or another. The town hushed as his coffin made its way through the corridor we'd formed. When it came within inches of me, I turned one-eighty, to face O'Malley's butchers.

'Shame on you, Maurice Hannigan,' Mrs Roche said, after the procession had passed.

'I'll not be made a liar of,' I answered, 'and don't look at me like you never cursed them like the rest of us over the years.'

'Your mother would be disgusted if she knew.'

'Oh, she knows, I told her that's what I was planning,' I said, muscling my way down the street, through the onlookers, who one by one, began to hear news of my crime as it trickled down the line. What I hadn't said was that my mother had made no reply when I told her earlier what I was going to do. She'd simply handed over her list of messages and turned back into the house in silence.

'Have you no respect for the dead?' Roche called after me, playing to the crowd, encouraging them to join her in my condemnation.

I stopped and turned to her.

'You blessing yourself as he passed isn't going to make them treat you any better, Mrs Roche. They'll still pay you the same pittance for the washing.'

'You're nothing but a scut. Someone will put manners on you one of these days, Hannigan.'

'I look forward to them trying,' I said, bringing an end to our public debate, turning once again for home.

'You're not a patch on your brother. He knew manners.'

I didn't look back to her final and cruellest blow but stretched myself as tall as I could and strode away. When out of sight, I closed my eyes. She was right, Tony was by far a better man than me. I didn't like to think of him up there despairing and ashamed of his brother.

'I couldn't pretend, Tony,' I offered in my defence, mounting my bike, with the few messages under my arm and pedalling my way home.

Even before he'd died the Dollard fortunes had been slipping. Some said it was gambling, others bad investments. To me, it was payback. By sixty-three we'd already bought Moran's land, then Byrne's and finally Stanley's, until my land surrounded Dollard's on three sides. Slowly, I began to eat into theirs.

The strategy for buying their land was the same as with any other man. Offer low. But with them, it felt extra exhilarating. Invariably, the price I paid was paltry. Every couple of years they sold off a little more and each time my offer got lower. Until, that is, the last time.

One evening back in the early seventies, I opened my door to a young man I'd never set eyes on before.

'Good evening, Mr Hannigan,' he said, with a smile so wide it caused me to wince. 'I know these things are normally left to the agents, but I felt I had to come talk to you myself about your recent offer on the Dollard land.'

'And you are?'

'Forgive me, I'm Jason. Jason Bruton. I'm married to Hilary.'

He put out his hand.

'Hilary?'

'Yes, Rachel Dollard's daughter Hilary?'

Let me go back, son. Thomas's sister, Rachel, who'd all those years before stood and watched her brother inflict that scar on my face had left the house as soon as she was old enough. Was she even sixteen? I'm not sure. Went off to marry Reggie, some English toff. Not wealthy as it turned out and so they ended up back at the house after a few years with Amelia, the mother, after the Dollard senior died. They had one daughter, Hilary. And this Jason Bruton was Hilary's husband. When I offered him nothing to this news of who he was, he continued anyway, pulling back his unshaken hand, looking at it to make sure he wasn't mistaken, 'as I was saying, this land business—'

'Business. Now there you have it – business, not charity. Just in case that's what you're here for.'

'Quite. Well, I'd like to call a spade a spade also,' he said, clearing his throat. 'Yours is the only offer we've received. I could stand here and say we have another buyer. But you are no fool, as is plain. Therefore, I've come to ask that you consider bringing up your offer, not of course to the selling price but to one that is more . . . reasonable.'

'Well now, Jackson—'

'Jason. It's Jason.'

'And tell me, why might I want to do that?'

'May I come in, Mr Hannigan? To talk this over further, in private,' he said, looking about him as if my house was right in the middle of a housing estate.

'You may not,' I replied, pulling the door in closer behind me, emphasising my position and ensuring Sadie might not overhear.

'I see,' he said, drawing in a considered breath and then laughing. 'They did tell me this was a waste of time. Rachel and Reggie. And yet here I am, wishing I'd listened to them.'

'How's your uncle-in-law?'

'My uncle-in-law? Thomas you mean. I've no idea. I don't hear much about him. Did you know him well?' he replied, clutching at whatever straw I was willing to throw.

'You could say that.'

'He's in London. Got married again.'

'Did he now? Did he murder the first one?'

'I . . . I . . .'

'Listen, John. You've no idea how brave you are to stand at my door asking *me* for more money for *them*,' I said, jabbing my finger in the direction of the house. I paused as we held the other's eye. 'Now, unless you're telling me something I don't already know about that land, I see no reason why I would "up" the offer.'

That fairly shut him up. Or so I thought. He swallowed hard, readying himself for the battle he'd never wanted.

'Decency, Mr Hannigan, that's why. Your offer is criminal, no other word for it.'

I hadn't expected that.

'I thought if we talked it over man to man you might see your way to being fair. But it appears I'm not always right. I know when to admit defeat.' And off he went.

I liked him.

'Five.' I called into the darkness.

'Pardon?' his voice replied, before his body stepped back into the reach of my porch light.

'I'll give five thousand more. For you, mind, and that pair of balls you have. Much more impressive than any Dollard male could ever boast.'

I hoped Tony was listening.

The land was worth so much more. I knew it. He knew it. A part of me wanted to invite him in, to have a whiskey and thrash it out further, but I got over that quick enough. He stood there, looking at me, ever so slightly dazed.

'I'll ring my man in the morning, to tell him of our gentleman's agreement. You might want to go back now and tell them how you wrestled it out of me,' I added.

But before he could take a step, I called him back.

'But tell me this, Jason. There's not much land left over there now. What's the plan, when this lot of my money runs out?'

He didn't answer straight away but looked at me from squinted eyes. Eventually, he said:

'A hotel.'

'A hotel is it? Well, holy shamolie. Now there's something this town could do with, what with all the tourists we have.'

'I'll have you know, Mr Hannigan, my family has been

in the hotel business for a century. If anyone can turn this God forsaken backwater into a tourist destination, it's me.'

I liked him even more.

I smiled and closed the door. Leaning up against its frame for a moment, I considered this new departure in the Dollard fortunes.

'Who was that, Maurice?' Sadie asked, coming out from the kitchen with you waddling behind her.

'That, my dear, was Jason, the hotelier. He's got big plans for this town. We're getting ourselves a hotel.'

When I met your mother, it felt like she'd filled a small piece of the hole that Tony'd left behind. Certainly, her love took the edges off his loss a bit. It was like bubble wrap in a way. Keeping him safe and settled within me, the sharpness gone. But as mad as it sounds, I sort of resented her for robbing that little bit of him from me.

Hand on heart, in all my years without him, not a day has gone by, without me chatting to him about the cows or the price of feed or whether I should buy or sell a piece of land. The Sunday game, now that's one of our big things. He sits on my shoulder, pointing out where the players are going wrong. Such a bloody perfectionist when it comes to hurling. Addicted to it, when he was alive. Gone, every Sunday and every summer evening to play on the pitch above by the church. He dragged me along with him, even though I hadn't the heart to tell him I didn't share his passion. I played alright, but not like him, not with that soul, that drive, like he was fighting for Ireland's freedom.

'You don't have to, Big Man, you don't have to come. I

get it,' he told me one Sunday as we set out for the pitch. I must've been about fourteen.

'What are you talking about? I wouldn't miss it for the world. Watching you make a complete eejit of yourself on that pitch is the highlight of my week.' He slapped me on the back and off we went, our hurls over our shoulders.

Only the other week when we were watching the Carlow–Westmeath match he said to me: 'You were good you know, Maurice, better than me, if you'd put your mind to it. I'd have given anything to have had your talent. But you couldn't've been arsed.'

But one evening, Sadie found me out at the car staring into space, looking all worried. We must have been married a good while by then. I don't know where you were, were you even born at that stage? I thought my mind was beginning to let him go, for good. You see, I was driving home and looking out over our fields that ran a good bit of the road before our turning, when I saw him. Bent down, his arms digging away. The old brown shirt on him, like he'd always worn. I jammed on the brakes. Just before the driveway. I walked back the way to look for him, but he was gone. When I drove up the final bit to the house, it struck me that I hadn't thought of him that whole day or the day before. His name, his spirit had not passed within one inch of me from the moment I'd risen until the apparition in the field.

'Maurice, what's happened?' Sadie asked, coming out the front door, looking at me. She must've heard me pull up and been watching from the kitchen window.

I hadn't realised I was crying until she lifted her hand to my cheek.

'Nothing, nothing,' I replied, coughing my tears away,

moving my head out of her reach, 'I'm grand, woman. It's just the wind.'

I couldn't look at her. I was convinced she'd replaced him. And I couldn't bear it. Couldn't bear losing what little I had left of him in that brain of mine. I walked away from her over to the sheds. Pretended at doing something, looking at the tractor, possibly. I waited until she'd gone back in the house and then I let those tears fall. Big bucketfuls of them. Holding on to the wheel arch, leaning in, feeling like the legs might just give way. One ear cocked for the back door opening again. No one came. Eventually, I pulled myself together and went off into the house to sit for the dinner and to give your mother the excuse of a flu for my puffy eyes and weary body. But the whole evening I couldn't even glance in her direction.

I stayed in the bedroom for the evening, left her alone with the telly. I pulled out the old shoebox I had from under the bed. Dug through it and found as many photos as I could of him. I sat there on the floor, old negatives and pictures around me, staring at my favourite one: the one where we were sat in front of the butter churn outside the upper-room window of the old house. A creamy haze of a photo, curled in so much by then that I had to hold the edges back to see him properly. His left hand was raised to block out the sun. I concentrated on his face, trying to embed it in my brain. But the more I tried the more I failed. I had myself in such a state that Sadie had Lemsips, paracetamol and Vicks VapoRub all lined up. In the end I gave in, took the lot and went to sleep. I dreamed of the picture that night – Tony sitting on our old kitchen chair and me standing to his rear. My lower half hidden by the churn, my chest puffed out, smirking proudly. My hand lay protectively on Tony's shoulder, holding on for dear life, refusing to let him rise, although he tried. In the end I remember his words like he was actually beside me.

'Alright, Big Man, let me be. I'm not going anywhere.'

The next morning, I rose, knowing he'd never leave me again. Sadie was amazed at my recovery. Quizzed me on the exact concoction I'd taken for future reference. For years after we had to abide by my made-up instructions of that supposed cure whenever any of us caught a cold or flu.

But it's his living presence I've missed the most since your mother's left. And no amount of talking to him in my head can take the place of being able to see the man, to touch the skin and bone of him, to hear him sup a pint in Hartigan's. What I wouldn't give for just one hour of his company. No need for much conversation at all. Our elbows on the counter. A bottle of stout each in front of us. Half empty glasses. Looking out at the town. Tapping our feet to the music on the radio or laughing over the madness of the world. The company of the trusted, what? Being understood without having to explain and not having to pretend all is fine. Being allowed to be a feckin' mess. The feeling of his pat on my back as he passes behind me to go to the jax. Is it too much to ask for a simple resurrection?

But I'm grateful for those years I had him. Isn't that why I'm sitting here? Giving thanks for a man who shaped me, guided me, minded me and, most of all, taught me to never give up. But he's fierce quiet today, son. Hasn't said a word in my ear this whole time. I wonder, has my plan finally baffled him into silence.

Chapter Three

7.47 p.m.

Second Toast: to Molly

Glass of Bushmills – 21-year-old malt

If there's one thing I like about the bar room of this hotel, it's the light; not that I've ever shared that compliment with Emily. Perhaps I should. There's something about how the evening creeps through those front windows. They're not the original ones, the windows. They're long, thin rectangular panes that stretch from top to bottom. You can't open them. I've only ever seen the like in modern churches before. At first, I didn't take to them but now I can't get enough of watching that light streaming in at the slanted angles, showing up the dust and movement of the place. I could watch it for hours. Hypnotic, it is.

The bar is fairly hopping now. The men nod in my direction as they give their orders and extend their elbows, allowing the counter to take their weight. The cavalry has arrived to help Svetlana. Emily and a lad. Whizzing up and down. They're all arms. You'd swear they'd more than just the two each, pulling one pint while reaching for another glass to start the pump beside it flowing. Their speed and efficiency are to be admired. I could watch this dance all evening.

I recognise most of the crowd. You would too, son. Crimmens joins me. Leaning on the bar, all serious, like he's bothered by something. I take a sip of this fine whiskey before looking over at him again. It's the suit that's troubling him. He looks about as uncomfortable as I would in that get-up.

'Let me get you a drink there, Mr Hannigan.'

'I won't, now. I'm grand with what I have.'

'On the whiskey, what?'

'Are you having one yourself? Here, Emily, could you throw on a pint for Crimmens here?'

'Don't be minding him. I've one over beyond.'

For the life of me, I can't remember the chap's first name. If you were here, you'd know it. I'm sure you would. I steer my way around my memory loss as best I can. It's the faces I remember no problem these days, but the names have me stumped. He's out of Lissman. Did some business together a few years back. One of the new breed, organic this and corn-fed that. I tried it for a while. But I've let it slip of late, like everything. Still, I have to hand it to these young farmers; they've a vigour and commitment to the land that'd make my father smile.

'Do you know much about the solar panels, Mr Hannigan?' he asks, after a moment of silence between us. 'I'm thinking of getting into it. There's lads over there in England who've made a fortune giving over fields and fields to it. What do you think, would I be mad?'

'You'd be mad not to. If I were a younger man you wouldn't hold me back. I'd have done it long ago and set my sheep to graze under them.'

'Is that right? I might look into it so,' he says, nodding his head to the counter.

And then we fall into our silent contemplation again. Happy with our wanderings over this farming life and all we do to keep the bellies of the world full and our own hearts and bank balances at ease. A gong booms in the background, making me near spill my Bushmills. I never knew the place had a gong, hardly surprising, I suppose. And true to Irish custom, the horde ignores its request. Each group has to be encouraged by the hotel staff to loosen their grip from their conversations and the bar. They herd them like sheep dogs, blocking all exits and means of escape, in the direction of their dinner. Gearstick would've loved this, giving it his all until he had every last arse sitting in their seats below.

'That's me so, Mr Hannigan.' Crimmens stretches out his hand and shakes it with a strength I envy.

'Good luck now,' I say, as I watch him and the last of the crowd make their way out of the bar.

'Can you believe they've actually gone in on time?' Emily says, proud that all is going to plan. A bit of her hair has fallen out of her tight bun. It falls down at her cheek in a curl that reminds me of Sadie.

'They'd be afraid not to,' I say, grinning, getting down off my stool and heading in peace to the toilet. 'And don't be drinking that when I'm not looking,' I say, pointing at my Bushmills before going through the door with a smile.

I remember the day I took my first sip of whiskey. I was no more than twenty when I had the notion to try it. My father never touched the stuff, but I was always drawn to that rich liquid sitting in the bottles behind the bar in Hartigan's. One day I felt the bravery and ordered a glass. Well, it nearly cut the throat out of me. Coughing and spluttering, I was. Mrs Hartigan thought it hilarious. I swore there and then, I'd never do it again. But the taste stayed with me over the following days, its vileness mellowing with the passing of time, so much so that I did indeed take another. The day I tasted the 21-year-old malt, I took my cap off in reverence to her magnificence. This one here, son, is for the sister you never knew – Molly.

One of the pictures in my jacket pocket is of you on your christening day. You're in your mother's arms, wrapped in your white cocoon of a christening robe. She's stood in front of our house right before we headed to the church. 'Course I'd pulled the old house down by then and built a brand spanking new one a bit further up from the road. I think I'd a Ford Cortina back then, a red one. Sadie in her pink tweed suit with matching pill-box hat. She loved that suit, hardly ever wore it. It was still in the wardrobe until recently. All packed away now with the rest of her stuff. She's looking down on you like you're the centre of her world, like no one else matters. I only remember her looking like that one other time, three years earlier, before you came along.

Forty-nine years ago, I met Molly, only once and only for fifteen minutes. But she has lived in this dilapidated heart of mine ever since. It seems your mother and me were never meant to have more than one child. Life was not on our side with that one. We had you relatively late. I was thirty-nine and Sadie, well, she must have been thirty-four. We'd been trying of course, from the get-go. Watched all around us have one baby after another while we were blessed with none. It was hard. I took my disappointment to the fields, to the dairy, anywhere but the house. Our silent burden. Month after month, year after year, we fell deeper and deeper into the quiet sadness of it. Sadie wouldn't talk. Despite my fumbling attempts to engage her. If I'm being honest, I was relieved at her silence. What, after all, would I have said when I didn't even want to hear my own pain, let alone face up to hers. But still, the guilt of that silence dogged me as I walked my lanes and turned the key in the tractor and blessed myself at the end of Mass. It sat on my shoulder, never letting me forget that I'd failed.

They say women are good talkers. If that is true, then your mother was the exception. I didn't know her to have many friends around; acquaintances sure, but no one really close. Early on I suppose, when we were just married, she may have spoken to her mother. But I'm not convinced of that either. Their relationship didn't strike me as being that type. There was a love but of the Irish kind, reserved and embarrassed by its own humanity. These days people are all for talking. Getting things off their chest. Like it's easy. Men, in particular, get a lot of stick for not pulling their weight in that quarter. And as for Irish men. I've news for you, it's worse as you get older. It's like we tunnel ourselves deeper into our aloneness. Solving our problems on our own. Men, sitting alone at bars going over and over the same old territory in their heads. Sure, if you were sitting right beside me, son, you'd know none of this. I wouldn't know where to start. It's all grand up here in my head but to say it out loud to the world, to a living being? It's not like we were reared to it. Or taught it in school. Or that it was preached from the pulpit. It's no wonder at the age of thirty or forty or eighty no less, we can't just turn our hand to it. Engineers are not born with the knowledge of how to construct a bridge. It has to be learned. But despite all of that for some reason, back then, with all that hurt and absence in our lives, I felt the urge to give it a go.

'So, how are you now?' I managed to say to Sadie one day, nodding in the direction of the bathroom from where I'd just come and seen the evidence of another failure, a blood-soaked napkin.

'Just leave it, Maurice.'

'Sadie . . .'

'No, Maurice. I can't do this now. Please.'

She raised her hand to stop any further efforts I might attempt and simply left the kitchen. Leaving me to land in my chair and run my finger around and around the wood-knot on the table. Listening to the incessant tick of the clock over the Aga that had never gotten on my nerves before. I looked at it and considered throwing the *Meath Chronicle* in its direction. It was killing me that I couldn't fix this thing, this barren nothingness of us. For a man accustomed to being able to solve anything once he threw enough money at it, this was bloody torture.

I didn't try talking to your mam after that. We skirted around each other's lives from then on. Coming together in the bed when we tried to rid ourselves of our burden, giving it another hopeless go. Until one night she turned away from me for weeks on end. Not wanting to try any more, exhausted by our collective failure. And so, the silence grew stronger and wider and took us over until there was nothing to say over the teacups of an evening.

That was until Doctor Arthur McRory arrived in Duncashel. His practice wasn't open a wet week and there we were, in line to see him. Where she'd heard this man could help us any more than Doctor Matthews in Rainsford, I had no idea. But I came home one evening to find her standing waiting for me at the door. I was barely through it and she had the coat and boots off me. I was escorted to the table where she sat me down and took a seat beside me.

'Maurice. We're going to a doctor.'

'We are, are we?'

'He's new. In Duncashel.'

'And why might we be doing that?' I asked, having a good look around to the stove to see if there was any sign of a rasher for the tea.

'For to see. You know,' she said, nodding her head below.

'Oh, right.'

'You'll go so?'

'Suppose.'

'Grand. Tuesday. Four o'clock. You'll have to have your bath Monday night so.'

Young and confident, he greeted us with a compassion that made me wary. I wasn't used to kindness, having never looked for or given it to those beyond my own. But Sadie grasped hold of it for all it was worth, trusting and believing all he said. She did the talking. I stayed quiet while she answered every question. He tried to engage me, but it was as if there was a boulder stuck in my throat, stopping me from telling him any of those intimate details that Sadie seemed only too willing to expose. Every time a question was pointed in my direction she laid a hand on my leg and answered for me. He sent us off with our instructions and promises of further interventions.

'Tests,' he said.

I did manage to say one thing to him just before we said our goodbyes:

'And how much will all this cost us?'

Sadie shoved me out the door.

Over the coming weeks and months, we had tests and charts and appointments coming out our ears. It drove me demented. 'Rhythm' fecking this and 'cycle' fecking that. I hadn't a clue. I just did what I was told. Performed when it was required and looked for nothing when the calendar had a big mark through it.

'Well, everything is looking very well, Sadie, I must say,' Doctor McRory beamed at her one spring day. 'The reports are showing no difficulties. If we keep going as we are [we? I thought], I'm hopeful that soon there might be news. Yes, it's all looking very promising.'

He hadn't lied. Within three weeks of that great proclamation, our teatimes came back to life. Sadie was indeed pregnant. She couldn't be contained for the joy of the news over the following months. And neither could I. Everywhere I turned the world was a nicer place. People were nicer. I was nicer. I bantered with Lavin, smiled at Nancy Regan in the street and even tipped my cap to the bank manager.

Our little Molly was to be born 9th of January 1966. Not that we knew it was a girl for sure. Or should I say, not that I knew. From the get-go Sadie was convinced of it. She'd bought pink and yellow bedding and a couple of wee dresses, as she said herself, home from one of her trips to Duncashel. The little heart was beating perfectly Sadie was told, at every visit to the Doctor. Limbs dancing and kicking away, elbowing her mammy to pure ecstasy. It was

a happy time. They say women glow when they are pregnant. It was no different with Sadie. The woman shone.
Everything about her seemed alive and triumphant in the
happiness of what was to come.

Things couldn't have been better for me workwise either.
I was powering away. All the bits of business, the cows,
the land buying was motoring better than I'd hoped. I had
gotten into leasing machines at that stage, combines and
tractors. I had a few on the go. I was putting the hours in
and seeing the benefits. I had a whole team of lads around
me, taking care of the everyday stuff while I was off making
sure the bigger picture kept expanding. They were good
lads, dependable. Things felt as they should be: a happy
wife, a new home and a baby on the way. I was doing right
by everyone. Making sure they would never have to worry
about anything and want for nothing, or so I thought.

I arrived home one evening to find Sadie sitting in the
kitchen staring at her eight-month-old bump, holding it.

'I can't feel her, Maurice,' she said, looking up at me.

'Sure, she'll be asleep.' I went over to her and hunkered
down, putting my hand on hers, on Molly. 'Having an auld
snooze.'

'But not now, Maurice. She's usually doing somersaults
at this time.'

'Ah, don't be worrying. I'll make the tea. You just go on
and have a lie down on the bed,' I said, distracted by a
meeting I had planned that evening with Jim Lowry, a
solicitor from Navan. He was selling some land up in north
Meath on behalf of the estate of a farmer who'd died a
few weeks prior. I'd gotten a sniff of it on the grapevine
and approached him immediately. I had plans to begin

leasing my machinery up that end of the county. No one else was operating there at the time. It wasn't a huge farm by any means. What I wanted were his sheds. Big and modern they were. Secure enough for my machines. The revenue would be good enough with Cavan, Monaghan and Louth on the doorstep. An opportunity not to be missed.

Sadie did as she was told and lay in the bed all evening, staring at our Molly's quietness.

At eight, I popped my head around the bedroom door.

'Just going out for a half hour, Sadie. You sleep, and I'll be back before you know it.'

I didn't wait for her reply, didn't respond to her worried face, simply marched my way out of there to secure another bargain. With not a shred of guilt or concern, I turned the key in the ignition and drove off down the driveway.

At around eleven I came home with the deal done. Happy out. I crept into the bedroom, tiptoeing to the bed only to find her still wide awake.

'Where were you?' she said, her voice unsteady. 'I rang every hotel in the county looking for you. You said you wouldn't be long.'

'It took a bit longer than I thought.' I was sitting on the side of the bed taking off my socks.

'She's gone, Maurice.' Her words steadier now – matter-of-fact almost. No tears, no hysterics. Was there blame, though? I can't remember the sting, even if she had intended it. Just – she's gone. 'We'd better go,' she added.

I got up and followed her to the car for the trip to Dublin. Not one word passed between us the whole way. They induced her the next day. Fifteen minutes, that's how long we held her. Our little porcelain doll with her golden hair.

Plump cheeks, a dimpled chin and a red birthmark on her lower lip, like she'd been sucking away at it for all that time in her mammy. Still and quiet, she lay in Sadie's arms with no breath to feel the rise and fall of, to awe over. But that didn't stop your mother rocking and singing to her. Her tears falling on the yellow blanket.

'Molly,' she said, 'that's who she is. Our beautiful Molly.'

I had to take her from your mother's arms. May you never, son, never have to do that. It felt as if someone had my insides in their hands and was squeezing them as tightly as possible, trying to drain the life and will from me. I felt the physical pain of it, as I gently took Sadie's hand away, cradling the bundle of our making in the crock of my arm. She was magnificent, that little thing, our magnificent Molly. I lay my lips against her soft cheek and let my body convulse in the grief of never having known her and of never being afforded the opportunity.

'I'm so sorry,' I whispered into her ear, into the crisp cotton smell of the blanket. Sorry for not having whisked her and her mother away to the hospital the minute I walked in the door the previous night, giving the mite the chance she'd deserved.

Despite her closed eyes and the anguish of my guilt, I smiled for her, showing her my endless, hopeless unquestionable love before giving her away to the midwife. I grabbed your mother's hand as our daughter left the room in the arms of a stranger. I knelt by her side and laid my head on her lap. She ran her fingers back and forth through my hair, before I felt the weight of her head on mine.

The funeral was small. We stood beside Molly in her tiny white coffin. Your mother closest, then me with my arm around her, giving support should she fall. There was my mother, your aunt May – the only one of my sisters who could make it back in time, although Jenny did come back a month later to have a few days with us – your granny Mary and grandfather Michael and your Auntie Noreen. Doctor McRory, and Robert Timoney senior, the solicitor from home. The chapel in the basement of the hospital smelled clinical, despite the best efforts of the flowers and aromatic candles. Three rectangular windows up high, let in the only light there was. It was a bright, crisp winter's day – blue sky and the whitest of wispy clouds skitting across it like they were in a race to something good beyond that I couldn't see. I remember watching them as the hum of the prayers and cars passing in the street above held the room. The hospital chaplain led the small service alongside Father Forrester, the parish priest from Rainsford. We brought Molly home to be buried. The same grave in which your mother now lies, five rows down from Tony and my father. I don't think I opened my mouth once, not in homage to the Lord nor to those who shook my hand as I stood by the graveside. Molly's loss had all but taken the will out of me.

During the year that followed, I returned to spending as much time as I could away from the house and Sadie. Me and my guilt stayed out until after midnight and rose before the dawn. Avoiding her eyes, her accusation, that she had every right to level. What a fool I'd been, what a damned stupid fool, allowing a piece of land and a handshake to rule me. The 'if onlys' tore at me in the day and in the suffocation of the night. Dragging on my breath and haunting my dreams. I watched Sadie from the corner of my eye, when I thought she couldn't see me. I saw her pale skin grow old before me. The worry-lines, digging deeper, taking hold. I was powerless, to stop the silver sneaking into her hair. I closed my eyes to it and left. It seemed those months were full of closing doors – me, always on the other side, running away from what I'd done.

Did she watch me too, I wonder? And if she did, what did she see? I couldn't even look in the mirror for fear of what I'd find there. So convinced was I, that greed dripped out of every pore, into the dark shadows under my eyes and the crevice of my scar. It felt as if my voice had lost its magic, and in its place, I croaked.

'We'll be grand, Doctor,' I said, the first day Doctor McRory called by, waylaying me in the yard, his case in his hand. It must have been a couple of weeks, maybe a month after the funeral. I didn't lift my head to him. But concentrated on the stick I held. Tapping it against the side of my boot. Waiting until he got the hint to leave.

'I'd like to see her, Maurice. To check she's OK. I take it you'll not object if I go on in.'

The stick tapped out its rhythm louder and longer, as we waited. Of course, I objected. Jesus, could the man not leave us to the awfulness before he came 'round, poking his nose in. But in the end, I lifted the stick towards the house, giving the permission he was looking for, and off I went down to the fields, saying nothing.

To be fair to him, his intentions were good and he never let up. If he hadn't, God knows how things might have ended up. I found evidence of his visits around the house when there was nothing further to distract me and keep me from going home. Pamphlets lay beside the kettle or on the little table beside my armchair where I put my tea and the handful of biscuits. They remained unread, covered in crumbs and teacup stains. But the more I ignored them the more they seemed to multiply. Eventually, one found its way into my jacket pocket. I pulled it out in the tractor one day, looking for a rag: *Working Through Your Grief.* She had put nothing in there about working through your culpability. I crumpled it up. Crumpled loads of them in fact, whenever I found one in the house.

'I want to try for another,' Sadie said, into the darkness after I'd crept into our bed one night some weeks later. Late it was, about two in the morning. It'd been past midnight when I came in. I'd fallen asleep in front of the telly and had woken to that awful hum they used to have on back when there was no such thing as all-night TV.

'Fine,' I replied, like it was nothing. It was anything but. Truthfully, I didn't want another, may God forgive me. I didn't want you. What madness had come over her, I wondered, as I stared above me into the darkness? Did she not know who slept beside her? A man whose greed was put before his child's life. Is this who she wanted to father another, if by some miracle it made it to us?

But I didn't deny her. I owed her.

I was as nervous the next night as if it was my first time. No, it was worse. I shook, unable to control myself. Petrified, I waited for her, as she got ready in the bathroom. When at last she arrived, I made myself look at her face and deep into her eyes. In that moment I begged her to let me be, to remove this burden. But she laid her hand upon my cheek, lowered her face to mine and kissed me, imparting a forgiveness so deep and honest that I had to fight back my tears of relief and gratitude. Her kindness flowed through me, saving me, bringing me home.

The nine-month wait for you was the hardest of my life, or so I thought back then. I didn't know whether I was coming or going, I mean that literally. I'd be halfway down the driveway in the morning and would turn back to make sure Sadie was OK. Or I'd call her incessantly from wherever I was. Like the evening I held up the phone in Royal County Hotel, when she told me she'd vomited.

'For pity's sake, Maurice. It was just the bacon we had for the dinner. It didn't agree with me, that's all. You're causing me more trouble every time I have to haul myself up from the couch to answer the phone,' she said, after my fourth call.

I hadn't wanted to go to the bloody meeting at all, but Sadie insisted, nearly pushing me out the door. And then there was the weekend she decided to visit her father to stay for the couple of days. I dropped her off with the intention of heading back after a cup of tea. But I couldn't make myself start the car. I ended up staying too.

And as for the Doctor's visits, I made every one.

'Maurice! Back so soon?' Doctor McRory said, on another of our weekly visits that I insisted on.

You made it in the end. Strong as an ox. Screamed your way into our life on the 20th of February 1969, like you were screaming for two. Maybe Molly had left a small bit of her breath in there for her baby brother. That's what Sadie said, and she laughing in the bed, holding you to her. I watched Molly grow, alongside you. With each of your milestones, I have imagined hers also. Her first step. Her first word. First day at school. Her debs. 'Course I never told Sadie a hint of the fact that her daughter has lived in my head all this time, loving her life; the picture of her mother. Blonde hair, though, with a little wave in it that Sadie would have envied. Slight but not too dainty, just the right side of it. Determined. Doing whatever she set her mind to. A great sense of what's right and wrong in the world. No middle ground with her. No grey area in between. I like that in her. But, for all her bravado, she has a vulnerability that's made me want to make the world just right for her.

Mad isn't it? There you were, my living son right in front of me, waiting to be noticed, but my head lingered with a ghost. My heart, missing a small beat of its rhythm. Not so unlike my mother after all.

It wasn't just me I blamed for Molly's death, you know. Our maker had to answer the charge also. It's true my faith was tested when Tony was taken but when He decided on Molly too, well, I called it a day. Your mother still believed. I'd walk her to the door of the church for Mass and there we'd part ways. I'd hang around outside or go back to sit in the car. I couldn't go inside. I wouldn't give Him the pleasure.

I made my peace with Him, in a manner of speaking, after you were born. He never received my full forgiveness, though. My faith never felt quite the same again. I know the theory: these things are put here to test us, with one hand He taketh and so on. But all the words in the bible and the placations of Father Forrester could never smooth the injustice of Molly's death. I've only crossed over the threshold of His house for funerals – Noreen's, not to mention your mother's but that's different. I did that for

Sadie, that's nothing got to do with Him. We have an unwritten rule now, Him and me. He lets me live my life as I see fit and in return I say the odd quiet prayer in my head. Our gentleman's agreement works. We've made a new one of late, His greatest test yet. But I can't be getting into that yet. There's an order in which I want to do this. Bear with me just a little longer.

Emily reminds me of Molly. Small, fair haired, precious looking. When she stood before me on that first day, all I could see was my daughter. Floored, I was. Could barely get the words out of my mouth, to book the rooms. Did I tell you that bit yet, about the first day I met Emily?

You see, true to his word back well after you were born, Jason Bruton, Hilary Dollard's husband and Emily's father, did the hotel conversion. It opened in 1977. We were invited to the opening but I purposely hid the invitation from your mother. She'd only have wanted to go. I'd seen Jason around the village over the years since our showdown. He'd nod in my direction or mouth a very curt hello. Always in a rush somewhere. In return I'd raise my index finger, not too high mind. Regret is too strong a word, but I wish I'd made an effort to know him. There was something trust-worthy in his bravery the night he'd stood at our front door asking me to give more money for the Dollard land. But even if I had reached across the divide and stopped for a chat on those days we passed each other by, I doubt he'd have given me the time of day. I wouldn't have, had the shoe been on the other foot. In the end, he possibly came out the better man. It was your wedding, nineteen years later in ninety-six that did that.

'Mr Hannigan, it's my absolute pleasure to welcome you

to the Rainsford House Hotel,' he said, standing at his reception, holding out his hand once more to me on the day of the viewing. 'We've had our doubters, but here we are, defying the odds, ready to spend your money,' he said, a big grin on his face.

Oh, he was good. It was like he'd been waiting for that moment for years. I couldn't help but smile. But it was you who shook his hand and drew him away. As I stood there looking over at the pair of you, I noticed his ill-fitting suit and the sunken cheeks. When I'd first met him he was a young man, handsome and strong, but now he wore more than signs of age. He held his hollow body, like it might cave in if someone were to grab his shoulders and push down. Cancer, not that I knew it then. He died three months later.

'The wedding! What about the wedding, Maurice?' Your mother shrieked at me the day she heard the news of Jason's passing. 'They'll still go ahead with it. I mean Hilary will still keep the hotel going won't she?'

'Might we let the man rest first, Sadie? Give his wife a chance, before you start badgering her.'

'Thank you, Maurice. Thank you for pointing that out to me because I was just about to march up there to ask her about it. What kind of woman do you take me for, Maurice Hannigan?'

When my full name was used, I knew to shut up.

'I'll ring Kevin. What time is it over there? I can never figure this out. Maurice? Maurice, what time is it over in the States?'

There was a deluge of calls back and forth. All sorts of scenarios were discussed between the pair of you from the hotel closing down permanently, to, the Lord preserve us, marquees – in our garden no less. I fairly shifted in my chair at that one. But after three weeks of speculation and worry and a massive phone bill, it all died down. The hotel went on as normal, much to my despair.

'Maurice, do you not care about your only child's wedding? It's like as if you wouldn't mind if the whole hotel went up in smoke.'

'If only dreams *could* come true, Sadie.' A clever man would not have said that. Instead, he would have protested at such an injustice being levelled, proclaiming his unquestioning support for his son's wishes.

'You and your stupid feuds. You're a petty little man, who can't see what he has in front of him. Your son, our beautiful boy, is getting married and wants to do so in that hotel and all you can think about is how mean they were to you when you worked for them. Well get over it. Bosses aren't meant to be nice. But you know who is supposed to be? A father. Yes, loving and kind, apparently. You're doing a grand job of that one now, aren't you?'

She rose from the chair, threw her knitting on the sofa, walked past me, slamming the sitting-room door. There was no dinner, or tea, or supper to be had in our house for seven long days thereafter. No stews, no scones, no freshly baked soda bread, although I did arrive home one day as its aroma wafted through the air. But as I could find no evidence of its existence I assumed my longing was playing tricks on me. As it turned out, however, while I ate shop-bought bread and butter sandwiches on the sofa, she enjoyed the soda bread in our bedroom. For it was there she was holed up in protest. Door locked and radio on. I slept in your room. How she had survived without the telly I've no idea. Although, I suspect, her being a dab hand with the VCR, she was taping everything in the evening and watching it during the day when I left. A clever woman. A woman in whose hands a grudge was respected and played out to its fullest potential. On day seven, I waved the white flag.

It had taken me the full week to think of something that would end the war. I ruminated on it in great detail, thinking through the pros and cons of each option with both Tony and Molly. Flowers and Dairy Milk chocolate wouldn't cut it this time. But after a glass of whiskey at Hartigan's, we had it. I slipped the envelope under our bedroom door, leaving a corner sticking out on my side so I'd see when she picked it up. And when I saw it disappear, I left her to it and went to my refuge on the sofa. She was down in less than a minute. Sat beside me and laid her head on my shoulder. We didn't say anything for a while, but our hands found each other. In silence, we looked across at the family photo of the three of us over the fire-place, soon to be replaced, I had already been told, once Rosaleen said 'I do.'

'You're a good father.'

'There's always room for improvement,' I answered, relieved at my reprieve.

'Have you told them yet?'

'Sure, didn't I ring them Thursday. It's all arranged. They'll be home in three weeks for a weekend treat in the hotel. It's all paid for.'

'And you arranged all that yourself?'

'I'm a grown man, Sadie.'

'I know, but that can't have been easy, going in there on your own and all.'

'Sure, I was fine. It took me all of five minutes to arrange the rooms.'

'The rooms? Maurice, you do know they're living together over there.'

'They can do what they like over there. But over here they'll have two rooms for three nights.'

There was of course a small lie in what I'd told her: it had bothered me, and bothered me greatly to walk into that place, voluntarily. But my desperation gave me the incentive to stand at that reception desk to arrange a weekend visit home for the pair of you. As the girl approached me from the rear office, I had to brace myself.

There she was – my Molly – or at least how I'd always imagined her, all confidence and smiles but with a lovely air of modesty dancing around the edges. I swallowed hard as my hands held on to the reception counter and I came to my senses. You see, despite it all, I could see them in her.

'Well, you have to be a Dollard,' I said, when I finally found my voice.

'No, I'm a Bruton. I'm Emily Bruton. My grandmother was a Dollard though, Rachel Dollard.' No more than twenty at that point, she had the most beautiful of smiles. Her voice was sweet and light, innocent almost.

'So you're Jason's daughter?'

'Yes, that's right: Jason and Hilary.'

'I liked your father.'

'He was a very good man . . .' She nodded and looked down at her hands, smiling as if a particular pleasant memory had come to mind. 'I'm sorry, I don't know your name. I'm only just getting to know everyone. Having been away at boarding school and university means I've lost touch a bit. And now, well, because of Daddy, I've come home to help.'

She looked at me with her kind brown eyes. I smiled back knowing this would all change once she heard my reply.

'Hannigan. Your neighbour.'

I paused, to let the news sink in.

'Ah. Mr Hannigan.'

As quick as you like, her bright eyes dulled with the mistrust and dislike of the man who'd bought up their land. 'Well, I see,' she said pushing her hair behind her ear, coughing, buying more time, 'how can I help?'

At first I thought I was going a bit mad, thinking she was like Molly. But over the months when I got to know her more, the feeling didn't change. In fact if anything, it got stronger. It was her character. Her graciousness, her courageousness with life. Thrown as she was into this place. Her life choices taken from her so young. There she was, her father having died, left with a broken-hearted mother and a hotel to run. Hilary, the mother, hadn't an ounce of interest in it, Emily told me later. Had been dead set against it becoming a hotel in the first place. In fact when she'd first met Jason in Dublin, in his family-owned hotel, she thought she'd found her way out. A way to be rid of the crumbling house. Rachel and Reggie, her parents seemed to hate it as much as her.

'If that's what he wants, Hilary, let him have it,' Rachel had told her daughter when she'd first heard of Jason's plan. 'Frankly, I don't care what he does, I just want heat. For once in my lifetime in this blasted place, I would like to feel warm. If he can manage that then he can build a bloody zoo.'

Emily's legacy – the Rainsford House Hotel.

Had she lived, Molly that is, I believe she would have lived her life, like Emily, always righting things and sorting things with that same selflessness. I feel she'd have taken her father in hand. I might be a different man altogether.

'I'm not the ogre they make me out to be, you know,' I said, that first day as I stood across from Emily. She lowered her head to the computer to make the booking for your stay.

'I didn't say you were.'

'You didn't have to,' I paused, searching her face, wondering if she might let me in at all. It was an odd sensation, this worrying about what others thought of me. 'It was all just business you know, buying the land. Nothing personal.' I coughed then and felt myself floundering around like some fish washed up on a beach. But somehow I got myself together and said this: 'It can't be easy with your father gone.'

She stopped what she was doing and looked at me for what seemed like ages, like she was trying to figure me out. She said nothing. I was a bit stumped as to where to go from there. It was then I noticed her tears. She leaned her elbows on the desk and sobbed. Funny isn't it, what you remember in those moments of panic. It was the sound of jingling coins. I must have had my hands in my pockets foostering with my money, while I stood looking at her like a mute gom.

'Ah, here,' I might've managed. Or maybe I stretched out my hand on the counter to attempt some kind of useless comfort. 'Wait there,' I do remember saying after a bit, when things weren't looking like they were getting any better, 'I'll be back.'

I went off to the bar, returning with two Bushmills only to find her missing. Bold as you like, I went around the counter and knocked on the office door. Not waiting for a reply, I opened it to find her with her head still in her hands at a desk.

'Drink this,' I said, as I placed the whiskey beside her. 'It'll steady you.'

She looked at it, then me. Finally taking it from my outstretched hand, she smelt it before taking some and grimacing.

'Takes a bit of getting used to alright,' I said, having a healthy mouthful of my own.

'They hate you, Mr Hannigan,' she said, after swallowing her second mouthful. 'You paid them far too little for far too much. That's what they've always told me.'

'They're not wrong. I'm a businessman. I'll not apologise for that.'

Surprisingly, she gave the briefest of smiles. She was more composed now, sitting back in her seat. She gestured to a chair opposite her at the other side of the desk. I took it and sat as she tapped her fingernails at her glass, watching the liquid shiver under the impact.

'It killed him. This place, this bloody dream of his. It killed my father,' she continued, not looking at me but at the whiskey before tipping it back, shuddering and laying the empty glass on the desk before her. 'We are in debt up to our necks,' she added, speaking to the empty tumbler. 'And my mother, well, what can I say . . . she's heartbroken and totally out of it. She can't face the mess. Losing money hand over fist in a hotel that no one will want to buy.'

'You're trying to sell?'

'Oh, it's not on the market. Not yet anyway. That's what I'm here for. To try to figure it all out. Mother's drugged up to the eyeballs. So it's just me. It's all up to me.'

She looked about her, surveying her empire. 'And look at the fine job I'm doing,' she laughed, as her hand gestured enthusiastically in my direction, while those big clear eyes of hers came to rest on mine, 'confessing all to the enemy. Does that make you happy, Mr Hannigan?' she asked, leaning into the desk, towards me. 'To know that we are at last about to fall.'

What more had I expected from her? To be forgiven for what I'd done to them. For the satisfaction I had felt as each piece of land they lost became mine. For checking the land registry in the county council every year or so to see my name as owner of what once was theirs. Did I expect this young girl, who I imagined as my own not ten minutes ago, to say none of that mattered? That her father's death could not be laid at my door. I sat there, my whiskey not yet gone, letting the silence, save for the hum of the computer sitting on her desk, fill the room. I swirled the last of the liquid in the glass, and watched it catch at the sides and fall to the bottom, before swirling it again and again and again, like a child with a spinning top, mesmerised by its simplicity. And when at last the time came to either leave, without your surprise holiday, or bite the bullet and reply, I looked at her, took the last of my whiskey and said:

'I worked here once, you know.'

'Yes, mother mentioned it.'

'It wasn't a particularly nice place. Your great-grand-father Hugh was not an easy man. And as for your great-uncle Thomas . . . Let's just say those men knew how to throw a punch. This here, see this,' I pointed to my scar, 'that was him.'

'Oh God.' Her brief glance and wince at my face was enough to lower her head and to give a sigh that felt more hopeless than any of her words gone before. She raised her fist to her mouth and looked off to a future, I imagined, she neither wanted nor asked for. I saw the tears well and glisten again. It was then that I felt regret for drawing her in on a history that was not really hers, to suggest a blame she had no power over.

'How much do you need?' I asked. It took her by surprise as much as it did me. But there it was.

'How much do I need, for what?' she asked, slumping back into her chair, wiping at her eyes.

'To keep this place going. You said you wanted to sell it. How much not to?'

And that's how it began, my foray into the hotel trade. As simple as that. Robert, the solicitor, was killed trying to get me to reconsider.

'Are you mad, Maurice? No one's investing in hotels. Not round these parts anyway. Stick to the machines man.' But he never turned me.

'Do it,' I told him, my fist landing on his desk, frightening the bejesus out of the both of us. Never challenged me again.

Emily, Robert and I have kept the secret of it. Sadie, you

and Hilary have never known a thing. But Molly, Molly knew. I told her. I met her not long after the papers were signed. Off out on one of my walks through the fields. She came up alongside me, then ran past me. I'd say she was twelve, nothing more. That is one of the things about her visits, I never know what age she might be. I told her as she twirled about me, her eyes closed, spinning and spinning, laughing with the dizziness. I thought she'd not heard me. But before she left, whirling off into her noth-ingness again, she smiled and gave me a thumbs up. It was good enough for me.

I hold a forty-nine per cent share of this place. Forty-nine per cent of this stool with a hundred per cent of my arse sitting on it. Forty-nine per cent for this scar on my face, for a robbed childhood and Thomas Dollard, an enemy for life. What would you all have thought the night of the wedding, had you known when we danced on its floors and ate its food and you, the happy couple, slept in its bed, that it was mine. It was my dark, shameful secret. It was nothing to be proud of. Nothing to boast about. Nothing I wanted the world to know. I have stayed away from it, not wanting to be reminded. That's what me and Emily agreed. I left her to it. The exemplary silent partner.

Emily has steered the place through. Even when the recession hit six years back, she managed to hold her steady. Robert has acted as my agent, allowing me my freedom to remain outside of it. Never allowing it to pull me into its lair.

But as much as my decision has weighed heavily on me over the years, I've always felt it has been far worse for Emily. After all, the only person with the potential to be offended on my side was me, and I seemed to be managing it, to an extent. But for Emily, well, that was a different kettle of fish. Surely for her it was a matter of betrayal. Did she feel her father turn in his grave the day she shook my hand? We never really talked about it after. Somehow it felt sordid. This place we found ourselves in was something that perhaps should never have happened had human weakness not stepped in our way. Over the years that followed we kept ourselves to ourselves, just as with our secret. All this time, never speaking about it again, until the day Robert came looking for me.

It was in 2006. Ireland was in the height of the boom. Money was coming out our ears, or so they told us. Personally, I couldn't have complained. My family was comfortable, more than, in fact. You and Rosaleen had Adam with Caitríona on the way. Your mother and me in our twilight years, working out as well as we might have hoped. So when Robert came waylaying me about the hotel, I didn't want to know a thing about it.

He'd tracked me down to a farm in Balnaboy where Francie was harvesting a few acres. I'd gone along to check all was going well. Best always to keep an eye. No matter how good your lads are, the odd spot check doesn't do any harm. I'd finished having the chat with Francie and was heading back to the jeep at the far end of the field when I saw Robert's Range Rover pull up. I watched him get out and walk over to my Jeep and lean his back against my driver door. He waved. I didn't bother to reply.

'Well,' I said on arriving within earshot.

'Maurice. How's she faring?'

I came up along beside him and stood at my rear door. We remained that way for a bit, looking out on the cut rows. Like a badly shaved head, they were. Tufts sticking up everywhere. But the gold being poured into those trailers at the top of the field was a sight to behold. The yield was great that day. When I saw them fill, grains rushing down the funnel like some powerful waterfall, my heart fluttered a little. Not that it was my own grain. But still, the sight of a yield such as that always gave me a thrill. Robert pulled at a forlorn stalk and started to shred what was left of it. I watched him take it apart until only flakes remained and fell from his hand into the wheel tracks below.

'Emily was over with me. She was wondering would you call to see her tonight.'

I looked at him, then out at the fields.

'No.' I said.

'An hour. That's all she wants.'

I watched Francie turn the harvester to begin on another row of oats. Inch by inch the crop was swallowed up. When he was a quarter of the way up the line, I'd had my fill of Robert waiting for me to change my mind and decided it was time to move on. I stood in front of him.

'Listen,' I said, 'that's your job to talk business with her. That's what I pay you for.'

I gestured for him to move. But he held his ground.

'Hilary's away, she said. It's nothing to worry about.'

'Well, that's alright then. Because we all know what a fierce man I am for the fretting.'

'Ah, Jesus, Maurice. An hour. It won't kill you. Seven, she said.'

And with that he left my door and opened his own. 'I'm

texting her now that you'll be there, on the dot,' he said, hanging out of his open window, his fingers already pressing buttons on his phone. He turned to me with a smile, pushed his last button, winked, and drove away.

I arrived at seven fifteen. The place was busy. There was a bit of activity around the reception desk so it was a while before I came to rest my elbow on it.

'Is she about?' I asked.

'Yes indeed, Mr Hannigan,' the young man said to me. I hadn't a clue who he was and was a little taken aback that he knew me. 'Let me show you the way. If you'll follow me.' He had an accent I couldn't place. He rounded the counter with a big smile. My hands found their way back into my pockets and I followed him. He led me to a wide, expansive meeting room. Long trestle tables were pushed to the sides, leaving one round table in the middle, all set for dinner.

'If you'd like to take a seat here. I'll let Miss Bruton know you've arrived.'

He held out one of the chairs for me but I waved away his offer. He gave a courteous bow and left.

I sauntered to the table, giving it a good once over. All she was short of was the romantic candles. An envelope with my name on it stood leaning up against the vase of flowers in the centre. I took it up, turned it over once or twice, before replacing it and moving away to the windows to take in the street. I inhaled deeply like I might be able to smell the evening air outside, but what met me was the smell of business. The crisp clean air of efficiency, washed fabrics and hoovered carpets intermingling with the slightest waft of the posies from the table. I watched the cars come and go over the bridge. At the far side of it, I could see two people make their way into Hartigan's, but I couldn't place them. To my left, the lights went out in Lavin's newsagents. I saw the door at the back of the shop that led to his private quarters close, pulling the last of the light out, leaving the place in darkness. The outside of the shop looked naked without its postcards and plastic toys that usually hung from the metal bars of his awning. When I heard the door behind me open, I turned my body a little in its direction, my head to the side.

'You know I'm a happily married man,' I called into the room.

'And a good evening to you too,' she replied.

I turned back to the road for a minute.

'Will you be standing over there for the whole evening or might you be joining me?'

'Robert said nothing about dinner. I've eaten already.'

I turned fully to face her now.

'Well, I'm ravenous.'

She was seated and raised her hand in invitation to the chair opposite. My hands still in my pockets, I walked back and sat like a man waiting for a bus that was about to arrive. I felt her eyes on me.

'Shall I put you out of your misery, Mr Hannigan, and tell you what this is all about?' she asked. I shrugged. 'It's ten years. Ten years since you gave me . . . since we went into partnership.'

I hadn't realised. 'Is that right?' I said, releasing one of my hands to take off my cap and run it through my hair.

'And, given this place is at last turning a profit, I thought it only proper that we should celebrate.' I raised an eyebrow.

'Robert tells me you never ask about the place. That you don't even care about your return, small enough though it's been over the years.'

I'm not sure what she expected of me. My head struggled with the various words I might offer, but I could settle on none. The door opened behind her and in came a waiter, again no one I knew, with two plates and laid them before us. A second waiter followed with a bottle of both red wine and Bushmills. He poured the red for Emily and the Bushmills for me, leaving the bottles down on the table. Emily smiled at them as she laid a napkin in her lap.

'Thank you,' she said beautifully, to the lads as they departed.

'It's steak.' Her attention turned back to me as the rich aroma did a good job at enticing me. 'I decided against a starter. I thought if I could hold you here for one course I'd be doing well. Please,' she said, gesturing towards my plate.

I reached for my glass. And drank down a hefty portion, settling myself. I played with the food. I had little room given the scrambled egg Sadie had handed up to me not an hour previously. But it seemed rude not to have something so I cut into the steak. The blood ran from it, the meat near bouncing at the touch. It wasn't charred to a crisp like you get in some places. I'll never understand the Irish obsession with burning the goodness out of a good hunk of beef.

'There's something there for you,' she said, breaking the silence. 'Just this once I wanted you to see what you have done. Open it,' she added, dabbing her mouth with the napkin and watching me.

I put down my fork, lifted my head briefly and reached for it. Her eager eyes followed my fingers as they fumbled to open it. At one stage I thought she might grab it from me, my progress obviously slower than she'd hoped. Finally, I pulled the contents free. It was a cheque.

'Our best year yet, Mr Hannigan. That's your share.'

I looked at her before replacing the cheque in its envelope and laid it down beside my plate. I moved uncomfortably in my chair and then sat back to consider it.

'I thought you'd be happy. It's a sizeable amount. I mean I've worked so hard and, well, I—'

'Emily,' I finally said, 'this whole thing,' I said gesturing to the room, 'the investment, it was never about the money.' I surprised myself. It was like I was listening to someone else, someone who genuinely didn't care about wealth. I sat there wondering how I could ever explain the many truths of it all, the motivation behind what I had done ten years prior when I didn't understand it fully myself. How would it have sounded? . . . I did it because you reminded me of a ghost.

'It was the wedding,' I said, instead. 'If you'd shut up shop there and then, Kevin would've been left without a wedding. I'd never have heard the end of. Probably would've ended up with a bloody marquee in the front garden.'

I smiled at her. She seemed to relax, buying the half-truth of it. She began to eat again and laughed a little, at what I wasn't quite sure, as she worked through the deliciousness of everything on her plate. When we finished the meal, with which I had surprised myself, finishing the entire thing, I took the envelope and handed it back to her.

'I don't want it.'

She took it, considering me and this madness that had come over me. It didn't seem right to take what had never been expected nor wanted.

'But you can't,' she said, 'you can't *not* take it.'

The waiters arrived once more and her bewilderment disappeared and was replaced by a gracious smile. They refilled our glasses before taking the plates and leaving. She held the envelope in her hand like it was a bad school report she could not bear to open.

'Listen,' I said, 'why don't you invest that back into the place.'

She lowered it, looking baffled and a little sad. A daughter hurt when her father hasn't given enough praise for a picture she's worked so hard on. Well, what can I say, that sent alarm bells going in my head. I was afraid of what I might do or say just to appease her and make her smile that magnificent smile again. I needed to nip my vulnerability in the bud quick smart or God knows what I would've bought this time.

'OK, the truth is someday I may need you to buy my share back,' I lied, 'so it would be best all round if you kept that, just in case,' I said nodding at the cheque.

'Why? Are you in trouble?'

'I'm just saying, you never can tell what's around that corner.'

I watched her and wondered was she swallowing any of this. She laid the cheque down where her plate had been, still looking at it like none of it made sense. I wanted to put her out of her misery, to offer her something she could do for me, to take the weight from her. I thought quickly and in the end this is what I asked:

'There is something you could do for me, though. In recompense, if that's what this is about.' She lifted her head then in hopeful expectation that the puzzle I had presented could finally be solved. 'You could tell me about why Thomas Dollard lost out on his inheritance because of that coin that went missing all those years ago.'

Her face dropped so quickly that it took me aback.

'Seriously?' she asked.

'Well, yes,' I said in return. 'I've been meaning to ask you about it for years. None of it ever made sense to me.'

She breathed deeply. Took a long sip of her drink and held the glass in front of her for a bit, staring at the remains. I didn't know where she or her smile had gone and I sat there wishing I'd never turned up at all. I'd been tempted to do just that, of course, to stay at home for once, with the feet up, beside my wife. Nothing seemed more inviting now than an episode of one of those soap operas she watched. I took a gulp of my own drink, still holding my tongue and waiting. After a while Emily put down hers and looked at the table edge, along which she ran her finger. Her nails a deep, rich purple.

'It's Edward VIII,' she continued, her hands now holding her napkin, her fingers running along its folds. 'Edward and Mrs Simpson, that Edward? It was him on the coin.'

'Is that right?'

'As the story goes, they were to mint six coins for the occasion of his coronation in thirty-seven. Apparently on the day he sat for them to get his likeness, not only would he not turn the right way, he demanded they make a seventh, for her, for Wallis.'

'What do you mean, "turn the right way"?'

'According to Uncle Thomas, the tradition was that the new heir must sit in the opposite direction to that of his predecessor. But Edward thought his left side the more handsome and so refused point blank to sit to the right. Anyhow, the point is that he bullied the minters and made sure he got his seventh. Apparently he planned to give it to Wallis on the day of his coronation. But of course that never happened. He wanted to marry her you see, but she was divorced. At the time, a King was not allowed to marry a divorcee. So he was faced with a dilemma. He gave up his throne for love in the end. Very romantic, I suppose.' She trailed off.

'But how did your family come by it?'

'Ah, yes, well, there I will have to betray some more of our family secrets. Perhaps I should whisper, sometimes I think these walls have ears.' She eyed all four, before continuing. 'Great-grandfather Hugh was a gambler. Poker. Was forever over in London and when there would spend his time in one particular den of iniquity, frequented by one of Edward's footmen. It was he that told Great-grandfather the story of the disagreement between Edward and the Prime Minister of the time, can't remember his name. Uncle could tell you. Begins with a B, I think. Balford, Bal—'

'Baldwin?'

'That's the man. Edward it seems had been trying to convince Parliament to give Wallis a lesser title than Queen when he became King, but the PM was having none of it. There had been one final row between the two this one evening after which Edward could not be contained and had flung the coin across the floor of his study. He told the footman to get rid of the thing. But instead, he kept it. Turns out that footman was in debt to Great-grandfather, owed him quite a bit, it seems. And that's what he gave him, to cover it. According to Uncle, Great-grandfather knew straight away what he held. And what's more important, that it would be worth a packet in the future. He brought it home and then, well, all that awfulness happened with Thomas when he lost it. Seems he loved it as much as his father. Had a real obsession with all things antique and so would spend hours looking at it, despite how it annoyed Great-grandfather. No one really understood why. I mean Thomas meant no harm by it.'

She paused and gave me a sad smile and continued:

'Uncle was never right after the disinheritance. He spent the rest of his life trying to find that coin. Not on the grounds I mean, although when he does come home I still find him wandering about looking down at the ground exactly where it fell, apparently. But no, he searches out there in the wider world. He's kind of lost it, if you understand me. Poor Uncle Thomas.'

It was then she realised who she was speaking to and dropped her eyes because of the sympathy shown to my enemy. I paid it no heed.

'They never called the guards, the day it went missing,' I said, 'never brought the law into it. We could never understand why.'

'Well, now you know. Great-grandfather could never have risked the scandal. He should never have had the thing in the first place.'

'The coin that ruined the fortunes of many, what?'

'If only you knew the half of it.' Her palm lay on the table, busy smoothing the invisible creases of the perfectly pressed tablecloth. 'Still that's enough of the family skeletons let out of the cupboard for one night, I think.'

And then she raised her glass across the table to me:

'A final toast, Mr Hannigan. To us.'

I smiled and raised my tumbler in return.

I didn't stay much longer after. And I admit I was eager to be away from the place to consider all that I'd been told. So I rose and thanked her for her kindness before taking to the air and driving myself home.

Sadie was still watching the telly in the front room but I didn't linger long with her and continued on down the corridor to my bedroom. After a bit of rummaging in the drawer of the dressing table, I pulled out the coin from where it had lain untouched since your Auntie Noreen had got her hands on it a few years back, but I'm coming to that. I looked at the King's defiant face to consider how far it had fallen from grace: from the splendour of English royalty, to the mediocrity of a County Meath dairy farmer. Sitting on the bed, I twisted it under the light of the bedside lamp to get a good look at him – the King. What did it feel like, I wondered, walking away from everything for love? Would I have done the same, were our roles reversed? I chuckled, as I pictured myself over there, in the splendour of an English castle and him back here, knee deep in muck and hay. It occurred to me, feeling the weight of it in the palm of my hand, that by rights that little beauty might well be considered mine now, given I had effectively bought it by virtue of my shares in the hotel. After a bit I replaced it and made my way to the bed with the madness of it all running around in my head. It didn't leave me, however, even in my sleep. Its beauty and wealth danced me through stately rooms and cowsheds. Faces I knew, and some I didn't, drifted in and out of confused scenes I couldn't remember when I awoke with a start.

'What is it you want?' I asked of it, as I closed my eyes for my final few hours' sleep with Sadie by my side.

I learned a new word the next day: Numismatics. There now. That's what the man in the antiques shop in Dublin told me was the name for the study of coins. I found this place on the corner of Sackville Row. Barringers, I think it was called. I looked it up in the Yellow Pages. Decided to take a trip, to kill a couple of birds with the one stone, as I needed to throw an eye over the few acres up Sword's direction.

'Edward VIII,' I said, sitting down in front of a man, no older than myself but with a stomach, the bulk of which could have fed a small village, 'there were sovereigns made. Do you know about them?'

'Ah, you mean, "the coinage that never was" as they called it in the papers of the day, how could one not?'

By the time I left, William Shaw had not only confirmed the existence and approximate value of the coins but that there was a rumour of a seventh, made more valuable because of its original intended purpose – Wallis Simpson. I didn't bring it with me of course, didn't want to start some kind of panic. It lay at home, back in our dressing-table drawer.

'There is of course no way to be sure if that one exists. Unless it turns up, that is. The other six are all accounted for at this point,' he told me, with that wide smile of his.

He was a pleasant man in a place I hadn't expected it. I had prepared myself for snobbery and coolness. In the end it was me who'd played that role, while he had been nothing but decent and charming.

'Who could put a price on that one?' he said, after I enquired about the value of this possible seventh. 'A six-figure sum is a given. You see, what will happen is, if it appears, public interest will start to rise, and who knows what price it might fetch by the time the hammer falls. Are you a coins man yourself, Mr . . . ?'

'Rogers. No, no interest at all. I'm more of a cow man,' I said.

I took my leave and thanked him for his time.

I never told Sadie the truth of that night with Emily in the hotel. Never told Thomas's story. She would have insisted I give the coin back there and then, and that was not my plan. To be honest I wasn't sure what I would do. In one way it felt like me and the Dollards were quits, having paid royally, if you'll excuse the pun, for the price of the coin by buying into the hotel and giving the money to a more deserving Dollard. But then again that blasted thing that I hadn't given a second thought to for years began to niggle at me.

And then one day I was sat in my car thinking over all Emily had told me again, looking down over Molly's hill as I called it. I had a few places I found myself when I was in need of some quiet time: nooks and crannies or open spaces, where the silence cured me, bringing a bit of peace to my weary head – Molly's hill was the most beautiful of them. Its rich green fields dipped down into a forested valley below. I sat above in the car on the road, watching Molly move among the grass, running and laughing or sometimes walking and singing. It was her favourite place to find me. In one sitting, I could see her at different stages of her life, as a youngster galloping about or as a pensive teenager sitting among the growth, barely visible, lost in her worries or as a mother herself running after my grandchild. At some stage she would always stop to wave up to me. It was my favourite part. That day, however, no wave came. Instead she sat in the long grass and turned in my direction, holding her arm to her forehead to block out the sun to look at me.

'But it's not yours, Daddy,' she said. A whisper in my ear, it was. Plain and simple. Her words had drifted up to me on the breeze that curved the grass in my direction.

'It's not theirs either, as it goes,' I replied. But, it was no use. My daughter, as always, knew right from wrong.

'But it still has one last job to do,' came her final words on the matter. She smiled then rose and moved on, far down deep into the valley, until I could not see her any more.

Chapter Four

There's just me and Svetlana alone again. She's taking the glasses out of the dishwasher. The clinking breaks the silence of us. Emily has gone to sort out proceedings below at the dinner. I'm getting a bit peckish myself.

'Any chance of a toasted special, Svetlana?'

'A toasted what?'

'Special?'

She looks at me like I've just asked for it in Irish. 'They'll know what it is in the kitchen.'

'I check,' she says, looking a little bothered by it all and leaving through the bar door.

It's back to just me and my reflection. Really, I wish it wasn't there. Reminding me this night's not even half over. Giving me that 'Do you really think you're up to this, Big Man?' stare. I ignore him. What the feck does he know anyway?

'They say yes, but twenty minutes.' Svetlana returns to lay her elbows on the counter in front of me, like she's worked here for years. 'They do dinner now so very busy. OK? I order?'

'Order away. And while you're at it, I'll have another of your finest bottles of stout.'

Stout of course always reminds me of Tony but it was my father who got me drinking the stuff in the first place. He wasn't a big drinker, mind. The odd time he'd bring home a bottle if he felt his day deserved it. Even more rare was the occasion of a drink taken in a bar. Never this one, of course, even if it had been operating back then, my father would never have crossed its threshold. Hartigan's, that was his watering hole.

'I think we deserve it, son,' he'd say, leading me over the bridge on the days the market had gone well. No further incentive was needed. I'd be by his side, smiling, working up a grand thirst.

'This here beauty, son, always remember she's fool's gold.'

He'd watch the stout settle in the glass, eyeing it like a heifer that's known for kicking. Putting off that first taste a little longer, he'd take out his pipe from his pocket and begin to pack the tobacco good and tight, his thumb pressing down into the bowl. And after, when he'd finally drink the first sip, he'd let out a sigh as if he'd battled winter winds all day and now stood at a blazing fire.

'If ever you have money, son,' he'd continue, 'don't indulge this jezebel. She'll empty your pockets and make a drunken fool of you.' He'd light up then and pull away at his pipe until a scattered orange glow peeped out from the darkness and he'd pap, pap, pap away for the duration.

Sermon over, I'd be free to drink in peace and watch Mrs Hartigan and whichever daughter might be around work at some pace, quenching the many thirsts of the winners and losers of the day. We didn't talk with any of them. I loved to listen to their conversations, though. That's what the old lad was at too – eavesdropping, picking up information we might somehow turn to our advantage. That's how, years later, we came across the first piece of land we ever bought. But when the chat could offer nothing, my eye wandered, falling often on the cobwebs hanging from the ceiling, thick as ropes.

'Are ya done?' my father would ask, after a bit. Then we'd tip our caps to our hostess and leave.

'Course, my father trusted no one beyond his own. Blood, that's where it was at for him. (How he ever got a wife was a mystery.) His mistrust followed him to the market and there he'd haggle his way to the best deal any farmer could hope for:

'Do you think I'm a fool, man?' My head bowed with the embarrassment of him, sometimes. But when his brusqueness pushed up his earnings, I paid attention. A master in manipulation. I watched his facial expressions and listened for his silences, counting the seconds until he spoke again. Learning his phrases, his hand gestures, his stance. I had it all by heart. By the time my turn came, I was ready. There were many who hated to see me coming but could not deny the quality I brought. Cows and sheep reared on the finest grain and grass. Tended closely. Ailments nipped in the bud before they had time to take hold. I stood at the stall gate knowing none other around had finer. I expected a good price and held my ground until it came. But there were times when even the best of what I had to offer fetched poor prices. I couldn't always fight the economic tide, try though I might. I was as much a victim to its whims as the next man. But unlike him I would rise earlier, watch longer and pounce quicker.

Fool that I was.

This pint here, son, is for your Auntie Noreen. If it wasn't for her I don't think your grandfather Michael would have accepted me like he did. And it was her who solved another part of the mystery of the coin. But, above all, it is because of how much your mother loved and struggled with her. Noreen was a woman forever on your mother's conscience.

I met Noreen and the rest of the in-laws not long after Sadie and me started stepping out. We were only a couple of months together when we boarded the bus that bumped us northwest to Annamoe in Donegal. Your grandfather Michael met us, a man taller than de Valera and broader than Churchill. Sadie hugged him like he was a big cuddly teddy bear, becoming lost in his coat folds, with only her shoes as evidence that he hadn't swallowed her whole. When they finally separated, she held on to him with one hand and with the other reached behind to pull me forward and make the introductions. I shook his hand firmly, meeting his unsmiling eye.

'Mr McDonagh,' I said.

No words were offered in return. He simply nodded, then released my grip. The jig was up, I was convinced. He knew, as all fathers did, the thoughts that raced through my head about his daughter. I silently pleaded for mercy with promises of never thinking those things again. So distracted was I that I did not see his hand reach across to take my suitcase that I gripped in terror. His arm tugged and his eyebrow raised but still I didn't let it go. We must have looked ridiculous, me most of all, stood there in this tug of war.

'Maurice! Daddy just wants to take the case. Would you not let it go?' Sadie's words eventually made it through to my panicked brain.

'The case? Yes. Right,' I said, looking down at it. And yet, there it remained, still firmly stuck to my sweaty palm. 'I'll put it in the trap. Where are we?' I strode off to God knows where with a foolish determination a man could only pity. I can still feel the trickle of sweat at my neck as I realised I hadn't a clue what I was at, at all.

'Maurice!'

I stopped, closed my eyes, steadied myself and turned. Sadie had a look as bewildered as my poor head, pointing to her right, and to a car. A car! I ask you? No one owned a car in those days. But there it was nevertheless, spotlessly clean, no hint that it lived in the countryside, with himself standing at its open boot like a bored taxi man waiting for his passengers to finally say their goodbyes and get the hell in.

'Even better,' I commended, like a man in the know, on top of things. I laid the case safely and finally inside, not daring even a glance in his direction.

'Sadie, you can take the front. Maurice, you're in the back – I hope you like dogs.'

I shared the journey to their home with Dinky, the sheep-dog, a temperament as good as Gearstick's, who looked embarrassed on my behalf. I searched his one silver and one brown eye for help but he offered me nothing. Thankfully the reception at the house could not have been more different. Your granny hugged me like I was a hero. Laughed and smiled, perhaps knowing by some Irish mother sixth sense, what had happened earlier and meaning to make up for it.

As we sat in the sitting room, Michael directed no conversation to me, only his daughter, enquired after her health and her job. She enthused away, delighting him with her replies. In an effort to build a bridge between the two men in her life, she spoke of my family, having met them by that stage, of course.

Actually, my mother had shown very little interest in meeting her when I first suggested it. My father, on the other hand, had been quite enthusiastic and insisted on coming for us in the trap. Sadie sat up front with him. Their chat, the whole way back out to the house made me proud. My sisters had the house gleaming. And the smell of freshly baked bread was inspired. They fluttered around your mother like she was a film star, admiring her summer coat, blue I think it was, and her dress and her pearls.

'Ach, would you go on,' she said, 'these aren't the real thing. My Aunt Maura gave them to me when I left home. She's comfortable mind, but the money wouldn't stretch to the real thing. But they do the job, don't they? I only wear them on good occasions.'

Jenny and May laughed at the honour. And I was sure a flicker of a smile passed my mother's lips as she bent to put another log in the range, holding its door with her apron. She said very little to Sadie, but she seemed to stay with the conversation, nevertheless, frowning and smiling at the appropriate times. We sat at the table, laid out with the best tablecloth and the willow china and my parents' wedding cutlery. The soda bread and tea tasted better than ever I remembered. Plates with ham and tomatoes, hard-boiled eggs and scallions, beetroot and cheese were passed up and down with laughter and enthusiasm. We finished our meal with a choice of apple tart or Madeira cake. Sadie tried both. Tittering away, as her slender fingers worked the silver-plated fork delicately, taking tiny forkfuls until her plate was empty. After, we decided to take a stroll up the road. And as my sisters began to clear up, Sadie stalled our departure, attempting to help but they shooed her out the door, laughing.

'They're a pair,' she said smiling, linking my arm, as we made our way on to the main road.

'They're not the worst, I suppose.'

'What are you like? Could a man want for better sisters?'

'I'd happily swap the armchairs for their bed.'

'What you need is an extension, a little bedroom of your own out the back. You could work wonders.'

'Is that right? Got your eye on the place already?'

'You should be so lucky.'

'Anyhow, they're heading soon. Bristol. We have a cousin there works in the Cadbury's factory.'

'Lucky them.'

'May's to go first and Jenny not long after.'

'I've never been to England.'

'It's Mam I worry about. It'll only be me left, other than Dad of course.'

On our return, the goodbyes were exchanged with wide smiles and firm handshakes. Except for Mam. Although she raised her hand politely to shake Sadie's, she quickly lay back against the chair's headrest and became lost in her own world, almost ignoring her. Jenny and May distracted Sadie by making a fuss about wrapping a couple of slices of cake in a tea towel for her to bring home. They stood in the doorway then with my father, waving, as we set off in the trap under the summer-evening light.

When I returned, I found my mother alone, still in her chair. I stalled a little, wondering what to do. But eventually I felt the bravery.

'Well, Mam, what do you think?'

'Tony would have loved her, son.'

I stood beside her, my back to the range, leaning against the tea towel rail.

'He'd have loved her,' she repeated.

Her hand surprised me and patted mine gently and quickly.

'I hope so, Mam.'

Silence fell, as we both, no doubt, thought of him.

'Was he sweet on anyone, Maurice, before he died? Was there anyone who'd turned his head?' she asked after a bit.

'He never said a word to me,' I replied, 'but I always thought him and Kitty Moran would've made a great pair, though.'

'A nice family, the Morans. Wouldn't that have been a good one now? Them married. The little blondie babies they might have had.' Her voice shook ever so slightly.

'Ah, Mam, stop now. This isn't doing you any good.'

'I know, son. I know, but sometimes . . .' she stopped and her eyes began to wander around the room, 'do you think he ever got to kiss a girl?'

'Mam!'

'I'd just like to think, he knew what that felt like before he went, that's all. It's a bit of magic, isn't it?' Quickly and shyly she smiled in my direction, before returning her gaze to her hands in her lap. I was stumped, unable to think of how to reply. Tony had missed out on so much and at that moment I felt the guilt of my love for Sadie deeply. If I could've sacrificed a slice of it for him, I would've. I bent low on my hunkers and put my hands on my mother's as the clock ticked from the corner.

'I'm fine, I'm fine,' she said after a bit. 'It's time for my bed, anyway.'

She removed her hands from my cocoon, leaving one to rest for a second on mine before getting up.

I sat in her seat, gathering up the warmth she had left, and watched her disappear through the door, her walk more noticeably stooped in recent months. I wondered how hard it was for her seeing one son pass life's milestones, while her other, cold in the ground, never got the chance. I felt a bit put out, if I'm honest, about how she was that evening. There I was, loyal and hardworking, had just brought home the best-looking woman this side of the Irish Sea, who was delightful and clever, but her conversation was all about Tony. 'Course I felt the guilt of that thought as soon as it entered my head. I sat arguing with it for a while before shrugging it away in disgust at myself, at my mother and at the world.

It wasn't until after the wedding, when Sadie moved in, and the lower room became ours, what with my sisters gone by then, that Sadie began to see how Tony's loss lingered in everything we did in the place. It clung in the very air, his name an afterthought of every sentence we spoke, until the day my mother died and she took its potency with her. We were left with a sorrow for her passing

and Tony's and my father's that felt normal, if you understand me – it was sorrow, simple uncomplicated sorrow.

I was proud on that first visit to Donegal to hear Sadie
speak of my family and our lives as if we were special.
Her efforts to impress her father seemed to be having little
effect, however. And to be truthful, I couldn't stand all that
praise for much longer. In an attempt to distract her, I
asked of her sister, Noreen.

'Noreen not about so, out on the town, what?'

Now here's the issue I had with all of what was to follow:
had a sister of mine been mentally unwell, I think I would've
found the time to tell your mother before she waded in
and made a complete fool of herself in front of my parents.
I'd told her about Tony after all and she knew to tread
lightly. But no, in her wisdom, she had told me nothing
about Noreen. My foolish, innocent question hung there,
like a grenade with the pin pulled out. I saw the panic.
Michael looked at me like I was some new specimen of
gobshite. Sadie couldn't even turn her head but stared at
the tea in her cup, her hands gripping the saucer in her
lap. While her mother glared at her daughter, wondering
how she had brought such a man into their home.

'I told you, Maurice, I did! I told you our Noreen was
a wee bit soft,' she whispered, as soon as her parents left
the room. Embarrassed by the whole affair, they'd gone to
gather their coats and things for the afternoon visit to Saint
Catherine's where your Auntie Noreen was living, apparently. I was livid.

'Yes, but I thought you meant sensitive, you know touchy.
And what's more, you didn't tell me she lived in the local
asylum!' That bit, a little louder than I'd intended.

'Would you keep your voice down.' Her hands flapped at me as she looked anxiously towards the half-open door. 'I thought I had. Honestly!' she continued, whispering again. 'And in fairness, that only happened recently, just before I met you, in fact. I've only been getting my own head around it. Mammy just couldn't cope any more. What with her hitting and all. And with Daddy out working and me away, well, they'd no choice.'

'What's wrong with her anyway – what do they call it?' I asked, my exasperation and voice mellowing on hearing what the family had been through.

'Melancholy, they say. And don't ask me what it means. All I know is she gets very down and can lash out when things aren't going her way. She was lovely as a wee one, a really cute little sister. I wish there was a picture to show you but we only have this family one. She's thirteen there,' she said, crossing the room and taking down a photo that sat on the mantelpiece. She studied it as if she'd not seen it in a long time, handing it to me. 'You can see it in her, can't you? The distractedness, the not all thereness.'

'So when did she start being like that? Did she go to school?'

'For a year or so. But she used to get so upset at the others. If they'd use her pencil or rubber, she just couldn't take it. That was enough. They knew then she was easy prey. Cruel, they were. Threw stuff at her in the playground or on the way home just to rise her. She'd be raging, crying and shouting. It was too much for her and me, to tell you the truth. The day Mammy and Daddy decided they wouldn't send her there any more was the happiest day of my life. Isn't that just an awful thing to say? But I couldn't have been more relieved. Not having to defend her and protect her any more. I could just . . . be free of her.'

Those final words were said so quietly that I almost missed them. A small little whimper escaped between the fingers she'd raised to her lips. I put my arm around her shoulder and pulled her to me and kissed her head. The sound of her parents' preparations in the distance moved towards us at a steady pace. Sadie ran from the room, out through the adjoining kitchen and the back door. I rose to follow but wasn't quick enough.

'Right, so. We'd better go,' her mother said, standing at the sitting-room door, with Michael behind her. 'Noreen normally expects us at three. She likes us to be on time. Where's Sadie?'

'She just popped out to the yard there. Said she'll be back in a second.'

'Well, while she's out,' her mother said, coming to stand beside me, 'me and Michael were just talking and we were thinking that it may not be the best thing for Noreen to meet you today. She can get a wee bit distressed with new people. We'll tell her you're about and see how we go, alright? You can wait in the corridor. The Nuns won't mind that at all, or you can walk in the grounds if you like. They have nice grounds there, don't they Michael?'

'Aye, nice grounds.'

'I just didn't want to say it in front of Sadie. She can get very upset about Noreen.'

'Of course. I don't want to be upsetting anyone. Whatever you think is the best, Mrs McDonagh.'

'It's Mary, Maurice. Would you go get herself, like a

good man so we can get going,' she suggested, nodding towards the back door.

I found her behind the shed.

'They're ready to go now,' I said, reaching out my hand to her arm, bending down searching out her face. 'Are you up to it?'

'Aye,' she said, looking as resolute as she could. Wiping away the residue of her tears, raising her two hands to her face, attempting to rub away her upset. I put my arm gently around her waist to guide her to the waiting car.

When we reappeared, her father was already in the car and her mother standing with Sadie's coat. On seeing her, she didn't comment on her upset and merely handed over her belongings before insisting I ride up front with your grandfather.

'Dinky, out!' she demanded of my former companion. He didn't protest and dutifully climbed out, his tail between his legs and head bent watching as we all climbed in and my front door finally closed. Sadie's mother chatted the whole journey; her voice like a radio in the background for that five-mile drive to Noreen, comforting and welcome but to which the rest of us paid little attention.

When we got there, I left them in the car park and took the path around the green in front of the hospital, walking as far as I could before turning to look back at the building. It was huge, monstrous really. About ten times the size of the Dollards' house. Long and wide with seventy, maybe eighty windows, looking back at me. Chimneys, I couldn't even count, there were so many, one stretching back behind the other. Turrets and peaks, and a set of big double doors in the front porch. Great thick heavy wooden ones. At another time, with another clientele, the place might have been considered beautiful. But back then it was pure ugly. Grey and dark, its loneliness spilled out of every crevice. Things must've gotten pretty bad for Sadie's mother and father to condemn their daughter to that place, with its 'nice' grounds, I thought to myself. One big circle of grass with one tree right in the middle – that was the height of it. Still, I reckoned, if it had been my own child, I might possibly have found solace in the simple things too.

Lost in my thoughts, I could hear shouting in the distance but it was a while before I realised it wasn't an inmate at all but Sadie, now halfway across the grass, trying to get my attention.

'You'll never guess,' she said, all smiles when she reached me, 'Noreen wants you to come up. She saw you arrive with us and was upset when you didn't appear. She kept saying "Him, him, bring him," and pointing outside. See up there, that's her room. Isn't that just great? Mammy's thrilled, will you come in?'

'Of course,' I replied, the two of us already making our way back across the lawn.

I'll admit I felt anxious. Inside, the building was as dark and dreary as it had promised. Long narrow corridors with closed doors on each side, and an eerie steady hum of machines and voices, pitted every now and again with a loud scream or laugh. At the end of each, residents gathered in communal rooms, overcrowded with chairs and little else. Some sat while others paced. Some rocked as others mumbled. And then some stood perfectly still. Pyjamaed people totally separate in their togetherness. By the door of one of those rooms, a woman sat with her suitcase. Smartly dressed in an outdoor coat.

'Did you see Frank?' she asked, holding out her arm to stop me as I passed. 'Did you see him? He said he was coming. He'd be here today, he said. Is he down there? He's taking me home, you know. My brother Frank, did you see him?'

Her lipstick had been carelessly applied. And the rouge on her cheeks seemed more liberal than was the norm at the time.

'Frank? No, I'm afraid I don't know him,' I said. 'He's coming for you, is that right? I'm sure he'll be here soon, so.'

'He's taking me home today. Frank. Did you see him?'

'No, Teresa, we haven't seen him,' Sadie interjected, taking my elbow and hurrying me on. Turning awkwardly, under the force of her grip, I raised my hand in goodbye to Teresa. But she didn't see me, having already turned to find someone else to ask.

'That's Teresa,' Sadie said, 'she's been waiting for her dead brother for fifteen years now. Waits there every day so Mammy says. Asks the same questions of everyone that walks by. She doesn't even hear the answer.'

At every door after, I saw Teresa's painted face. The hopelessness of her fate dogged my steps as I followed aimlessly behind Sadie. Twisting and turning with the yellow speckled corridors, nearly colliding with her when she finally stopped to knock on Noreen's door.

'Only us,' she called, as we entered.

I followed anxiously, expecting to find a younger, sadder Sadie. But the woman before me, sitting by the window bore no resemblance to your mother at all. Smiling broadly, her face didn't seem to fit with the family. Her dark hair was worn straight to her shoulders, with a fringe. She was plump with sallow skin and brown eyes that suggested a youth and beauty that could've been foreign.

'Maurice!' she said, rising from her chair, coming to embrace me as if we were old pals. I looked to the others for guidance, but each looked back at me completely baffled. I patted her shoulders cagily.

'Lovely to meet you, Noreen. You seem well.'

She said nothing. But still held on to me, her head on my shoulder.

It was Sadie who came to peel her away when she stayed in that position longer than was comfortable. She didn't protest, but neither did her eyes leave me. They clung on. She insisted I sit on her bed beside her as she sat at the window. And while she said very little else, every now and then her hand would stretch over to my arm, where she would leave it, feeling the fabric of my shirt. It didn't upset me and I was in fact comforted by her touch and so when I saw Sadie rise to intervene, I motioned for her to sit. I glanced at her parents and they, like Sadie, seemed ill at ease with Noreen's goings on. They sat on the edge of their chairs, tense and ready to pounce.

But after a while, they settled, their conversation growing more natural. I sat listening to the news of the village, becoming lost in it, enjoying learning about Annamoe and all who lived there. Every now and again, I began to feel a slight tapping or it was more like a tickle against my leg. I paid no heed at first, as it was so brief. But then it began to annoy me and I looked down to swat away what I was sure would be a fly.

'Noreen, no! Mammy! She's at it again. Noreen, take your hand out of there,' Sadie protested.

The level of disgust was such that I didn't associate it with me, at first, but on following Sadie's eyes, I saw Noreen's hand lift out of the pocket of my jacket that had lain over my leg. Drawing her hand close to her face, she peered at what she had taken and laughed. Of course, you can guess what she was at, how well did you know her games.

'Sparkle, sparkle,' she said, like a little girl whispering a secret.

'Noreen! Oh, Maurice I'm so sorry. She does this. She loves money. Coins. She was forever going through our pockets at home like that. It's the silver ones really. Now Noreen, give those back to Maurice, they're not yours,' Sadie said. She was up at this stage, in front of Noreen scolding her.

'Sparkle, sparkle,' Noreen said defiantly, turning to the window, ignoring her sister. She stared at the shilling she held in her hand, letting the coppers fall.

Sadie and her mother leapt to rescue my farthings and ha'pennies as they hit the hard floor.

'Maurice, I am so sorry. We've tried to teach her,' Sadie's mother assured me.

'There's not a bother, Mrs McDonagh. Don't be worrying,' I said, joining the bent heads scrambling around for my few pennies.

'Now Noreen, it's not yours. Give it back.' Her mother's muffled instruction rose up to her daughter, who I noticed, was having none of it. I turned an amused grin to the dark-haired divil beside me.

'You like the shiny ones? Well, aren't you clever, going

for the ones that are worth more? It should be you working in the bank and not your sister,' I said, laughing a little.

Noreen's laugh erupted. Nearly blowing me back with the force of it. Such a fine appreciation of my wit, I thought, before realising she hadn't even heard what I'd said. Her happiness was about the coin, nothing else. As the others returned to their chairs, her manic laugh continued. They sat as tense as before like runners waiting for the race to start. Mrs McDonagh glanced at the father and tilted her head towards the door and to the help that might be on the other side. It all seemed a little extreme to me. But what they knew, which at that stage I didn't, was that the return of the shilling would be a hard-won battle, should I ask for it back. Suddenly with no warning Noreen stopped laughing, its abrupt halt as startling as its eruption. Then her free hand reached for my arm, to feel the shirt fabric once again. Despite all the worried stares, I put my hand on hers.

'You keep that, Noreen. I might not always have one to give but you can have that now as my gift. Sparkle, sparkle, what?' I patted her hand.

'Sparkle, sparkle,' she replied, and laid her head on my shoulder.

To this day, despite the many conversations had on the subject, no one could quite figure out why Noreen took to me as she did. No stranger was ever given the welcome of our first meeting.

'It's my irresistible charm. It worked on her sister didn't it?' I offered in explanation as we drove back to Annamoe after the visit, taking a sneaky peek to my right at your grand-father, breathing an internal sigh of relief on seeing him grin.

Noreen had worked a miracle that day: having walked into that hospital a condemned man in my future father-in-law's eyes, I walked out a hero. She had changed everything. From then on he paid attention to me. Listened to what I had to say. Even agreed with it occasionally. Either way, I felt I had his respect from that day on. And so it was when I came to ask for your mother's hand, he said:

'Her mother would kill me if I said no, not to mention her sister. You have my blessing, Maurice.'

We married on the 3rd of October 1959. Noreen was to be bridesmaid, making the wedding a very tense affair. With everyone saying any amount of novenas that we might not have the bad luck for the ceremony to fall on one of her off mornings, the threatened rain didn't even get a mention. It was Sadie who had the idea that I should drive the car to collect her on the morning. She'd always loved the jaunts, she said, and so I was dispatched at seven in the morning to get her to the church for the ceremony an hour later. Weddings were in the mornings back then, you see.

The prayers seemed to have paid off. Noreen was delightful. She laughed her way there. At what, I wasn't sure but nevertheless she infected me with her cheerfulness. By the time we reached the church I bounded out of the car, much to the general relief of her family, who had, apparently, spent the entire hour worrying about whether we might both make it there alive.

In the absence of Tony it was the McDonaghs' neighbour, Diarmuid Row, who stood for me. I knew very little about him. He was a few years older than me and had a car. Don't ask me what had them all so rich in Annamoe, but everyone around seemed to have one, so he seemed the perfect choice being able to drive the family to the church, while I fetched Noreen. If I wasn't mistaken though, I saw a hint of something in his eye when he looked at Sadie that morning. She was admittedly breathtaking. I had my suspicions.

'Would you go away,' she said, when I mentioned it later. 'Sure he's engaged to Annie Mulligan.'

'I'm just telling you what I saw, is all.'

The day went perfectly until it was time to bring Noreen home. After the ceremony we had gone back to the house in Annamoe for a breakfast and, as it turned out, a lunch. The morning grew into afternoon and things began to wind up as the various guests headed home, including my parents; my father had borrowed a car for the day, from who I haven't a clue. But Noreen had other ideas about going back to St Catherine's. And when her mother rose to get her ready, she clung on to me, then the door frame and finally the kitchen table. In the end her father had to pull her away. She must've had some grip on it because they were propelled against the wall when he finally managed to release her. He was pinned there, under her weight. We leapt to his aid but weren't quick enough to stop her turning and digging her nails into his face. It took the three of us, her mother, Sadie and me to detach her. By then blood was streaming down on to his suit, which only seconds before had still boasted the freshness of being newly cleaned and ironed. Reaching into his pocket he pulled out his handkerchief to stem the flow.

'The chair. Get her to the chair.' We struggled to get her seated as her mother instructed. She had some strength in her.

'No!' Noreen screamed, thrashing at us with her arms and feet.

Meanwhile, the father sat defeated with his head in his hands, holding the handkerchief in place. His wife glanced back at him trying to assess the damage.

'Michael!' she shouted, over Noreen's protests, 'you'll have to go for Doctor Kenny. Michael!'

He looked back at her dazed, nodded and then rose.

'Should I go instead?' I suggested, taking in the state of the man as he left the kitchen.

'No. You stay,' Mary said in a low voice, watching him leave, 'he needs to get away from this. He can't cope with it. He'll be fine once he's on the road.'

And then a miracle occurred. Mary bent low to Noreen's ear and began to whisper. She kept at it, five minutes or so, until slowly Noreen's screams lessened under her murmuring.

'There, there, little one. There, there.' The quiet words seemed to calm her daughter's distress, coaxing it to a whimper. 'There, there.'

She continued at that over and over, lulling even me into a stupor, never mind Noreen. I stood mesmerised as her hand moved back and forth on her daughter's head, caressing it to the rhythm of her refrain. Noreen leaned into it like a cat, moving with the waves of her words. Time ticked on as we all stood watching and waiting. Michael may only have been gone ten minutes but it felt like a lot longer before we heard the sound of the car returning and doors opening and closing.

'Maurice!' Sadie said, calling me back, when she realised I had relaxed my grip.

'You'll need to be ready!' she warned, nodding towards Noreen.

As soon as the door opened and the Doctor and his medicine case appeared, we were thrown into Noreen's raging storm again. As if there had been no lull, no calming of the seas, she rose again, greater and more vicious than before. She shouted out all kinds of profanities as she kicked and threw whatever limb she could at us. She glared at the Doctor as he readied the syringe. He moved to my side.

'Tightly now,' he instructed.

I held her hand against the armrest with all of my strength. In it went, pressing down through her screams. Her eyes turned on him, red with anger, like you might imagine the Devil himself, boring into him. She spat and cursed and writhed. Slowly then she began to quieten, but not as before. No, this time she was frightened. Terrified that she was losing the battle, that something more powerful, more dangerous was taking charge. My tight grip eased to a caress and in that moment her eye caught mine and pleaded for help. It's a rotten thing to feel power-less but even worse to feel like a collaborator. Rotten, Kevin, rotten. At last, her screams stopped. One by one we let go as her eyes closed. None of us felt relieved. Each stood looking at her, ridden with guilt.

When I met your mam it had been her intention to make her way home to Noreen, to be there to help out with her. She hoped to get a transfer to Donegal at some stage. But I scuppered her plans. Failing us moving there, it was Sadie's wish that in later years Noreen would come to live with us, once your grandparents had passed. She told me once that she hoped this would coincide with medicine making such advances that Noreen might mellow, becoming at last the doted-on little sister of her longing. Only one wish was fulfilled when Noreen moved to Meath in seventy-four. Your Granny Mary died first with the father remaining to make the daily drive to Saint Catherine's. It was a flu that was his downfall in the end. You don't hear of that much these days, someone dying from flu, but it took that bull of a man. Noreen, to everyone's surprise, didn't seem at all upset by the prospect of a move hundreds of miles away to the brand spanking new nursing home in Duncashel. In fact, the day we arrived to pick her up, she beamed at us, not bothered by the recent loss of her father it seemed and delighted by the prospect of a new bedroom.

'New room, new room,' she repeated, intermittently as we drove south along the Donegal coastline, then east towards home.

Sadie was silent. I imagined a whole host of emotions churning around inside her. Sadness to have lost her father, fear that Noreen mightn't settle, and concern that she, the big sister, might, once again, not be up to the job. You know what a worrier your mother was; she had herself in a state in the weeks building up to the move:

'Maurice, what if she hates it? What if it sets her off on one of her fits and she doesn't recover? I don't know what I'd do. Would we have to bring her to live in the house with us then or what? Sure, we couldn't bring her back to Donegal. Ach, are we doing the right thing at all?'

She sat in the passenger seat staring ahead the day of the move, like a scared little girl, needing to explain and defend this woman, merrily chatting away to herself in the rear. I reached my hand to hers as they writhed in her lap.

'We're in this together, Sadie,' I said.

I think she nodded. My hand didn't leave hers until the gears cried out. I felt her own hand move in under my left thigh then, where it nestled for the rest of the journey until we arrived on the gravel driveway of Duncashel Care Home. I'd barely stopped the car before Noreen was out and past the nurse standing waiting to greet us. We ran after her as she scurried down the corridors.

'New room! New room!' she chirped, louder and louder until the nurse finally caught up and escorted her to the yellow wallpapered room with its neat single bed and locker. And a large window at which she was to spend much of her life, looking out at the car park, waiting for us to arrive, or so your mother always thought.

Sadie cried buckets that night on leaving. It was utter relief, of course.

It became the tradition that Noreen came to our house every Saturday, thereafter. Most days, depending on her mood, she'd stay over long enough to attend Mass and then have Sunday dinner. You were about five at the time. You called her Auntie No-no.

'No-no,' she'd squeal, and so would you when you saw each other.

She wasn't always a saint with you mind. Do you remember the rows? It was like having a second child. She was such a rummager, loved to poke about. One minute she was beside us and the next gone, and might have been for a while without us knowing. She was crafty in her escapes. In the early days we let her wander too much.

'Auntie No-no, NO!' we'd hear you scream from down the corridor.

We'd arrive to find some Lego thing you'd been building broken in bits on the floor. Your mam would stay with you and help set everything right again while I got Noreen out and back down to the sitting room, where she'd sit and watch the match with me, twiddling at my sleeve. In the end we had to lock your door when she came to stay. You'd take out a few toys to keep you going while she was there, bits that you didn't mind sharing. She didn't seem to care that your room was out of bounds. But still she'd check the door every time, in case we forgot.

You played endless games of Monopoly together.

'What kind of rules are they playing in there at all?' I asked your mother once, when I came in to find you both sprawled out on the sitting-room floor with *It's a Knock Out* on the TV in the background. You had hotels and houses everywhere, in the jail, on the free parking, in the middle.

'Their own,' she said, smiling at me, laying the Saturday-evening fry in front of me.

It all ended in tears when she'd started to pocket the iron and the hat, not to mention the dog, your favourite.

'Would you go see where that one is?' Sadie said, this one Sunday when things seemed a little too quiet in the house. She was bending down to turn the roasting tin around in the Aga at the time. The aroma of the meat wafted around the kitchen, making my stomach howl. Reluctantly, I laid the sports section of the *Sunday Independent* down on the kitchen table and ventured forth.

'Any sign of No-no, Kev?' I asked, putting my head around the door of the sitting room to find you on your own, watching telly, giving it loads, pretending to be part of the action of the cowboy movie on screen.

'Don't let your mother see you on the back of that couch,' I warned, as I left you to it.

'Noreen,' I continued, making my way down the corridor leading to our bedrooms, 'are you there?'

I detected movement and tracked it to our bedroom. I opened the door and straight away wished I hadn't.

'Sparkle, sparkle,' I heard from the window beyond, in front of which stood our dressing table. Sadie's pride and joy. Purchased beyond, at great expense in Shaw's in Duncashel.

'Oh dear. What have you found?' I said, optimistically enough until I took in the disarray she had created. 'Ah, Noreen, what in God's name are you up to?'

The room seemed in shock from the hurricane that had just swept through it. Coats and jackets that rarely got any outings, some of which I was sure I'd never seen before, lay strewn on the bed and floor and anywhere else that might support their weight. Drawers stood open, the contents half in, half out.

'Sparkle, sparkle!' she answered.

'Sparkle, sparkle my arse. Your sister will kill you, not to mention me if we don't get this lot cleared up quick smart. Noreen! Noreen! Are you listening to me at all?'

Where things got put in our house was a world of magic and wonder to me. We lived in a house of order that was Sadie's domain. Now, here I stood with a heap of mess, with neither wand nor wisdom to know where to begin. I had two choices: call in the big guns or make a stab at it myself. For reasons I cannot fathom, I chose the latter. And so, while I charged about bravely, folding and hanging and pushing and squeezing things into spaces that were blatantly too small, Noreen continued to stand with her back to me, entranced with whatever it was she had. Even if I'd wanted to know what it was, I couldn't have reached her, such was the mountain of chaos between us that I'd have needed one of those Sherpa lads to guide me through.

My longer than expected absence from the Sunday paper had obviously aroused suspicion and before I knew it, I heard Sadie approaching. Despite my innocence of the crime, I felt as guilty as Noreen should have when Sadie entered the room. I all but cried out *'mea culpa'*.

'Jesus, Mary and Joseph. Maurice, what in God's name . . .'

Now, let me just say that this was a first – never in her whole life had your mother ever cursed so much as she did that afternoon. Generally, that was my department. I don't even think I could do justice to what she actually said. Had I not been so terrified myself, I would've been rather proud of her rage.

'It wasn't me. It was your sister!' the idiot that was me said, pointing in your auntie's direction.

'Noreen. Noreen. Look at me right now,' Sadie barked.

I closed my eyes because I couldn't bear the wrath that that poor woman was about to endure, however much she may have deserved it.

'Sparkle, sparkle, Sadie.' Noreen turned and held aloft the treasure she had unearthed.

'You and those bloody coins! Noreen, what were you thinking? Look at this mess! Look at it . . . And who is going to clean it up? Not me I can tell you. If you can pull it out you can put it back. And you can do it right now! Maurice, come on out, come on. Would you just climb over that and stop foostering. Leave her to it. No dinner until this is done. Do you hear me, Noreen?'

No dinner until it was done! I was too afraid to enquire if this 'no dinner' punishment was to extend to me – sure that would have meant we'd have been eating that lovely big lump of beef at teatime, or later. My stomach was not accustomed to that. I was strictly a one o'clock man, always had been. This was a disaster. My shock meant my exit was slower than Sadie would've liked. But in my slow retreat, I had time to see what had caused the whole debacle. Now remember, son, this was years before Emily told me about the history of the coin I'd stolen from the Dollards. By this stage, I hadn't seen it in over twenty years, but there it was. Noreen, having noticed my interest, stretched it out in my direction.

'Beautiful sparkle. Gold sparkle!' she shouted enthusi-astically, hoping I would share in her joy.

'Gold?' I said. Not knowing then what I know now, I'd never believed the thing to be real gold, but it wasn't the time for a debate. 'Where did you find that, Noreen?'

'Here.' Noreen pointed to a small drawer of the dresser, left of the mirror. For the life of me, I couldn't remember putting the coin in there. What's worse, if I'd been asked before that moment whether a drawer even existed there at all, let alone a coin in it, I wouldn't have known.

'That's not mine, Noreen . . . well it is, in a way. But you can't have it, you understand, it's not mine to give. You'll have to give this one back.'

'Maurice's sparkle?'

'Yes. Well, no. It's complicated. But you must put it back.'

'Noreen will mind Maurice's sparkle and then put it back. OK? I only mind it, Maurice, OK?'

'You promise to put it back, Noreen? I'll have to check later, before you go. You'll put it back – yes?'

'Noreen put it back.'

She nodded and smiled. I left the room dubiously. It was the first time I'd ever denied her a coin, but for some reason it would have felt wrong to have parted with that one. When I got back to the kitchen I found my poor wife with her head in her hands.

'What was that thing she found, anyway?' she finally managed, after we'd been sitting for some time at the kitchen table, me with my arm around her in an effort to show support with my stomach howling.

'Mammy, I'm starving, when's dinner?' you said, coming through the door at that very moment along with the sounds of a Comanche attack from the other room.

'Hold on a wee while there, Kevin. What was it, Maurice?'

'But Mammy . . .'

'Ah, that,' I said. 'It was that coin I found a long time ago. You know, the Dollard one. I'm sure I told you about it. Forgot I had it. I told her she couldn't have it. She said OK, but you know yourself.'

'Kevin, will you stop with the jiggin' and pulling out of me?' Sadie said. 'That yoke? I thought I told you to give that back a long time ago. And now look what's happened. Sure we'll never hear the end of it now. She'll always be wanting it.'

Everything had suddenly become my fault. I looked at my paper as my indignation breathed in the smell of the roast beef and felt wholeheartedly sorry for myself.

'How long should we leave her in there do you think?' Sadie said, not a hint of regret at her unfair treatment of me. 'Kevin, will you stop? I can't hear your father. The dinner will have to wait.'

'But I'm starving,' you appealed. I could've kissed you.

'In fairness Sadie, I reckon my stomach can't hold out much longer either,' I bravely added.

'Alright,' she said, taking pity on the sorry sight of her two men, rising to take the meat out of the Aga. 'We'll sort it all after the dinner so. But she'll help us.' Sadie stood over the beef on the counter, shaking the carving knife at me, like I might protest. 'Kevin, start setting the table and Maurice, go call Noreen.'

Noreen did help to clear up in the end, in her own way. And to my utter shock she was true to her word about the coin. It was back in the drawer when she left for home that night. No battle, no war of words, no injection this time. Over the years there was less and less need for those, thankfully. As she grew older, she actually mellowed, or maybe like the rest of us, her energy gradually waned.

Svetlana puts the toasted special down.

'Sorry for delay. "Bedlam," Chef say, I don't know what that is but there you go, that's what he say. You OK for everything. You need sauces?'

'No, you're grand now,' I say, and watch her push her way back through the doors, disappearing into the kitchen.

I look at it and wonder what was I thinking. As the night has drawn on, I haven't the heart or inclination for more food. But not willing to waste it, I take a tentative bite anyway, wary of the lethal burn of a hot tomato. But as I chew, I know it's no use. I lay it back down and push away the plate of this, my last supper.

It was twenty-seven years later that I learned the origin of the coin from Emily at that special dinner she'd arranged. But even then she'd been holding back. And it wasn't until a year after that again that I found out the real consequence of its theft. And it was all because of Noreen, would you believe.

It was another Sunday, and Sadie, Noreen and me were in the market for a lunch. In those days we'd begun to have the Sunday dinner out. We were in our seventies by then and were deserving of some treats, or so your mother had told me anyway. There we were on the road after Mass debating our destination.

'Hotel,' Noreen stated from the back. She always wanted to go to the Rainsford. I blame you and your wedding on that. One of the happiest days of her life.

'And what about Kenny's over in Duncashel, would you not prefer that? You like the chips there.'

'Hotel,' came the reply, a little more forcibly this time. It was not one of her good days.

'How about Murtagh's?'

'Hotel,' she roared.

'Ah, for God's sake Maurice, would you not be upsetting her. We'll go to the hotel, Noreen, don't you worry.'

The force of Sadie's words could've turned the steering wheel all by itself. I dropped them off at the door of the place, while I went to find a parking space. Delaying as much as I could, I stopped into Lavin's to pick up the paper.

'Hannigan, it's yourself,' Lavin bellowed, as I put the paper down in front of him.

''Tis.'

'Great day, now. Are you in for the bit of lunch? I saw you drop themselves in there. You can't beat their steak. That's my recommendation any way. How did the sheep go for you Thursday?'

'The sheep? The sheep are my business Lavin and none of yours.'

'Tell nothin' to no man.'

'Shall I pay you for the paper or are you giving it to me free?'

'Wouldn't I be the fool if I did that?'

'Far be it from me Lavin . . . Here, I'll get next Sunday's free, so,' said I, landing a fiver on the counter before leaving.

By the time I arrived in the foyer, I could see all was not well. The place was heaving. Sadie was standing at the dining-room door looking in all worried, perhaps there was no room, I thought. Hope for me yet. I risked a smile. But it didn't last long when I remembered it was the thirtieth anniversary of the hotel's opening. Robert had told me about it but I'd forgotten. My stomach lurched when I considered it quite possible Thomas might be home from England. Ducking like a big eejit behind some class of a tree in the foyer, I peered out cautiously. No longer a well-built brick of a man, instead a terrified boy of ten still fearful of the master. Coming to my senses, I near knocked the tree down as I stepped out from behind it. Attempting to settle myself, I allowed my eye to wander, to pretend an interest in the decor. It was then I saw a photograph of Rainsford House in its heyday, hanging on the wall nearby. I'd not seen it before, certainly it hadn't been there at the wedding or I'd have noticed. I leaned in to get a better gander. There was a date – 1925, a bit before my time. A man was standing in the foreground looking directly at the photographer. His face was familiar, but I couldn't place him. A Dollard alright, but not one I recognised. I stood there for some time lost in the puzzle of him, annoyed that I couldn't figure it out, until an exasperated Sadie found me.

'It's full. A private function apparently. What will we do now? She'll not be happy. You'd better tell her. She accepts things better from you.'

'Like in the car, you mean. She's your sister, you tell her.'

Sadie turned away, betrayed. I looked at the picture one last time, making sure my memory couldn't produce a name, but nothing came in the end and I walked off defeated. When I found Sadie again she was standing at the entrance to the bar, flummoxed, looking about her.

'Well, where is she?'

'If I knew that, Maurice, I wouldn't be standing on my own now would I?'

Back firmly in my box, I surveyed the crowd, but couldn't make her out in the hustle and bustle. And then, there arose a familiar sound.

'Sparkle, sparkle!'

We moved quickly. Scurrying through the crowd, we followed its summons, wondering whose pockets she'd rifled or whose change she'd stolen this time and how we'd talk ourselves out of it. We arrived right where I am sitting now, to find none other than Thomas Dollard attempting to wrestle a coin from Noreen's hands. She, of course, was having none of it and was batting him away with her powerful swipe.

'Madam! I beg your pardon. Give me back my coin at once. Madam!'

Had Sadie not rushed to Noreen's aid, or perhaps it was Thomas's she was more concerned with, I'd have gladly stood back to watch that pantomime for as long as it lasted. Priceless. A grown bully, wrong-footed by a woman half his size who, by the looks of it, was winning the contest.

'Noreen!' My poor wife's pleas called me from my reverie of Noreen punching him in the face.

'Noreen, give it to me. Noreen! Maurice! Could you help, please?'

But before I could take a step towards them, Noreen was before me, having bounded over, even more excited than was normal with one of her discoveries.

'Look! Your sparkle. Your sparkle, Maurice,' she said, holding her fist far too close to my face.

'My sparkle? Noreen, how's it my sparkle?' Smiling, I placed a calming hand on her shoulder and lowered her fist so I could focus on what she held.

'Come over here and show me,' I said, leading her to a nearby table, the occupants of which had quickly left to give us space.

Sadie instinctively knew to hold his highness back, throwing him a warning glance to leave me be. He danced an infuriated jig at the bar, while keeping his eyes firmly fixed on me.

'Right, Noreen, show me my sparkle, so?'

She unfurled her fingers and there I saw my, or rather, Thomas's, coin. Time stopped as I swallowed hard. He'd found me out, I thought. Somehow, he'd broken into my house and ransacked it until he'd retrieved the only evidence of the theft – the coin itself. There could be no other explanation. The Gardaí were possibly outside at that very minute, waiting to take me away. Or perhaps something more sinister, perhaps Thomas wished to finish what I always suspected he had truly wanted – to kill me and now he had the justification. I placed my hands over Noreen's, closing them, willing the thing to go away, willing time to transport me back so that I could keep walking, never bending down to pick up the blasted thing in the first place.

'Uncle, what is the matter?' Emily passed by me, making her way to Thomas, bringing a momentary distraction, a relief.

'Your sparkle Maurice, in my pocket,' Noreen added excitedly.

Releasing her hands from my grip, she proceeded to pound one hand against my chest, while her other rummaged in her pocket. She made no sense, nothing made sense.

'Uncle, are you alright? You look awful. What's going on?' Emily's eyes followed her uncle's to where I sat. 'Oh, it's you, Mr Hannigan.'

'That, that . . . lunatic has taken my coin, Emily. The family coin! She's a mad woman.'

It amazed me that the man hadn't recognised me. Not even my name rang a bell. After all those years of beating the living daylights out of me, he hadn't a clue who I was. My name, my face, had mattered nothing to him after all. For a moment I felt slightly offended, but then realised his ignorance gave me an upper hand. I was ready to unleash the charm. I smiled as I rose and approached this woman of reason who held sway with the brute rearing and snorting behind her.

'Emily,' I said reassuringly, 'there's nothing to worry about—'

'Nothing to worry about! I beg your pardon—' I held up a hand to halt Thomas's protest.

'As I was saying, *Emily*, all will be fine. I merely need a moment with my sister-in-law here and the issue will be sorted. She . . . if I could just have a quiet word with you over here,' I suggested, taking her by the arm and leading her to the corner of the bar, beckoning Sadie to take my place by Noreen. 'As I was saying, my sister-in-law is, what you might say, a little . . . slow, if you get me, and she has a love of all things shiny, well, actually a love of shiny coins and—'

'Oh, God, don't say any more, Mr Hannigan. It's that bloody sovereign isn't it? I had hoped he might have left it behind for once. But to my horror I saw him prancing around with it earlier. If I hear one more time about how valuable it is and how we lost and found it, I'll scream.'

'Found it?' I asked, still trying to remain as calm and composed as I could, and no doubt failing, 'what do you mean found it? You never told me he'd found it.' I hadn't meant to give such a forceful response but my head was so confused that I couldn't help myself.

'Never mind that now,' she said looking a bit hassled herself, 'what do you need to get this thing off your sister-in-law?'

'A quiet room should do us,' I said, trying to sound in control, hoping my voice wasn't letting me down, 'five minutes tops, Emily, and he'll have his coin back.'

'Right, follow me.'

She made a quick stop to explain the situation to 'Uncle', which allowed me time to retrieve my wife and Noreen. Before long we three were in the meeting room Emily had used the night of the dinner if I wasn't mistaken. This time the tables were set up in a U-shape. Fizzy water sat at each placing of 'Rainsford House Hotel' stationery. As soon as the door closed, I fell into a chair, like I'd just run a marathon. Hyperventilating, I pulled at the neck of my shirt, trying to release my tie. I managed to get up and open a window.

'Maurice, oh my goodness, are you alright?' That was your mother. 'Oh my Lord! I'll get help.' But I held her back with all the strength I had in me.

'Sit,' I commanded, opening one of the bottles of water laid out around the board table and taking a seat myself. I gulped at it. I feckin' hate fizzy water.

'Sadie, did you tell him who we were? Do you think he has any idea?' I asked, a bit calmer now.

'What are you going on about Maurice, who?'

'Your man, Thomas. The man Noreen took the coin from.'

'I certainly didn't say anything. Oh, that's him isn't it? He's your bully from all those years ago.'

'And that's his feckin' coin as well, the one Noreen has in her hand.'

We glanced over to where she sat by the window engrossed by it, eyes for nothing else.

'But Maurice, did you give the coin back to him? I thought you still had it? That is, despite my feelings on the matter. I always said—'

'But this is the thing, Sadie, I didn't give it back. And what's more, I don't think he recognises me, 'cause if he did he'd possibly be screaming that here's the thief who stole the feckin' thing in the first place.'

'What do you mean "stole"?'

'Found, whatever, does it matter?'

'But, Maurice. This doesn't make sense. How could he have it, if it's still up in our house?'

'I don't know!' I blasted back at her, rising to pace the room.

I'd figure out this man's game if I had to stay there all day, drinking posh fizzy water and listening to Noreen's damned 'sparkle, sparkle' over and over again. It took all of my power not to roar at her as I passed behind her seat of reverence to the bloody thing. I looked down, mouthing a curse at her and it. And that was when I had to grip the back of her chair to hold myself up for fear of falling down. I leaned in closer to ensure that what I thought I saw was in fact the case. In her hand she held *two* identical coins. I looked and looked at them, as she turned them over. There could be no denying, they were the same. Two gold coins, with the same heads and markings.

'Noreen,' I said, when my power of speech eventually returned, 'there are *two* coins.'

'Maurice's sparkle and Noreen's sparkle.'

'Maurice's sparkle?'

'Yes, Noreen took Maurice's special sparkle and now Noreen has her new sparkle.'

'OK. So, Noreen, let me just get this straight, you borrowed my one from my drawer and then you got the other one from the man outside, is that right?'

Noreen nodded.

'Noreen's sparkle,' she added.

The penny finally dropped and I slouched in the chair by her side with utter relief. Laughing, I wiped the worry away and explained it all to my confused wife. Noreen, I told her, must have entered the hotel with my coin in her pocket, having 'borrowed' it again from my drawer and had then come across Thomas parading about showing an exact replica to all in the bar. What a man, I thought. Never to be outdone. Never to admit defeat – he had to get a copy of the thing, well crafted though it was.

'This one, Maurice's. This one, Noreen's.'

She handed over mine, as it were. How she knew the difference, I didn't know.

'Now Noreen, you do know you have to give your one back.'

'Noreen's,' she stated, hiding it away from me in the folds of her coat.

I looked to Sadie and recognised the panic. Sadie rounded the table and sat the other side of her sister. Flanked from both sides now we started our negotiations. We walked out of that room ten minutes later with a deal under our belts. The coin was to be relinquished to Thomas in return for Noreen keeping mine, on the understanding that it would always live in her bedside locker in our house, with an additional sweetener of three two Euro coins that we scrambled together between my wallet and Sadie's purse.

'Where's himself?' I asked Emily, as soon as I found her, twirling his coin around in my fingers.

'He was around there a moment ago. I see you've managed to retrieve it then. I can give it back to Uncle,

Mr Hannigan while you and Mrs Hannigan have some lunch on us. I'll set you up in the snug. It will be nice and quiet for you there.' Her face bore the worry of what might happen should we men meet again.

'I'll gladly take you up on the offer of some lunch. But, if I promise to behave,' I said, as charming as I was able, 'would you allow me the honour of returning this personally to your uncle? It's important to me.'

She looked at me, searching my face for evidence of trustworthiness. I smiled in return, hoping that whatever my lips were attempting, it was enough to convince her that here stood a man of his word; a man who would not upset the day of celebrations. She didn't appear wholly satisfied but nevertheless turned to Sadie and Noreen, ushering them into the snug, telling them the menu as she went. But as I took my first step to enter the bar to begin my search, she was by my side again, whispering in my ear, laying an urgent grip on my arm.

'Mr Hannigan, please, that coin has sent my uncle to hell and back. We have had enough torment in this family. If he knows who you are or if you start to taunt him then I'm not sure what he might do. Please, Mr Hannigan, just give it back to him and say nothing else.'

'Who I am, Emily? What do you mean, "who I am"?' I asked. Perhaps I hadn't got away with it after all. Perhaps somehow she knew what I'd done with the coin all those years ago.

'The land, the . . . You know what I mean. We don't need to go over that now. Please, just don't tell him who you are, just give him back the coin and be done with it.'

'Ah, I see. *The land*. I'll not antagonise him. It would

157

seem there are too many women here that would never forgive me if I did. I'll be good, you have my word.'

I patted her hand and then removed it from my arm, but held it not letting her go just yet.

'One more thing though, Emily. What was that bit about your uncle "finding" the coin again?'

She looked at me and I knew from her that she was too tired and exhausted from everything to go into it there and then. And really I should have let her go. But I squeezed her hand, impressing my curiosity just a little bit harder. Her face relented into resignation. She looked around her, then whispered:

'It's not the original, not the one he lost, I mean. It's one of the other six. He bought it about ten years ago. Before my father died. Used his second wife's inheritance. She divorced him after, when she found out what he'd done. We were forced to borrow, to settle the law suit she'd threatened.'

'Is that a fact?'

'I don't expect you to have any sympathy but he really isn't well. He's totally blocked out the truth of it all. Firmly believes the coin he has is Great-grandfather's original. He's created this make-believe world in which Great-grandfather was a gent and he, in turn, was the proud loyal son. We never speak of the disinheritance. Perhaps we'd have all done the same given . . . well.'

She stopped abruptly and closed her eyes on something she seemed unwilling to share. Her hand rubbed her brow.

'So when I met you that first day,' I said, calling her back to me, 'and you told me about the debt, was that because of the loan? Was that why you needed the money?'

I couldn't help but smile at the irony of it all. I may as

well just have handed back the coin there and then and saved myself the bother of investing the cash. Emily studied me, her face becoming serious.

'Why, would you have had second thoughts had you known it was all because of him and the coin?' she asked.

I had no answer for her. Not then anyhow. Not even now, if I'm honest.

'What's done is done, I suppose,' I said, 'but you told me he still looks for the coin when he's home. Why would he do that if he has one?'

'I suppose he still lives in hope.' She gave me a tight-lipped smile.

I nodded and patted her hand, not flinching for a second and headed in search of Thomas. I simply followed the loud laugh and greying head of hair sticking up above the crowd. I took his elbow without a word, hauling him to one side, away from the man he was speaking to.

'Dear God man, what in hell do you think you are at?' he protested, as he stumbled to face me, spilling his wine in the process. His face was old. Up close, I could see a vulnerability, a weariness that caught me. I had expected to feel hate, not pity. His eyes squinted in suspicion, bringing me back to myself. I hardened my stare and raised the coin in front of his face.

'Ah, at last! I thought for a moment there, I would have to call in the police. Only for young Emily, I would have, I'll have you know.'

'She's not a lunatic or a mad woman.'

'What? What are you going on about, man?'

'Noreen, my sister-in-law. She's not a lunatic or a mad woman and I'll thank you not to call her that again.'

I concentrated my eyes on his, trying to pour as much hate into them as I possibly could. Tony had always told me no matter what happened, to always look him straight in the eye. I wondered, did he know me now. Did he recognise his handiwork in the scar on my face. Did he see the child turned man capable of tearing him limb from limb. He showed no sign.

'I have no intention of ever meeting her again,' he said looking down, trying to maintain some dignity. 'If I have my way, she will not be permitted in our hotel again.'

There he was – the conceited bully of old.

'Your hotel is it?' The blood inside me boiled as I considered telling him just whose hotel it was but then I remembered my promise to Emily to go quietly. Instead, I told a different truth. 'Yours? And not that of the sweat of your grand-niece. Holding this crumbling place together with luck and borrowed money. Where have you been for the last fifty years? Swanning around Europe, is it? Only for that young lassie and her father before her, this place would be long gone. Yours my arse.'

That left him open-mouthed. I let my eyes linger on him for as long as physically possible before turning to rejoin the women.

Look him in the eye, Maurice, always look him in the eye.

Nothing more was said on the matter through lunch. We left as soon as our food was eaten. But when we got home, Sadie would not let it rest.

'Can you just not get rid of it to be damned, Maurice? Sure what use is the coin to you? It means nothing to us, when obviously that man is obsessed.'

'He got the better of me when I was a youngster, but he'll not do it now.'

'What are you, ten? Noreen has more sense than you sometimes. Bring it back and tell him you found it on the land a couple of years back or something, and it was only seeing his one today that reminded you.'

'Right so, and while I'm doing that are you going to tell Noreen that we're reneging on our bargain? 'Cause I'll tell you something for nothing – I'm not.'

My hand thumped the table, spilling the tea from our cups into the saucers. We watched the rest of the Sunday game in silence, not mentioning another word about it for as long as she lived. Meanwhile, Noreen sat in her bedroom with her newest treasure, among her many others, oblivious to the storm she had created.

I'm not a hundred per cent sure what Noreen did with those coins day in day out. Pour them on to the floor, sift through them and then put them back in again, I suppose. She had such a collection. Jar upon jar, full to the brim. At first those jars were very ordinary and then as the years went on they got more refined. Sadie'd often come home from shopping having found some fancy one that she'd wrap, but not before dropping in a fifty-pence piece, or whatever the shiniest one might be at the time.

You loved her obsession. Do you remember when you were small you insisted Aunt No-no got pocket money just like you? You'd give it to her on the Saturday when you got yours. And, of course, at Christmas, there had to be the special trip to Dublin to buy the finest of jars for her. You'd be so proud arriving home with the latest one.

'Well, now isn't that grand,' I'd say, when you waylaid me in the kitchen later that evening.

'This is the best one ever,' you'd beam.

And you were right, each year it was. And each year Noreen would not disappoint you and would squeal with laughter, opening her jar and looking inside to see what coin she had. And when you moved away, you never forgot her. It became as much of a pastime for you as for Noreen – the jars and the hunting down of new and different coins especially as you could get your hands on all kinds of interesting foreign ones by then. There was no one like you in her eyes at those moments when you produced some unusual specimen. I often felt my halo slip a little when she hugged you.

When she died, she left us her legacy of almost one hundred and fifty jars. When alive she only ever travelled with her three favourites: an old jam jar her mother had given her when she was five; a jar engraved with her name that Sadie had given her on her fiftieth birthday and then finally that one that you and Rosaleen gave her at your wedding. It was a beauty, I have to say: a photo of the three of you on the front of it. You and Rosaleen on either side of her taken on the settee at home in the front room when you got engaged. It was full to the brim of dimes and quarters. You must've been saving them for years. And to give it to her at the wedding, that was a stroke of genius. There it sat awaiting her arrival at her place at the top table. We all stood back to watch her reaction. Even the pair of you had slipped in to see it. She didn't disappoint and hugged you both until you had to disentangle yourselves in order to go back out to make your official entrance.

Of course, we lived in fear of those precious jars

breaking. Sadie worried constantly about them and therefore so did I. We were like parents tormented by the loss
of a child's favourite toy, the one they had to have to go
to sleep at night. I remember thinking that exact thing
when years later, on a visit home from the States, young
Adam, who was possibly no more than three at the time,
lost his toy duck, 'Ducky', a soft teddy yoke, on a shopping
trip to Dublin. Will you ever forget it?

'They rang everywhere they'd been, Maurice,' Sadie told
me when I came in later that evening. 'But no one had
sight nor sound of it. Kevin had to go back up to every
shop until he found it down the side of one of those kiddie
rides in the shopping centre, you know, the big one on
Stephen's Green. It was like they'd won the lotto, when
Rosaleen saw him come in with it. My goodness, I could
hardly take the stress of it,' Sadie said, holding a hand to
her heart.

After that Rosaleen scanned the Internet to find an exact
replica for fear it might happen again. She never needed it
in the end but says now she'll keep it and give it to Adam
when he has *his* first baby. Well, Sadie thought that was
just a lovely idea. But then again there was very little
Rosaleen could do that Sadie didn't approve of. You don't
hear of that much now do you? Mothers and daughters-
in-law getting on like that.

In the end we bought a case for Noreen's three special
jars. There they sat, safely enclosed in bubble wrap, ready
for any journey. Noreen would carry that case proudly
across the car park to where I waited to bring her home
for the weekend, with Sadie following on behind with life's
actual essentials, that Sadie, not Noreen, had packed. She

was a ticket. Her own woman, as they say. She pretty much ruled our lives, but truthfully her burden was light.

Noreen died in 2007, not long after the incident in the hotel. She was seventy. Fell on her way to her breakfast with the carer by her side, the one she liked the best, Susan was it? Collapsed into the woman's arms. Blood clot in the brain. The loss hit your mam hard. She became lost in a silence I hadn't witnessed since Molly had died. It was months before she smiled properly again or was able to laugh about the things Noreen got up to.

You'll remember it was a small ceremony, her funeral. Just us, you and Rosaleen standing each side of your mam, holding her hand, a few neighbours and some of the people who looked after Noreen from the home, and of course Jenny and May returned from England. We brought her home to Annamoe to be buried with her parents. I think Sadie found that bit the hardest, being parted from them all. At first we made the trip to their grave every second weekend and then it lessened as time went on and we got older. I know Sadie did her best for her all through her life, but I'm not sure she agreed with me on that. She was so self-contained that sometimes I think I missed the full extent of the hurt and guilt. I did my best to be on guard for it. But having spent half my life distracted by what was outside – my deals, my empire – I often forgot to see what lay inside and how precious it was.

Chapter Five

9.20 p.m.
Fourth Toast: to you, Kevin
Jefferson's Presidential Select

You've always been good at sending me the rare whiskies. On my birthday, I've been assured of an unusual beauty waiting for me on the kitchen table when I get in. When she was around, Sadie would stand there all proud, like she'd flown it over the Atlantic herself.

'Look what's arrived,' she'd say. Always that. Her eyes dancing with joy – her smile as bright and warm as a day for foaling.

She'd sit and watch me unpack it. And then 'ooh' and 'aah', once the wooden box was opened. Running her fingers up and down the bottle, over the label, her hands lingering on the silky material covering the plastic casing. She'd take it between her fingertips and rub it gently with her thumb. There was that one where the material was deep orange, you might remember it yourself.

'Isn't it lush, Maurice?' she'd said. 'You could bite into that and almost suck the goodness out.' Sometimes I wondered what was going on in my wife's head. Can't remember which bottle it belonged to. She kept all of them, the boxes, would you believe? Piled up in the back of the wardrobe, apparently. I never knew until I came across them after she'd died. I sat on the bed the morning of their discovery, with the door open for a while, just staring. Fifteen in all. All that pride packed away behind her coats. Days and weeks it took me, to decide how to keep hold of what those boxes meant to Sadie. Ladders. That's what I thought in the end – that they could make the nicest little steps for Adam or Caitríona. Up to those big bunk beds of theirs. So I took them out; sat on the old footstool, the one Sadie used to put her feet up on while she watched her soaps, do you remember it? An old wooden packing box that a spare part for the tractor came in one time.

'Are you using that?' she had asked, having come into the shed one day with a letter that had arrived for me.

'That?' I said, pointing at the wooden crate. 'I was going to break it up for the fire.'

'I'll take it. I have a bit of old carpet that'll do just the job to cover it.'

'For what?'

'A footstool. The price of them is just ridiculous over in Duncashel. No, this will do nicely.'

Forty years we've had that footstool. Still perfect. The carpet is a blue flower affair, offcuts from your bedroom. So I sat there on it, the night I cleared the wardrobe. Each box I took out I spent time over, trying to remember when you'd sent them. When I opened the box where the orange silk had been, I could see it was gone. Stripped of its lush lining. The inner plastic laid bare like a chicken picked clean. I couldn't figure it out. I just sat looking at it, turning the box over as if the very act might give me a clue as to why Sadie had done it. And then it occurred to me, I'd seen that orange material somewhere different. But it took me a while to find it in my memory. In the end I only had to turn my head and lay a hand to the dressing table and there it was. A purse in which she held her hair pins. That's what she'd made – something practical and something where she could touch the lush softness every night. I've kept it. Saved it from the storage boxes. It's with me now, in my bulging pockets alongside my father's pipe. If anyone were to frisk me now they'd wonder what in the blazes I was at.

Francie is making the ladders for the children for me. He's working his magic as we speak. They'll be ready in time for when you come, which won't be long now – a matter of days.

For me, though, it wasn't just the drink but the literature about the making of the whiskies that was important. Each leaflet I read from cover to cover. I wondered what it felt like to be a distiller and to have created such perfection. Master craftsmen, all. Creating beauties at which men sighed. I wondered at their lives, their names: Dan and Rust and Carter, I imagined. I saw them all as quiet men, contented in their simplicity, sitting on porches, rocking in chairs, listening to radios and crickets as evening turned to night. Hands as big as shovels but nimble as stonemasons'. Before I took that first sip, I always raised my glass to them, off there sitting on their stoops – men, alongside whom I'd have happily passed the time. 'God bless the hands,' I always said, when I held their creation up and watched it move with grace and balance around my Waterford cut-crystal glass, a wedding present from Sadie's

Aunt Maura, she was always at pains to point out in that worried voice of hers whenever I held it. 'God bless the hands.'

You gave me this bottle of eighteen-year-old Jefferson malt last Christmas. It's been hiding in the bag at my feet all evening.

'Here, put that behind the bar,' I say, handing it to Svetlana, when she comes to clear my barely picked-at plate.

She looks at me like I'm stone mad.

'I'll be wanting a swig of that, when I get back.'

I attempt to jump down from the bar stool but it's more like a slow motion topple. Still, I make it safely to solid ground and off I go. I look back at her still staring at the bottle looking very worried.

'I cleared it with Emily, you'll not lose your job.' Of course, I never mentioned a thing to Emily, but I'm sure she'd have had no objections. And even if she had, well, I'd have done it anyway.

She looks at me and smiles, a smile that says she knows I'm lying but she takes it anyway and puts it under the counter.

'You know those people at the awards are on dessert, now? Seriously, how you Irish not all get indigestion. You eat too fast.'

It's a funny thing walking these corridors. The place has changed a lot since my day – extensions and renovations heading off in different directions. But still there are parts I recognise. Like this corner here. There is the smallest of dents. If you weren't watching out you'd miss it. That was me. One day when they were short-handed in the house they asked me to bring wood to the main drawing room. I had to take my shoes off before they let me through. Thankfully, my mother had only darned my socks the previous week so I didn't make a holy-show of her. As I made my way down the corridors I became distracted by the furniture as big as myself, and pictures, great massive jobs spanning whole walls, with men in red coats on horses. There was a big grandfather clock in the main hallway that I couldn't take my eyes off. I couldn't believe clocks were made that big. We had a clock that sat over the range at home, small thing that never made an impression on me. Not like that one. I watched the pendulum swing, ticking so clearly, so grandly – announcing its importance to the world. Possibly would've stood there all day had the basket not begun to weigh me down. As I hooshed it back up and moved off, didn't Big Ben decide it was time to chime, it having hit the hour. Well, I jumped. The wall saved the basket from falling, but not before it made this little dent right here. I remember brushing at it as much as I dared. Not sure what I was trying to achieve, it possibly only made it worse. But I moved away quick smart before I was caught and hanged. That must have been the day I ended up getting lost, opening up Dollard's library door by accident. I'd forgotten that.

'Not here, next door, on the left,' he said, lifting his eyes from his desk.

'Sorry, sir,' I managed, before backing out. And now that I think of it, it was the only time I remember him not scaring the hell out of me. He seemed almost normal and, if my memory isn't playing tricks on me, I think I saw him get up in an attempt to help me with the door. But I was gone so fast, he didn't need to. Well now, isn't that a turn-up for the books? Isn't it interesting what the mind chooses to remember, or forget, for that matter?

'Well, Maurice, is all going to plan?' Robert is sitting there at the bar waiting for me when I get back. 'No, I'm not stopping,' he says, lowering my hand that I raise in the lassie's direction.

'I can't buy anyone a drink tonight, it seems.'

'No, honestly, Maurice, I can't,' he continues when I give it another go. 'Yvonne needs me home. Am just in for an hour or so at the awards. A bit of business you know, thought I'd catch some of those lads on the hop.'

'Sure aren't you every woman's dream getting home and the evening only beginning.'

'What can I say, Maurice? Have you not moved on to the champers yet?'

'Not yet. You ordered it so for herself.'

'I did. And tell me this, have they figured out it's you?'

'Figured out "it's me" what?'

'I reckon they think it's someone turning up for this gig. I wish I could be here when they realise it's farmer Hannigan and his mucky wellies who's their VIP.'

'Where're you going with the mucky wellies, sure don't I have my Sunday best on?'

'You do and all. Very smart, altogether.' I run my hand over the front of my green jumper. 'Listen, have you the forwarding address of this nursing home of yours, for the files like?' he asks.

'Did I not give it to you? I'll drop it over tomorrow before I head.'

'Good man yourself,' he says, stepping away from the stool he's been half hanging off for the last few minutes. 'Listen, enjoy the rest of the evening,' he says, with a big wink. 'We'll be talking. Drop by tomorrow before you go, so. Good man.'

And with a slap on my back he's off.

'Svetlana,' he calls, knocking on the bar and then waving to her as she stands at the other end, doing something with her phone.

She waves back before he disappears through the door.

'Do you know that man, young Robert?' I ask, nodding my head after him.

'Oh Robert, yes, yes,' she says enthusiastically, coming over to me, leading me to regret my question.

'He helped me with problem I had. He is very nice, very kind.'

'He is that. You're not from here then?'

'Me? No!' she says, as if it were madness to think any sane person could possibly be born, bred and still live here.

'Latvia,' said so proudly, it makes me smile.

'What do you think of working here then, at the hotel?' I ask, determined that she will drag nothing else from me.

'Yes. It's nice. Busy. Emily, is very nice person.'

'Ah, Emily. Yes, a lady.'

'Yes. Emily is lady,' she states, like she's confused at how I could possibly mix up her gender.

I smile more to myself than to her and think what an even richer man I'd be if I could bottle and sell that ballsiness of hers.

*

When you were small, no more than four, I came in late one evening. The kitchen was empty. Spick and span as it always was straight after the dinner. I knew Sadie would've been elbow deep in soapy water, scrubbing the kitchen back to order, not an hour before. My place lay set at the table. As I lifted the saucepan lid off my dinner and stuck it in the Aga, I could hear your voices from down the hall. I sat to the *Meath Chronicle*, perusing the market news. Try as I might not to let it, the laughter got the better of me in the end and I left the paper down and headed in your direction. The bathroom door was open, and as I passed it I could see the bath still quarter full, with a couple of surviving suds and a yellow duck floating among them. I held back in the hallway peering in at the pair of you next door in your bedroom.

'Kevin, I love you. Your Mammy loves you,' Sadie said, marking every word with a kiss to your tummy as you lay on the ground being dried. 'She loves every bone of you, do you know that?'

'Hmm hmm,' you replied, happily watching puffs of white rise from the Johnson's baby powder container every time you pressed its middle.

'And does Kevin love Kevin?' Puff upon puff of whiteness filled the air. *Does Kevin love Kevin*, I repeated in my head.

You didn't reply. Instead you turned the talcum powder upside down, shaking it vigorously on to your tummy and the floor.

'Because if you love this wee boy,' she continued, dispersing the powder all over you, 'and are always kind to him and always try to understand him then I think he will be the happiest little man in the whole wide world.'

She used the corner of the bath towel to rub the white smatterings from the carpet. 'Will you do that, will you love Kevin for me? Will ya? Ya rascal,' she asked, administering another tickle that let loose more squeals of laughter.

I never disturbed you but made my way into our darkened bedroom and sat on the side of the bed looking out at the silhouette of our trees and the hills against the night sky, brightened by one of the biggest moons I'd ever seen. It was too much even for me, a man of forty-three to try to comprehend what Sadie had said, let alone a child of four. Loving yourself? The very thought. I reached for the bedside lamp, fumbling to find the switch under the shade. I pulled the curtains closed and stood looking at the brown flowers with their orange centres, one after another, row upon row. My finger rose to follow the pattern of the petals. My blackened nail and layers of hardened skin that had no hope of feeling the fibre circled anyway.

'Oh, you're home?' Sadie said, from the door behind me.

'Thought I'd change out of these,' I said, my fingers pulling away from the flowers, pretending at taking off my jumper.

'A first for everything, I suppose. I left the dinner for you.'

'I saw that.'

'This man's off to bed.' Her head nodded in the direction of your room. 'Are you coming in to say good night?'

'I'll be in now.'

How many times did Sadie talk to you that way, I wonder. And is that why you are the man you are? So sure and happy in your life?

*

173

You never wanted the land, not even one bit interested. I tried. Made you work alongside me, from early on, out in your rain gear and boots. She'd have had you in bubble wrap if I'd let her. Aren't children supposed to love the mud and getting themselves dirty? Not you. There were times I got so frustrated. That moanie head on you. Miserable you'd be. Wet and feckin' miserable. Picking at the straw with your fork, like it was diseased.

'Come on. Give it a bit of welly,' I'd say, demonstrating how it should be done. You'd stretch the fork a little further, but that would be it. Soon you'd be back to picking at the edges.

'Go in,' I'd say, 'go in to blazes. I'll do it me feckin' self.'

Off you'd go then, back inside, bawling. I'd see Sadie bend to comfort you through the kitchen window, unfurling you from all of your protective layers.

'Ach, Maurice, he's only wee, can you not be a little kinder?' I didn't need to hear what she'd have to say on the matter. I knew it by heart. I knew to leave well enough alone and not go in straight away, even if I'd been inclined. I bulled on outside, cursing your softness. I gave up trying after a few years. Left you to your books.

'How do you read them yokes?' I asked you once. 'The size of them.' You must have been in secondary by then. Sitting at the kitchen table when I came in, always at the books.

'I dunno. I just do,' you said. 'They're interesting. This one's about the Mongols. One of their greatest weapons was that they smelt. Seriously, it says that no one ever wanted to be fighting downwind of these guys. That's just hilarious.'

'Yep. Hilarious,' I said walking away from you, wondering where I'd gotten you at all.

Do you remember the time you came into the shed one evening and started mucking out? Fifteen, maybe you were. You stood right beside me and got stuck in. After years of hating muck and manure, you worked the whole evening in it. I looked at you out of the corner of my eye to see what you were at. Kept waiting for a question or something to explain this change of heart. But nothing came.

'Will I start on them logs, Dad?' you asked, pointing at the pile ready for chopping.

'Go on so,' I said, delighting in the idea of watching you struggle with the axe. On the other hand I was worried about what your mother would say when I'd tell her you'd lost a finger. But you fecker, you took up that thing as if you'd always worked one, a minor miracle. Lobbing the pieces into piles like you were some kind of lumberjack.

'Anything else, Dad?' you said, when you'd finished the lot.

'No, you're grand now. Come on, we'll call it a night.'

I walked across the yard behind you wondering when it was finally going to come: the big reveal.

'Tea?' I asked, when we reached the warmth of the kitchen and I began to fill the kettle. You gave me the warmest of smiles, like I'd just handed you a hundred pounds.

'Sure, go on so. Mine's a coffee,' you said, slouching into the refuge of one of the kitchen chairs.

'Since when did you start drinking that stuff?'

'Carl Bernstein only drinks coffee.'

I opened the press door and stood there looking at it like I was looking at a knitting pattern. I took down the

Lyons then started to move the packets of soup and jars of jam and marmalade around, looking for the coffee.

'Yeah, Bernstein, one of the greatest journalists alive. Nixon and all, Watergate?' you said, raising your voice a little above the clatter. 'Bernstein was one of the boys that broke the story.' You were off your chair by now leaning on the counter right beside me. 'That's who I want to be. Well, when I say who I want to be, I mean—'

'Got it,' I said, pulling a blue Nescafé jar free. Looking at it, I rounded you to get at the kettle.

'Did you know you can do a college course now to be a journalist?'

'One spoon or two?'

'Just the one. There's a place in Dublin, Rathmines, where you can do a cert.'

The kettle clicked off.

'Milk?'

'No, I take it black.'

I brought the mugs to the table, with a handful of Fig Rolls, not bothering with a plate as I knew your mother was doing the ironing in front of the TV next door. Thursday was ironing day.

'So, yeah, I was thinking I might look into it a bit more. See what points you need like.'

I sat sideways to the table, staring at the back door, while you started to slurp at the dark liquid. I could feel your eyes on me the whole time. In the background the kettle emitted little mini clicks, like sighs after all its exertions, as it cooled down.

'Is that right?' I finally said, 'And tell me this, do you get extra points for drinking your coffee black?'

My son the journalist. I mean how the hell did that happen? I can just about manage to read the GAA results and the mart prices in the newspaper for Christ's sake but write *whole* pages, give my opinion to the world – are you mad?

'I hear himself wants to be a journalist?' I said, to Sadie later, as we got ready for bed.

'What?' she said, looking in the mirror, concentrating on securing a wayward strand of hair into her curler.

'Himself and the mucking out earlier? Turns out he wants to be a journalist.'

'He's told you so. I was wondering when he'd get around to it.'

'How long has this been going on?'

'Ah, Maurice, you know he's always been into reading and writing.'

'I know, but a career in it? Are there any jobs even?'

'There's no jobs in anything these days. Isn't that what the teachers keep telling them? They'll have to emigrate. Can you imagine, Maurice?' she said, turning to me, looking horrified, as I sat in the bed. 'Our little man leaving.'

'Sure he'll never make a penny at that game.'

'Did you not hear me? It's not about money, Maurice. We're going to lose him. England or America.'

She turned from me with one of her exasperated sighs.

When you went off to college, the mourning went on for weeks. Even though you were only a few miles up the road in digs, where you were rung every evening and from which you came home every weekend with your backpack full of washing. But on a Saturday, I have to hand it to you, you still rose early to work alongside me.

'Well?' I'd say, 'How are the books?'

'Big,' you said once, looking a bit hassled over the exams that were only a couple of weeks off.

'Sure, didn't I tell you this words business is a cod.'

When the exams started, I worked alone. I missed you then. Never told you but it was never the same. And when you decided to move to America in eighty-nine, when you graduated, joining the thousands of others doing the same, well I thought Sadie'd never recover.

'But Maurice,' she said to me one night over the dinner before you went, you had your tickets booked at this stage, 'you have to know someone up there in Dublin who could give him a job. You're always going on about your connections.'

'If it was herd of cattle he wanted, that'd be no problem, Sadie. But no, I don't know anyone of those tycoons who run the papers in Dublin or London.'

As it goes, I did enquire with those I knew had their fingers in many pies, just on the off chance that one of them might be a newspaper. But it was to no avail. But I never told your mother I'd tried. Never wanted to get her hopes up.

You left us after your graduation, a matter of days. Your mother cried through the ceremony and every night until you left. The airport was something shocking. Do you remember how she held on to you? How you had to actually take her arms from around your neck as we stood at the security gates.

'I'll be back, Mam. This isn't forever,' you kept saying, patting her back. Fair play to you; I would have lied too.

We watched you move inch by inch away from us in that line of young people, still teenagers some of them. Waving, until you disappeared behind the glass screen. But your mother wouldn't leave straight away no matter how much I reminded her about the price of parking.

'Just one more minute, Maurice,' she said, 'in case he's forgotten something.' So we waited, it must've been about fifteen minutes. In truth, I knew she was hoping you'd change your mind.

You did stay for good. And so your mother decided if you weren't coming home then she was going to you, as often as she possibly could. She took to the travel big time. Loved to get over to you if not every year then every two years. I only went the once. A year after the wedding. You had the house by then. The size of it. You'd swear you were planning to have ten children. Five bedrooms, not to mention a basement as big as our house. But sure that's the way of it over there, isn't it? Rooms the size of a semi-d in Dublin. I rather the comfort and security of small spaces. There's a warmth to them, not to mention the convenience of having everything right beside you.

'Did you ever think of knocking the kitchen into the sitting room, Dad?' you asked, about ten years ago now when you were home. We were all sat around the kitchen table. Rosaleen was there too. Was Adam even born then?

'And why would I want to do that?'

'The space.'

'Do you think, Kevin?' Sadie replied on my behalf, looking around her, considering the partition wall.

'It would be more airy and freeing, you know.'

'D'ya know you're right,' I said, 'it gets fierce cramped

alright in the front room when your mother and me are both in there watching the telly at the same time. I can't lift the remote without elbowing her. And when she brings in the tea, sure I have to stand in the hall.' I suppose that was a bit harsh, son. But you took it gracefully, or so it seemed. But then again, you're good at hiding your frustration with me.

I liked your local post office over there. Every morning when we were with you, I'd walk to it. Six a.m. in the heat that felt like a summer's day in Ireland, I went out for my stroll: down the driveway and left up along Mervin Avenue until I hit the church, the bank and the post office. And there I'd sit on the bench outside. The post office was white, wooden and spotless. I had to take a picture. I wanted to show Lavin when I got back what a real post office looked like, not the skit of the thing he has hidden at the back of his newsagents. Inside was tidy and clean, with a rail that shone and snaked its way to the counter. I was only actually in it the once, having volunteered to go get the stamps for the postcards. Apparently there were at least twenty people back home who needed telling of our trips to the shopping outlets. I liked to sit on the bench watching this foreign world wake up on those early mornings. I never got to stay too long as I had to be back for whatever excursion was planned for that day. I trundled along after Sadie and Rosaleen or you, whichever of you had taken the day off. All I wanted was the nearest seat in the shade and a cup of tea, if, that was, I could stand the queues and endless questions about how I took it. Medium, regular, with the milk on the side – I got it soon enough. I liked to stroll around the alien streets, listening to the alien voices. Never knew I was that much of an ear-wigger. Could've hung around those street corners all afternoon, if I was let. It helped me realise we were no different from our American cousins – the same things matter the world over: saving face and money.

And then there were the fancy restaurants. That one – Rolinsky's up in New York. Rosaleen drove us and we met you there. You knew the owner. Same guy who owned the paper you worked for. Spick and span it was. Toilets as big as bedrooms, cloth towels for drying your hands. You couldn't scratch yourself at the table but the waiters were over to check everything was OK. And as for the menu, that was huge too. I was exhausted before I even opened it. I laid it down not bothering to attempt.

'Are you not going to have a look at the menu, Maurice?' Rosaleen asked.

'No. I know what I want.'

'Would you not have a look. You should see the size of the steak. They do this surf and turf thing, it's to—'

'I'll be having plain chicken breast with mash and gravy.'

You reached a hand and laid it firmly on Rosaleen's.

I got my chicken.

'Pan-fried chicken on a bed of mash covered with "maple jus",' the waiter said, when he put it down in front of me.

For a while, I stared at the plate, as big as a hubcap as I recall. I knew you were all watching me watching it. After a moment I scraped off the brown liquid from the chicken and transplanted what was left of it to my side plate. Next, I scooped away the soaked outer layer of the mash with my fork and lifted out any whiteness I could find underneath, putting it alongside the chicken. The hubcap, I pushed into the centre of the table and proceeded to eat my dinner from my side plate, refusing to look at any of you.

'Is everything to your satisfaction?' the waiter asked, arriving back to us after a bit.

'Dandy,' I replied, on our behalf.

'Excellent. I'll just take this for you,' he said, reaching for the forlorn plate in the middle of the table. Not a flinch out of him. Professional to the end.

By the time dessert was finished, a very creamy affair as I recall, all I really wanted was to get out of there. I needed the air. But you wouldn't hear of me having a stroll.

'I thought this was one of the safest cities in the world?'

'But let's not take any chances tonight, OK, Dad? The coffee won't take long.'

I was all set to protest when Len or Lenny or was it Lev, the boss, arrived. He pulled up a chair beside me and seemed mighty interested in what I thought of the place.

'It's grand,' I told him, throwing in a smile, knowing I was on show.

On the other side of me, Sadie enthused enough for the both of us, so I sat back and let her at it while my fingers drummed on my napkin.

'You've got yourselves a fine boy here,' Lev said, pointing over at you, smiling, showing off his perfect white teeth. 'He's going to be big. You heard it here first folks, that boy is going places.'

Sadie clapped her hands in delight. You beamed and laughed, and Rosaleen stretched her hand to yours. Me? I nodded to the tablecloth wondering how much longer. But I wish now I'd smiled over at you, given you a wink that said, 'Sure, don't I know.'

And then you took me to meet Chuck Hampton. It had been Lev's idea apparently. He suggested I might like to go meet his friend the farmer. We left early one morning, passed the bench outside the post office and it wasn't even light yet. We must've been on the road about two or three hours, listening to flashy news stations that seemed more interested in selling us things rather than news coverage, before we pulled into his place. I wasn't sure if we were even in New Jersey any more.

'You're mighty welcome, sir.'

I was barely out of the car when that greeted me. I looked behind and a man of around sixty approached with an outstretched hand. I shook it. That hand said all I needed to know. The rough feel and the strong grip told me I'd found a piece of home. He spent the day with us, well me, anyway. You sat on the man's porch with your laptop. I don't remember at what stage it was, but you came running down to us in one of his red-painted barns saying you had to go for an hour or so to get better Internet coverage.

'You need to go to Sully's café. Three miles north, turn left at the tree stump.'

You looked at Chuck with a quizzical smile.

'You'll know it when you see it. Just head on out that way.'

'Don't be worrying, son,' I told you, as you ran off waving your hand with that laptop in your other. 'You take your time. I'm in no rush.' I turned back to Chuck and all he was telling me about the heifer standing in front of me.

We drove his land. At times we got out to walk it. Picking up fistfuls of the soil and smelling it.

'Lots of good Pike County sun and rain. No pesticides, just love and care.'

I reached for some and rubbed it, not the same richness as my own, drier and less dense but I couldn't deny the man its quality. We walked among corn stalks and wheat and grass to see his herds beyond. You could've left me in those fields for the rest of the trip and I would've been happy to sleep under the stars with a smile on my face. Listening to the foreign sounds of that world. Coyotes instead of foxes, crickets instead of owls. It was into the afternoon before we returned to the house where I met his wife and a most welcome bowl of soup with what they called 'biscuits' on the side. Turns out they were scones, I corrected them on that.

You came back around four, all apologies.

'I was just about to put this man to work,' Chuck laughed, coming down off the porch to shake your hand.

'I tried to call but I couldn't get a signal.' You held your phone up to the sky.

'Yep, it's a bit hit and miss out here. Come on in and have yourself a bite to eat.'

We sat on the porch for another half hour or so, with me mithering that poor man over prices and co-ops and seeding.

'The big boys have it sown up, Maurice, if you'll excuse the pun. Can't use our own seeds no more. They sue anyone who does. Have to buy theirs. Good friend of mine Kurt Lettgo, a seeder out Mission way, was put out of business. His family been doing that for four generations.'

'So let me get this straight, Mr Hampton,' you interrupted, taking out your pen and that notebook you always carried, 'you are *compelled* to buy someone else's seeds?'

'God's honest. Go look it up. It ain't no secret. It's the law.'

Turned out it was that story 'Seeds Unsown' that won you that big award two years later. You sent us a framed picture of you being presented with it. Needless to say it got pride of place beside the telly. On the back you wrote:

To Dad with thanks. I'd never have gotten this if it weren't for you.

It's in the storage boxes, Kevin. Wrapped and packed safely.

'Well, now this is some holiday,' I said getting back in the car and waving to Chuck as we reversed. Chuck, who promised he'd take a trip to Ireland so I could return the hospitality. Never came, of course. But we exchange Christmas cards every year. His wife died a while back, a few years before Sadie. Still lives on the farm, although his nephew has taken it over. I wouldn't mind a catch up to see how he's fared. See if he's handled the abandonment better than me.

When our holiday was over, I shook your hand with everything I had at the security gates in the airport. One of those ones where you hold the elbow as well. We stood there like that for a second until it got awkward.

'Sure, we'll see you back over beyond sometime,' I said.

'Absolutely. Christmas, hopefully. I'll let you know.'

'Do that,' I patted your hand and released it, turning to put an arm around Sadie who sobbed her way through the security gates.

Sadie lived for your newspaper articles. Whatever you wrote, or said for that matter, she'd be telling everyone. Gone off to the library to find out more to confirm just how clever you were. Forest fires in California, Hubble, the purchase of Alaska. Me? I never asked a thing.

'Is that right?' I'd say, when she produced whichever paper you worked for back then. I'd lay it in front of me above the dinner plate and read the first line. I can still feel the cold sweat of my forehead even now as I sat there wishing instead for the simplicity of the price of sucklings. See, I never admitted to either of you about me and the dyslexia. Oh yes, I found out I wasn't thick after all about ten years ago. A young one on a helpline I called after hearing Pat Kenny talking about it on the radio. Ten per cent of the population, she said. Would you credit that? But, it's not that I can't read, I can after a fashion, at my own pace with no one standing over my shoulder. I always found a way 'round things. I was a great one for losing the glasses at the right moment or complaining about the small print.

'Isn't that great now,' I'd say, pushing your article away after I'd given it an acceptable amount of time. That was another good one of mine – lying.

'Where did he get the brains from at all?' Sadie might gush, then.

'That would be your side.'

'Do you think?' she'd say, giving me her best modest smile.

You still bring me your articles when you come over. Putting them on the couch beside me or on my footstool. When I'm out of the room usually. But you never say a thing. Never ask if I've ever read them.

Since your mother died, I've noticed your trips home have become more numerous. Two or three times a year now. Checking up on me, what? Mostly it's just you but sometimes herself and Adam and Caitríona come as well. When you're on your own it's only for a weekend or so. I always put the heat on in your old room to make sure it's aired the night before and I leave the immersion on so you have the hot water whenever you want it. That's a thing I remember about being over in the States, hot water whenever you like. Of course, as soon as you're down the driveway on your way back west, I switch it off.

It's been hard trying to hide my plans from you with you home so regular. But you've not asked, when you've seen the odd box here and there. I reckon you think it's all her stuff, your mother's. Maybe you didn't want to think about that. Me, packing her away, getting rid of her like that. I left the packing of your room 'til I was sure there was no chance of another visit before now.

Do you look forward to coming home, son? I'll admit, the idea of having a living being in the house with me, as Gearstick wouldn't grace me with his presence, is appealing. And each time, I swear to myself that this time will be different, that I'll make the effort. That I'll ask about your job and what you're working on. And I promise myself I'll listen to you with my whole body and every ounce of concentration in me. I'll hang on your every word. And then I might even ask another question. But as soon as you walk in the door sure it's like a bolt closes over my mouth. And in you come, all bags and bustle. Landing on the couch with a big grin on your face like you've just arrived from the Bahamas. You hand over the bottle of whiskey and sit forward, elbows on knees, hands together, looking about the place, then over at me and you say something like:

'Well, what's the news?'

'Divil the bit now.'

'Didn't the lads get a thrashing in the finals, though? Some match. That full forward, Kirwan, is it? He's some man to go.'

'Not a bad team now.'

'How's the farm? Still buying and selling all 'round you?'

'I'm not doing too bad.'

'Did that business with the piece of land over in Lissman work out OK?'

'What was that?'

'You remember the last time, your man was trying to push down the price.'

'Oh, that. I sorted him.'

'All well with the Bradys?'

'Not a bother.'

'I see Tommy Brady is off out in Australia?'

'Is that right?'

'Saw it on Facebook. There's a load of lads from around there now. A whole gang of them. Times have changed; it was the States in my day, now it's Down Under.'

'Aye, that's the way of it.'

I'd watch your fingertips bounce off each other.

'Rosaleen and the children well?' I'd manage.

'Great. Adam's gotten into the rugby big time. It's getting popular in the States now. Plays every Wednesday and Saturday. Here, I have some pictures.'

You tap at your phone, then come hunker beside me and slide your finger so I can see him in action, mid-flight, the picture of determination. There's other photos too like that one of Caitríona and Rosaleen, sitting on your back porch eating ice creams. Caitríona's eyes closed and tongue extended, laughing trying to reach the ice cream on her nose.

'That was Labor Day,' you say.

I nod and smile. I'd like to sit over them a bit longer but I don't like to take the phone. And when you've finished, you sit back down and look around again. And pull out a few more questions. When you start asking me about Lavin then I know we've scraped the bottom of the barrel.

'Sure I might take a walk down the fields,' you say, rising, no matter what time of night. When Gearstick was still around and it was bright, I'd watch you from the kitchen window. Gearstick racing along beside you, so excited at the speed and distance. You throwing a stick and him bounding off after it, happy to have time with a younger model. Poor old Gearstick, when I was out and about myself with him towards the end there, it was more him waiting for me.

For the time you'd be around we'd have the dinners out. There'd always be a row, of course, over who pays for the dinner.

'Dad, you paid the last time.'

'I did in my eye.'

'You did, do you not remember? Sure it was only yesterday and it was here for Christ's sake. Here, I'll ask the girl.'

'You do that now and I'll never go for another bite to eat with you.'

'I'd just like to pay the once.'

'Can't you pay tomorrow?'

'Until tomorrow comes and you'll swear blind it's your turn.'

'Can a father not buy his son a dinner?'

At teatime, though, we'd have the soup at home. I remember

you bought some homemade stuff from SuperValu once. I ate it alright, but there's nothing like the packet.

You do a round of the house. Checking the rooms for damp and leaks and locks. I dread that. God love you but you never had the DIY gift. You spend the days mending things. I can never watch. There's more cursing and fingers injured than in a county final. I have to get out and tend to whatever I can, even if it's only my sanity, when I see you coming with my toolbox.

'Where are you going with that yoke?' I said, the first day I saw you with it, traipsing through the back door.

'There's a shelf in the bathroom that's a bit loose.'

'It's been that way all its life.'

'But we don't want it falling on you.'

'Do we not, now?'

'While I'm here I may as well be useful.'

'Is that what you call it?' I said to myself, as you disappeared through the kitchen doorway.

You like your lists, alright. You show me the list of all you've completed before you leave – so 'my mind is at ease knowing they're sorted,' you say. And then there are the lists of jobs that I could 'get one of the lads in to tackle', like I haven't been tackling them my whole life myself. But I bite my tongue. Later, when you're back home, the phone calls come: have I got them done? How long did it take? Did it cost much? Sometimes things are done and sometimes I lie and let the broken whatever alone, until right before your next visit home. If I'm pressed for time then Francie is hauled in. It's always amazing though, how, despite all of that mending, there's another list assembled as soon as you walk through the door.

Do you think things have gotten better between us as the years have gone on? I can't tell any more.

You never once mention your job, when you're home. You just work away on your computer, 'remote access' you say. Do you remember when you got the Internet hooked up to the house?

'What's this?' I kept asking.

'Wait, Dad, wait,' you said, stepping away from the flashing light on that box in the hall.

Amazing stuff. The world right there with one tap of a button. I'm not as fast as you now, banging away on the keys all speedy, but I get there. I usually boil up the kettle for a cuppa and set myself up, glasses and all before I finally get online. But you're all biz. Silent, save for the tapping. Hunched over, that serious clever head on you. I could watch you for hours from the armchair in the kitchen and you at the table, staring into the laptop like it has some kind of spell on you. I swear I can see the steam rising from your head, all those brain cells you must be burning up.

Maybe, I'd have been happier if you'd been a gobshite. Chip off the old block. Then maybe I could've talked to you. Feck it, son, you really pulled the short straw with me. A cranky-arsed father who can't read for shite.

Two years ago, my plan hatched, I made a list of all the things I needed to do. I began to sort them into stuff I could do that day, the next week, the next month, and so on, you get the picture. All that organising fuelled me, pumping me up so much that I nearly left the house in my pyjamas one morning. That would have been great now, wouldn't it? Walking down Main Street in my Dunne's best. It was only a matter of months after your mother's funeral. Only for the mirror over the hall table, I would've done it, too. I halted my gallop long enough to go get dressed, then make a cup of tea and a half slice of toast at the kitchen table where I'd spread out my lists.

My list for that day read:

1. Estate agents
2. Emily/coin

I walked into the hotel an hour later. My hand in my pocket, turning the coin over and over. You see, despite Molly's insistence I give the thing back six years earlier, I still hadn't managed it. That day, however, I was determined to tick the box. But as I stepped into the foyer, I had the strongest urge to turn and run. A small part of me seemed unwilling to give the thing back at all. Somehow, it felt as much a part of me and my history as the abdicated King or Hugh Dollard or Thomas, for that matter. It had, after all, lived with me longer than any of them.

'Are you wondering who that is?' Emily's question confused and startled me. I hadn't realised that I'd stopped in front of that picture of Rainsford House of old, again – the one with the mystery man I still couldn't place.

I turned to look at her, resting my eyes on her profile for a moment, buying myself a little time before what was to come.

'I know it's one of your lot alright, a Dollard I mean, the nose and the long face,' I said eventually, my finger gesturing lazily in its direction.

'It's Thomas's father.'

'Really? I always thought of Hugh Dollard as a heavier-set man, fuller in the face.' She didn't answer me but looked away from the picture quickly, like she regretted starting talking about it in the first place.

'And to what do I owe the pleasure, Mr Hannigan? You don't usually join us for breakfast or for anything for that matter,' she said, smiling at me. 'You're looking well.'

Emily pointed me in the direction of one of the seats in the foyer but I kept on to the bar. I made my way to a table far into the corner of the lounge. Well, I had to be careful, you never knew who might be about listening in, despite the early hour. I sat and rubbed a hand over my chin wondering where to start.

'We have a bit of unfinished business, you and me,' I said, 'well, me and your family, I should say.'

'I don't like the sound of this. Are you finally calling in the loan?' she asked, sitting opposite, looking fierce worried.

'It's nothing like that. No, this goes back even further.'

I tried to order the words jumbling about in my head. But they scurried about like a pack of frightened sheep, not one of them brave enough to take the lead. I eyed the bottle of Bushmills on the shelf and wondered would it be rude to ask at this hour. But I thought better of it. I could hear my fingers drum the table and, in the distance, the pots and pans clattering in the kitchen behind the bar. The odd time a silhouette passed the frosted window of the door. I looked at Emily one last time as she shifted in her seat, her hands clasped together under her chin, leaning eagerly forward, elbows on the table, waiting for me to finally spit it out. In the end I simply reached into my pocket and set the coin free at last. King Edward VIII sat on the table in front of her.

I watched and didn't watch her, if you get me, kind of half-watched, glancing every now and again at her silence and her eyes as they darted between it and me. My hands did a merry dance between my pockets and the curve of the table. My lips pursed and started some mad airy whistling. I felt as much of a gibbering wreck as the day I stood in Berk's line up when the coin first went missing. Emily finally picked it up and gave it a good once over.

'But this, this . . .'

Her eyes turned on mine.

'Aye. It's the original. The one Thomas lost.'

'Oh dear God!' She dropped it and it bounced under the table. Emily shot up to standing as if she'd touched a live cable. She kept staring at the spot where it had been and backed away. Her hand to her mouth, lost to me. I'd have happily left right there and then. Skipped out of the place never to see it again. But, you see, that's the thing about here, isn't it? This bloody place, it keeps reeling me back in and I keep letting it. After a bit she came forward a little, then backed away again. Her own private waltz.

I reached to retrieve the coin. Not so swiftly as the first time a Dollard dropped it. I held on to the table with one hand and stretched my other under, my fingers wriggling about trying to locate it. I knew if I had to resort to kneeling, there was a danger of my never getting up again, at least not with any dignity. Arthritic knees. When I brushed against the metal, I grasped it and put it back, dead centre on the table.

'It was me that took it. I've had it all these years. It

wasn't a deliberate plan to rob it, Emily.' My eyes looked for her. 'I didn't even know what the bloody thing was or that it was valuable. It was simple, childish revenge, that's all.' I waited to see if she would offer me anything in reply but when she remained silent, I gave it another go. 'He wasn't the nicest of men, Thomas, back then . . .'

I fingered the scar on my face; coughed, a bit ashamed of my childish attempt at an excuse; got up to go in around the bar to pour myself some water, the Bushmills still seeming a step too far. I gulped down the coldness of the liquid and, when there wasn't a drop left, I made a slow return to my seat, peeking at her every second step or so, bringing two full glasses with me. I laid them down.

But still, she didn't budge.

'Water,' I commanded.

She considered me for a second before making her way back. I watched her feet until they disappeared under the table as she sat. I admit I couldn't hold her eye and looked off at the long window at the end of the room to see the beginnings of the town's waking. Lavin standing at his open door raising a hand to the newspaper deliveryman's truck that spluttered away down Main Street.

'But all this time, Mr Hannigan,' she began, calling me back, 'all this time, with the hotel and me, you knew you had it and never said a thing.' She kept up the staring, boring into me like I was some massive disappointment. I sipped at my water and found Lavin again, carting his papers into the shop. 'And even when I told you the story of what that bloody thing has done to us, to Thomas, you never said a word? Not a word. Just let me blab on like a fool.'

She looked away, unable to bear me.

'Emily, I've never considered you a fool. I have nothing but the greatest of—'

'But that's what us Dollards have always been to you – fools, to be used for everything you could get your greedy hands on.'

I stared at the table and felt my own anger rise. Greedy. I'd heard her alright – greedy. The coin looked small now. The thing that felt heavy in my hand for years, was like a halfpenny shrinking away from danger. I tapped the base of the glass on the table. My foot began to keep pace as the water in my glass jumped and lapped at the sides. I thought of Tony, dying in his bed, hiding the coin under his sweat-soaked pillow. Tony's funeral. My mother, my father, terrified of losing all they had. The beatings. And Molly and you. And Sadie. Oh God. Sadie. All I had lost came back at me. A big tsunami of hate and sorrow. How sorry I felt for myself. Out beyond in the foyer, I heard the voices of the reception staff, greeting their guests, giving instructions on how to get to the dining room for breakfast. The smell of fried bacon reached me. My stomach howled but I kept tapping. My dentures bit down on my lip holding it all in.

'I mean, we've all nearly lost our minds because of this, because of you.'

Emily shoved the coin in my direction. I watched its un-wantedness spin towards me and hit my elbow, rico- cheting away from me before landing just on the edge of the table. The coinage that never fecking was – how much I really wished that were true right at that moment.

I'm ashamed of what I did next, but I felt as mad as a

raging bull. I took that bloody thing in my hand, bounced it once then threw it across the room, hitting the bar counter, propelling it back on to the hardwood floor.

'You'll forgive me, Emily,' I shouted, heaving myself up to standing, my fist hitting the table, 'if I was busy burying my wife and wasn't thinking about the Dollards for once in my bloody life!'

The words spat out of me as I leaned over the table right into her face. Blood pumping, veins straining, on the verge of some furious meltdown. Instead it was the tears that came. Big sobs of the stuff. I grasped hold of the sides of the table to stop myself falling. And I looked at her, through my welling eyes, a helpless fool, my wall tumbling down.

The door behind the bar opened.

'Sorry to disturb you, Miss Bruton, but Kerrigan's are on the phone looking for the order,' a young one said. Kerrigan's, my arse. The lie of this heroine, come to save her boss, waited for a response. My hands rose to my face wiping away what I could as I felt my head thump like someone was inside trying to fight his way out. Back I fell into the chair.

'I'll call them later, Donna,' Emily said, to the floor not looking behind her to address the girl at all.

'Is everything OK?' young Donna asked quietly, looking at the back of her employer's head, then at me.

Emily also looked my way. Just like Molly, just like that last time I saw her. Beautiful, kind, wise eyes.

'Everything's fine here, Donna,' Emily said, getting up and turning to the girl, picking up the coin on her way over to the bar, 'nothing to worry about. You go on now. Hold any calls until I'm finished here.'

She came back to me then, so quietly and laid the coin down in front of her and there was silence for a minute or two. A silence in which I closed my eyes as tight as I could manage, so there was just me and Sadie locked inside.

'I'm sorry, about Sadie,' I heard her say. Molly's sweet voice. 'I was there, at the funeral. I didn't say anything. I didn't want to intrude. I'm not the best at funerals but I sent a card.'

I leaned into the support of my elbows on the table and thought of your mother. Thought of what she'd think of me now. About the show I was making of her. A sigh that seemed to come from the very feet of me washed up through my body, stilling the mad beats of my heart.

'You did, Emily. I got it, the card.'

I watched her fingers resting on the table for a minute or two.

'Coffee, I think I need a coffee,' she said eventually.

I didn't have the energy to say I never drank the stuff. So I let her away with the clanging and clinking and boiling of it. I never looked up for all that time, just kept staring down at my finger making circles on the mahogany table, your mother's name filling my head.

The spoon shook in the saucer that she put it down in front of me.

'Oh, blast it, milk,' Emily said, about to turn and go back.

'Not on my account,' I said, 'I drink it black.'

And then I laughed quietly to myself, as I thought of you and your coffee drinking.

She sat to her seat again.

'Shall we start again?' she asked, looking at me like she might a child who's just bumped their head.

I nodded and waited, not willing to make the effort just yet.

'Why give it back now?'

Her voice was so gentle, almost a whisper.

I coughed and waited and then said:

'I was clearing out Sadie's stuff last night and I came across it. Forgot I had it and now here it is.' I needed the lie to offer her some logical explanation.

'But it was you who kept asking me about it all these years.'

I looked at her and imagined the guilt she could see on my face. But still I offered no further explanation that would be forgivable. She watched me anyway, hoping.

'And what am I to do with it now?' she asked when she eventually realised nothing else was forthcoming. 'What plan did you have? Am I to keep it or . . .' she said picking it up and looking at me, 'am I to tell him?'

I took a sip of the coffee and winced, I mean how do you drink that stuff? There's nothing nice about that bitter muck. But still, I persevered, happy to have the distraction of its torture for a moment or two. And mad as it may sound, it felt like I had a bit of you with me, an ally, I suppose.

'It's up to you,' I said, 'I'm done with it now.'

Her face grew sad and worried.

'He's very ill you know. Uncle Thomas. Pneumonia. He's in hospital. Mummy and I are going over soon. I suppose I could bring it.' She looked at me like I was the wise one among us. The one with all the answers. Did she not know by now how disappointing I was at that?

'Whatever you think is best.' Selfishly, I felt lighter in

myself, a burden lifted, finally ready to get on with my own plans. I drifted off to them for a moment or two, continuing to drink the coffee. And when only half of the black stuff remained in my cup, I managed the words I should have offered long ago.

'I'm sorry for taking it, for keeping it. For everything.'

She said nothing, just nodded and looked down at the King that never was, once more before I took my leave.

I didn't hear from Emily for some weeks after. But one evening my mobile rang. I'd been expecting a call from Anthony, my newly appointed estate agent, and so I hit the button eager to hear about his progress in selling me off to the highest bidder.

'He's dead, Mr Hannigan, Uncle Thomas is dead,' was all she said. 'Can you come over?'

I parked the jeep outside the hotel even more badly than was my wont of late. I'm not the best at judging spaces these days, have had a few near misses, but until I actually hit something I'll not worry too much. When I got inside, Donna, the young one from the last time, led me through the reception office and down a warren of different hallways until I couldn't tell which way was north. She put me into a cosy lamp-lit room.

I took my seat in a chair that must've been from the time of the old house. It still bore a trace of luxury. Its red flowers and cream background hadn't lost their colour but the armrests were beginning to strain under their years, and the thinned fibres rolled easily under my fingertips. I let them be. Not wishing to add to the chair's demise, I rose slowly and awkwardly, the lowness of the cushion having all but swallowed me up in its comfort. For the life of me I couldn't place this room in the house. I made my way to the window, to give myself some bearing. But to no avail. It would've meant turning off the lamps.

'It's the old pantry with a little bit added on,' Emily said, when she arrived, catching me squinting through the window, my hands cupped over my eyes, trying to block out the light. 'Daddy converted it. It's tiny I know but it suits me. It was his office.'

Emily looked pale and exhausted as she stood in the middle of the room holding two glass tumblers in her hands.

'Here, we'll need these,' she said, putting them on the low table that sat between my seat and an exact replica, opposite. I made my way back over, and took my Bushmills.

'I don't remember the pantry much,' I said, looking around, putting off the inevitable a little longer, 'though my mother would have. She worked here too, you know.'

I lowered myself wearily into the chair.

'Yes, you've told me.'

'Of course. One of the many pitfalls of being old: the brain can't recall how many times it retells the same story.'

I took a good deep swallow, letting the whiskey warm whatever bits of me it touched. I sighed at the pleasure.

'Was it the coin that did it, Emily?' I said then, finally taking the bull by the horns.

She looked down at her drink, the air of the room beginning to ruffle at the edges as she shifted in her chair. She lifted her hand to her mouth, her elbow leaning on the armrest. Her fingers began to pull at her lips.

'He didn't see it at first,' she began, still not looking at me but at the floral patterned rug that spared the pink carpet that had seen better years beneath. 'I held it in my hand trying to show him as he lay in the bed but he wouldn't look. I had to call him: *Uncle, Uncle look. Look at what we found.* But he didn't, he just kept his eyes on Mummy. In the end, I had to take his hand and place it in his palm. Instant recognition. Instant. He got so agitated, though. Began to struggle, moving his head from side to side, whimpering like a baby. *Emily, what is it, what have you given him?* Mummy kept asking over and over, getting equally worked up. *What's he looking for? Emily what's going on?* It dawned on me that he was trying to see that I wasn't playing a trick on him. He was looking for his own one that he'd hidden under his pillow. I freed it from its black velvet box so he could see at last the two, side-by-side. He cried. I watched him. He didn't smile like I'd hoped he might. His face just wrinkled in utter pain, not relief, not joy, but pain. He closed the coins in his fists and pulled them to his heart and cried, long, loud heaving sobs until . . .'

She swirled her drink, watching it go around, and then drank from it. I took a sip of my own in the silence of the hiatus. When the liquid had quietened, she continued:

'Until no more tears, no more pain, no more breath. He died there and then. Dead. Instantaneous. Heart attack, they said. It killed him just as we always knew it would. I didn't know what to do. Mother was shouting and wailing in my ear. I just ran out to grab someone who could make him come back, make him be alive again, make it so I hadn't killed him. Somewhere in my naivety I hoped that coin's resurrection, its return, would give him peace.'

She laughed ironically, and with a sigh said: 'Instead, it tormented him to death.'

She took out the black box and laid it between us. I

glanced down knowing what it held but not wishing to see. She put down her glass and opened it and I didn't stop her, as much as I'd have liked to. There, facing me sat the abdicated King, doubly defiant.

I didn't quite know what to say. Was I there to stand trial for Thomas's death, was that what Emily had wanted, was that why she'd summoned me? There were times in my life I admit I had wished that man dead – a horrible, painful death. But as I sat watching Emily twitch with guilt and sadness, her tears falling steadily, there was no solace, no joy that he, at last, was gone.

About a year ago, son, I was following a Volkswagen Golf, Dublin reg, down our road. Evening it was, about seven. When it came to our gate, it braked, went by real slow, and then sped up again on its way. I didn't like it at all. These rural robberies, son – Dublin gangs targeting old people in their own homes, cash, that's what they're after – it's not right. The next day when I was standing in the front room, Cup-a-Soup in one hand and slice of bread in the other for the lunch, didn't I see it pass again. Bold as you like. Broad daylight. I rang Higgins straight away. 'Course it rang out. Cutbacks. Possibly over doing his shift in the Duncashel station. Then, as I tried Robert, didn't the fecker pass again, slower this time. Stopped right outside the gate. Sat there, the car idling, looking up at the house.

'Some Dublin fecker's out here scoping the place,' I told Robert's voicemail. 'Can't get Higgins. Call me.'

With the lace curtain between us, I saw him edge slowly on and pull into the gate of the field opposite. Right in, good and tight. The door opened and out he stepped. He started to cross the road, his hand patting his left pocket. From the other, he took out his phone. Over the cattle grid he came, making his way up the drive, doing a three-sixty once or twice. I backed away from the window, reached for my shotgun and made my way to the back door. I hunkered down to Gearstick, looked him in the eye and held his snout so he'd know to be quiet. And then we were gone, taking a right along the back and then up the side of the house. Gearstick kept pace as I held the shotgun tight. At the corner, we stopped. Me, pressed up against the wall, and Gearstick at my leg, my heart pumping away like I was running to catch the 109 to Dublin. I poked my head out, quick like.

'Yeah, it's the place alright,' I heard your man say, mooching around my front door. 'Looks quiet to me. I'll call you back.'

I watched him stick his mug up against the sitting-room window. His hand over his eyes, having a good butchers. He switched sides then, starting on the bedroom windows. I pulled back in as he made his way down to where I was waiting, looking through each window as he passed. Slowly, I took off the safety catch and raised the gun high. Gearstick's quick panting body pushed against me. I imagined his ears pricked forward. I heard the steps close in, three more I reckoned; I nuzzled the stock on my shoulder. Three, two, one:

'What the fuck do you want?' My hand, steady as a rock.

'Jesus,' he shouted, jumping back.

Gearstick unleashed the best bit of barking he had in him, pushing the fecker until he stumbled and fell on his

arse. Stood over him, his teeth bared, ready to launch once
I gave the command.

'Don't move,' I yelled, as he attempted to reach his hand
inside his zippy.

'No, man. No. It's cool.'

'Don't fecking "man" me.'

'Listen man, sir, I mean, sir. You have it all wrong. I'm
David Flynn from the Seniors' Club in Duncashel. I have
a badge and leaflets.'

My phone rang in my pocket. ''Bout feckin' time,' I said
to Robert, jamming it between my head and free shoulder,
'I could be dead out here. This lad says his name is David
Flynn, from Senior something or other, in Duncashel.
Check it out and call me back. You might want to hurry,
my finger's getting fierce sweaty on the trigger.'

I looked at the boy. That's all he seemed now, a terrified
boy. I lowered the gun slightly. Gearstick, no longer interested in frightening the bejesus out of him either it seemed,
began to sniff at his shoes.

'What does this Seniors' Club do when it's at home?' I
asked, as we waited.

'We run groups.'

'Groups?'

'Groups. Like friendship groups. And arranging for
people to call by to see how you're doing, like. Although,
that mightn't be your thing,' he said looking at the gun,
'there's bingo. And yoga. And outings and . . .'

My phone rang. Robert again.

'Aye. Right,' I said when he'd finished telling me all I
needed to know about this boyo on the ground. I pressed
the red button to end the call.

'And tell me, is this what they teach you over in Duncashel, how to frighten the shite out of prospective clients?' I lowered the gun to my side. David's head dropped as Gearstick whined and licked his ear. And as true as I am sitting here, the boy reached out his hand and petted him.

'I'm new,' he replied, as my hand lowered to pull him up.

Only I felt I owed him, I might never have visited the centre in Duncashel. I decided the bingo was the safer bet. They offered to send the bus to collect me but it was best not to take the chance. Always important to have a means of escape. I sat outside in the car for a while, after I arrived wondering what the feck I was at. This loneliness was pushing me to lengths I'd've never considered before your mother died. Like reading the notices on the Community Board in the SuperValu:

Seniors' Bridge – Duncashel Amenity Centre. Thursdays
10 a.m.
Bereavement Support Group, Fridays 7 p.m., Presbyterian
Church Hall – call Anna
Medjugorje Pilgrimage – August 2014

Even to stop in front of that yoke at the back of the tills was risky. Anyone could've seen me. I had to keep pretending to look at the car section, to be on the safe side. I've imagined myself at every one of those bloody things, son. Pictured myself sitting among the strangers, nodding, making small talk about the weather and the price of things and the curse of computers. Or worse, crying my eyes out. I promise you, I've willed myself to live this worn-out life of mine. I even called 'Anna'. Encouraged me to attend 'even the one meeting. What about next Friday?' she said. 'I'll think about it,' I said. I watched the clock tick by on the mantelpiece the following Friday. The hand hit half past, then twenty-five to, then twenty to. My heart thumped and my hand rubbed away at my forehead, forging another worry line as it reached quarter to. In the background the weatherman on the telly gave the forecast for ice with the threat of snow showers. Ah, here, I said to myself, I'm not risking those roads.

But sitting there in the jeep in Duncashel, waiting to go in to David and his Seniors' Group bingo, I wondered might I really do it this time. Might I really be able to take the leap of faith into a world that offered me a bit of hope, even at this late stage? It struck me then, that maybe David was heaven sent. Maybe he was your mother's doing. Maybe she'd sent him to force me into trying to make it on my own. Next thing I knew I was pushing my way through the door. My palm laid flat on the 'Fáilte, Welcome, Bienvenue'.

'Maurice. Good to see you, man,' David called, coming over to shake my hand.

'David,' I replied. 'You've recovered after the other day, I take it.'

'What? Ah yeah, no bother, man. Sure, me Da was in stitches when I told him. Said he'd love to have a pint with you.'

'Did he now?' I said, scoping out the Presbyterian hall that I'd never been in before. Four long gridded windows faced each other over a scuffed wooden floor that looked like it had suffered one fête too many over the years. Pairs of depressed red velvet curtains, orange and frayed at the edges hung on each. Up on stage, behind the white bingo machine, a gaggle of unwanted chairs and benches clung to each other on the verge of one massive avalanche.

'You're not from around these parts?' I asked, although I was sure I'd possibly asked him the same thing the first day. Still.

'Me? No. Finglas. We came down here after the Ma died three years ago. Me Da said it just wasn't the same without her. Wanted a change, you know what I mean?'

Twenty or so plastic black chairs, the uncomfortable kind, were lined up at the front of the hall. And there, in pockets of twos and threes, in front and to the side of them, stood my great hope: my peers. Those who would pick me up and stick me back together again. My stomach lurched and my heart slowed with the effort of it all.

'What has you working here anyway?' I managed. I breathed in the mustiness of the place and it caught in my throat.

'It was the Da. He read about it in the *Duncashel Topic* and started to come every Thursday. Then it was a Tuesday too and sure, he may as well've moved in by the end. I used to drop him off. The odd time I'd come in and help out a bit with the setting up and I'd get chatting. Fidelma, the boss, got me on Job Bridge a month ago.'

'And is he here, your father?'

'Da? No. He died there last year. Reckon he just gave up. Couldn't hack it without her, you know.'

He looked at me all-sheepish, like he was considering whether I could be trusted with a secret. 'I talk to him all the time in me head. Stupid, I know, but . . .'

I looked at him, son, and I swear to God I could've hugged him. A man who knew what it was to talk to ghosts.

'So this is the lone ranger.' A woman of no more than five foot and almost the same wide announced, approaching me from the front of the hall. Her step near shook the boards as she made a beeline for me.

'Fidelma Moore, Mr Hannigan. I hope you left the gun at home today,' she said grabbing my hand despite it not being offered. 'We had a great laugh in the office over that one. What were you like at all, at all?'

I considered her with a stare, while I heard David shuffle nervously beside me. I looked at him, then back at her.

'You don't live alone then,' I said, 'in the arse end of nowhere, with only a gun to protect you from the gangs who steal your few bob and leave you half dead?'

She didn't reply but moved a hand to her chest as her eyebrows rose and her forehead concertinaed.

'Well, now, I'm sure I didn't mean to offend you . . .'

'No,' I said, leaning down to her, 'but you did.'

I turned from her then, and watched the bingo caller play with his balls, setting them up at the top of the room while your woman decided what to do with me. Rocking back and forth on my feet, I concluded that even if it was my wife's divine intervention that had me there with these people, eviction was still fine by me.

'They're just about to start,' she said finally, her words having lost their earlier confidence. 'David, take Mr Hannigan up like a good man.'

I know her eyes watched me as I made my way to the back row, where I sat on my own at the edge. I felt old that day, son. Looking around, watching those white-haired men and women with their dried-out, droopy skin, and teary eyes and fading clothes, wasting away the afternoon with neon highlighters. I don't know how I managed to sit as long as I did. I didn't even bother marking down the numbers, just pretended every now and again. I'm sure David noticed, standing to the side, running up and down, doing the checking of those who called 'house', shaking their books in the air like they were drowning. Mostly, I rubbed at the floor with the sole of my shoe.

Before half-time, he came over and bent to my ear:

'I have to get the tea now, Maurice, alright? But I'll sit beside you after. I reckon if we play our cards right that box of Roses is ours. Bags the hazelnut whirl, though,' he said, patting me on the shoulder. I nodded.

When the bingo caller announced the break, my fellow senior citizens passed by, getting a good look at the new boy. Some smiled. I looked away, unable for it. Unable for the lie of a man I would have to become to make my way into their circle. To be accepted, to belong. But here's the thing, son, I only ever wanted to belong to one person and she wasn't in that room. And in my heart I knew that even if I was a man comfortable with all the small talk it would take to break into that new life, I didn't want it. I simply did not want it.

I took out my phone to check a few non-existent messages as they milled about the table. David there among them, smiling and laughing, scratching his head. Filling cups, pouring milk and offering biscuits. And when I was sure he was far too distracted to wonder about me, I left. Got into the Jeep and drove straight home. Locked the doors and drew the curtains.

David called round a couple of times after. Some talker. Entertained me with his life story: Eamo and Deco and Gizzo, his mates back in Dublin.

'Drugs,' he said, 'that's all they're into now. Selling drugs. Wasn't me. Had to get out, man.'

I told him bits about you. Not much, but bits. He was calling you Kev by the end.

'So is Kev planning any visits home?' 'How many kids does Kev have again?'

'Two,' I said, 'Kev has two.'

But after a while I didn't answer the door any more. Couldn't face him. Knowing how desperate he was trying to keep me connected to this world, when I wanted nothing more to do with it. I knew for sure then, I had no other choice, but to find your mother.

Chapter Six

10.10 p.m.
Final Toast: to Sadie
Midleton Whiskey

I've left the best 'til last in every way.

Svetlana places my final drink down in front of me: Midleton, you can't fault it. Majestic stuff. I look at it like she has just handed me the keys to a new harvester. It's the autumn colours that get me. It's the earth of it, the trees, the leaves, the late evening sky. Its smell, so full of life that it catches in my throat before it's even touched my lips, sending a shiver down my spine.

Do you know it gives me a dead shoulder every time I drink it? Sounds mad, I know. I'm convinced it doesn't go down my throat at all but creeps along the muscles of my neck, over to my shoulder, numbing it. Doesn't do it with any other brand, mind, knows when I'm on the good stuff. I asked the Doc, the new one – Taylor, what that was all about. He told me cutting back was the only cure he knew of.

'I didn't ask for the cure,' I said.

'Drink isn't the way to deal with loss, Mr Hannigan,' came his reply.

Loss – what does he know about it, I ask you? He's

barely out of nappies for Christ's sake. I'd say the closest he's ever come to loss was his virginity, and even at that I can't be sure he's old enough. No one, no one really knows loss until it's someone you love. The deep-down kind of love that holds on to your bones and digs itself right in under your fingernails, as hard to budge as the years of compacted earth. And when it's gone . . . it's as if it's been ripped from you. Raw and exposed, you stand dripping blood all over the good feckin' carpet. Half-human, half-dead, one foot already in the grave.

Jesus wept.

Sadie liked to have a sip of the good stuff herself. She wasn't much of a drinker. But she always made an exception for Midleton at Christmas. Who in their right mind wouldn't, eh?

So, the simple truth of it, son? The reason for me sitting here on my own talking to myself is her, how could it not be. I want your mother back. Plain as. I can't do it on my own any more. I never dreamt the day I met her that there would come a time when I'd find it hard to breathe because her toothbrush no longer sits beside mine in the green, sorry – avocado, I always got that wrong, apparently – tumbler on the bathroom sink or because I can no longer hear her giving out when I set the fire wrong in the grate or that there is nothing – no breath, no heartbeat when I stretch my hand to her side of the bed in the morning. But I can't. I can't. And now it's time to sort this mess of the last two years out and find the woman that claimed my soul the day we met.

Trouble is, son, I'm worried that she mightn't want me back at all.

*

She worked in the main bank over in Duncashel. This of course was when you went into a bank and could engage with living people. These days I refuse to take any more of their time-wasting. When I go in now, I walk past the machines to find the nearest staff member and tell them to get me the manager.

'Do you have an appointment?' the newbies ask.

'Tell Frank to check my bank balance before he decides how long he'll leave me,' I like to reply as I take a seat.

'Course, I've told him nothing about me having taken well to this online banking that they are at pains to get us all doing. Wasn't it you that set me up. I had you pestered the first couple of times I tried, crawling my way on to it, marvelling every time that I could see my accounts just like that. By the time you were headed home, I was flying. Not as fast as those young fellas you see around the town, tipping and sliding their way around their gadgets I'm sure, but good enough. I still like to visit Frank, when I have the time that is. Sometimes I just make up stuff for him to do, like cashing a cheque. Once I handed him a cheque for €500 and asked him to cash it and when he handed me the money, I changed my mind and told him he could lodge it. Don't be feeling sorry for him, he gets paid well enough with my bank charges.

Granted, back in your mother's day, the bank queues in Duncashel moved fierce slow, but every five or six steps you got to one of the pillars lining the route for a bit of a lean. Then there'd be a pile-up forming behind you, until you pushed yourself away again, freeing it up for the next man. Magnificent building, you wouldn't remember it. They had it knocked down and rebuilt by the time you toddled along. Thick doors that required your whole weight to open them. High ceilings and red-flecked marble counters. I'd have taken that over a church any day.

So the day I met her, I was stood there in the queue, minding my own business as usual, counting the black tiles of the chequered floor for as far as my eye could concentrate, when I heard this delicious Donegal accent trickle down to me from the counter up ahead. I didn't lean against another pillar or count another tile after that, but stood to attention, a lot more interested now, trying to get a glimpse of whoever owned it through the heads. I could see her neck clearest of all. Elegant, it was. Like the slope of a scythe. It dipped and bent and stretched with grace. Strong too. I couldn't wait to stand in front of her, to unleash my charm, which to that point I wasn't acquainted with but was sure was in there somewhere. I pushed on, rear ending a few in front, hoping I'd be lucky enough to be top of the line when she called 'next'. I even let Nancy Regan ahead of me, over to the other one serving beside her. I racked up my best attempt at a smile as I made the final leg over to the counter, to her sweet voice, her perfect skin and, as it turned out, her narkiness.

'A bank draft?' she asked, like I'd just produced my penny jar for counting. 'We don't do bank drafts after three.'

Even with that thick head on her, she was still beautiful. Light-brown curly hair with little wisps of red through it that matched her lipstick. White milky skin. Chocolate freckles scattered over the bridge of her scrunched-up nose, as if she'd only stood at the mirror that morning painting on their perfection. Eyes as blue as a clear Meath summer sky.

'Just in time, so.' I nodded at the wall behind her. 'Your clock there says a minute to.'

'That's slow,' she replied, not even bothering to look.

'You're new?' I tried.

She let her eyes linger on me for a second then looked down at my book and docket, her red lips gathering in a good juicy pout. She frowned, held the docket up, then down, squinting even harder at each new angle. I shifted about, wondering what I'd misspelt now.

'Is that a T or a C?' she asked, pushing the slip back across, her pink nail pointing to the cause of her distress. Her nose was scrunched up like the unwanted Sunday paper my mother used to feed the range.

'C. Con Dolan. It's to be made out to Con Dolan.'

'A C?' she said, her voice rising with the incredulity of it all. 'It looks more like a T.'

'Ton's the brother. I don't owe him a thing.'

For my efforts, I received the tiniest of grins. I ran a proud hand through the big head of hair I had on me, back then. And beamed my broadest smile, hoping she'd notice. But to my disappointment, her head dropped back to her work.

After she'd finished correcting my handwriting, she got off her chair with a big sigh, to go sort the draft.

'I'll have to check if the manager is still about.'

Off she went. I watched her small little waist and her skirt swish about her shapely legs. Why did the pretty ones have to be such hard work, I wondered, like the man of immense experience I surely wasn't, as I settled in for the next five minutes, my elbows up on the cold marble counter, having a gander behind me, seeing who might be in.

'Was he over in Hartigan's?' I asked, when she finally returned. 'He's fierce fond of that snug.'

Another small smile. But this one was wounded and sad. Her ferocity gone. I tried to find her eyes to read what had happened but she refused to raise them. She fumbled with the paperwork again before stopping, taking a breath and saying:

'Mr Grigson has asked I tell you that bank drafts can only be done before three o'clock. On this occasion he has signed it but will not be in a position to do so again.'

My mouth gaped as I struggled to find some kinder words for the man too afraid to come and tell me all that himself, choosing instead to terrify this beauty before me.

'Sure a man would have to start queuing at one o'clock to do that,' I said, with a laugh that I realised, as soon as it had left my lips, was more sarcastic than the jovial tone I'd intended.

She busied herself with the bank draft and my book, putting them into an envelope. As she passed them back across the counter, the light caught her eye and I saw the tears welling up. I froze. Angry bank managers were no problem, but crying beauties? I was dealing with a whole different field of oats now.

'Ah lads,' I said, my fingers stretching in as far as they could go under the brass bars. 'Look I'm sorry. I didn't mean . . . I've an awful tongue on me sometimes.'

The backs of her hands tried to stem the flow bulging in her eyes, but she was losing the battle.

'I'm fine, I'm fine. It's not you,' she said looking up, attempting a smile. 'It's just all so new and . . . well . . .' her face began to crumble again.

I had no handkerchief to gallantly produce. Well, I did, but let's just say it would have made the situation worse, it had been a while since washday. I looked about me to see who was watching. Nancy, bloody, Regan. She was loving this, itching to get out of the place to tell the world that Maurice Hannigan was harassing innocent women.

'Listen, I can't leave you like this,' I said, 'I'll hold this crowd off for a minute while you go powder your nose or whatever.'

'I can't be doing that, sure they'd have me fired.'

'What'll he know? I'll tell him I asked you for some more lodgement dockets or something.'

She bit her lip, considering my proposition.

'Two seconds, so,' she said, and was gone.

I smiled at Nancy as she left the counter, giving me a good long stare before tottering away in those heels of hers.

Sadie was back before I knew it, tissue in hand, looking a sight better.

'Thanks,' she said hopping back up on her stool.

'All better now, what? So are you ready for this lot, so?' I inclined my head to the queue to my rear. 'I can't promise they'll be as charming as myself, now.'

She nodded and gave me a small vulnerable smile that stayed with me long after I'd left the counter and gone back to work the fields. That evening my sisters looked at me like I was ailing as I played all the wrong cards in the game Jenny dealt. Mind you, their concern didn't stop them filling their pockets with my pennies. The following day I seemed incapable of doing anything right what with me putting too much milk in my tea, tripping over the front door step that had been there since the day I was born and burning my hand on the range when I put it down, thinking it was the kitchen table. By Sunday I knew I had no other choice but to go back. After the dinner, I announced my intentions of visiting the bank again the following Thursday, giving the family enough time to gather their few coppers together.

By Thursday I stood before her with a fresh handkerchief in my pocket and five bank books in my hands.

'Hello,' she said, quietly, a little embarrassed smile rising to her face once she recognised me.

Now, son, you know I'm not one for sentimentality but I swear to God the woman just took my breath away. I mean she looked no different from the first time I saw her, granted there were no tears, but this time, this time it was like she had multiplied all of that gorgeousness by ten. I reached inside myself, past my shock and from somewhere pulled out my voice.

'Grand day, now. It must be hard on a day like this to be cooped up in here with the sun splitting the trees.'

'Oh, aye. What I wouldn't give to be out for a stroll right now.' She laughed, looked at me ever so quickly, took the books I offered and got stuck into the counting straight away. I ran a hand over my flattened hair.

'Maurice,' I said, 'the name's Maurice Hannigan.'

'Well, Maurice,' she said looking up from the books, 'you Hannigans are great savers.'

She looked below again, writing and totting away. And then, I heard her name for the first time:

'Sadie McDonagh,' she said, her face flashing up briefly to mine.

'Things seem better today . . . Sadie. I mean, I'm glad to see you're looking better today . . . I mean . . . it's not so busy.'

She looked up and laughed again. Pitch-perfect laughter. Her work completed, she tapped the books efficiently together on her counter and passed them back to me.

'Things are much better, thank you, Maurice.'

I took the books and paused for a second wondering if now was my chance. And as my eyes seemed unable to lift to her face, staring at the black tiles instead, I wondered where my charm had decided to feck off to. I tipped the books to my forehead, and had begun to walk away when she said:

'See you again next Thursday, I suppose?'

'Well,' I said, stepping back to face her fully now, 'unless, that is you'd like to take a stroll with me later. Maybe even a bite to eat?' There he was, Mr Confident, back to save the day.

'Well, I . . .' she stumbled as I waited, my toes crossed in my shined Sunday-best shoes, 'I would love that. I finish at six.'

'Six it is, so. I'll be outside.'

I think I actually winked at her before I left her counter. I near ran from it, convinced that I couldn't've been that lucky and any minute now she'd call me back to say she'd changed her mind. I don't think I took a breath until I got outside and leaned up against the wall wondering how I'd managed that at all.

'It's a big thing getting a job in the bank,' she told me later, in that Donegal lilt of hers after we'd given our order in the Duncashel Central and handed back our menus.

'I couldn't believe it when I passed the exams. Neither could Mammy and Daddy. I mean it's not something you can say no to, is it? Permanent, pensionable and all that,' she said, moving the salt and pepper cellars around. 'I know it sounds ungrateful but . . . I don't think it's me. I haven't an ounce of interest. Money's a nasty business really,' she added, leaving the condiments, now happy with their new positions.

Is it? I thought.

'You're a long way from Donegal, alright,' I said instead.

'And that's another thing, I'd rather be nearer home. To help out and that.'

'Farming people?'

'No. My father's a guard. No, it's just . . .' She looked like she was about to say something further but stopped short, thinking of Noreen no doubt, not that I knew about her then. 'Well, you know yourself, there's always work to be done about the place, farm or no farm.'

'True, true,' I said, not wishing to dig any further at such an early stage, 'it's back north for you, so? No way we can keep you down here?' I said, giving the condiments a good going over myself.

'Well . . .' She smiled over at me with a gorgeous shyness.

'Well, what?' I asked eagerly.

'You never know, I suppose.'

Our eyes met for a brief second before our blushes forced us to look around. The tables were a mixture of all sorts: a single bachelor, eating his fry in silence, looking out to the passers-by on Patrick's Street; a couple, more experienced than ourselves in the ways of relationships, sitting opposite us, him with his paper held up and she reading the adverts on the back page. There was one family, all dressed up for their Thursday treat. The children with their knee socks pulled right up, the boys with their Brylcreemed hair, the girls in pigtails with green polka dot ribbons. The mother keeping a watchful eye over their behaviour as the father chatted across to her. Every now and again he gave a big neighing laugh and hit the table with his hand, making the cutlery protest as he looked around for the appreciation he felt his joke deserved.

'Do you come to this place much?' Sadie asked.

'I like to take all my girlfriends here.'

She laughed too then. But hers was a laugh that felt precious and dainty, quite the opposite of the father, three tables down. Her eyes met mine, just long enough not to embarrass us but to acknowledge our beginning. I knew for certain then, that there, sitting across the red Formica table, with the perfectly placed condiments, was the woman I was ready to love until the life went out of me.

I never attempted to kiss her on our first date. I wanted nothing more than to hold her hand, but as we left the Duncashel Central, I decided against pushing my luck. I walked her home to her lodgings. I was glad she lived the other end of the town. We chatted comfortably all the way to her door and stood doing the same once we'd arrived. We could have been there an hour for all I know. I'm sure it was just a matter of minutes before she started to root in her bag for her key. I'd lost all sense of time, you see, couldn't have given a damn if it was five in the morning and it was time to milk the cows. I would've done it, happily. That's how she made me feel, happy with the world, with myself.

'Go on in, so,' I said, fighting the urge to hold her just

a moment longer. 'Mrs Durkin's hand must be getting tired holding back that curtain there, as if we can't see her.'

'Ssh! Make no mistake she knows you can see her. That's what she's aiming for. She knows all about the likes of you.' She laughed, and I smiled too, feeling the cheekiness of her statement egging me on. I took hold of her free hand as her other turned the lock. I looked down at it and asked:

'Might you be free for the dance, so, on Saturday? Over in O'Reilly's hall, it's a bit out the road but I can come get you on the bike – nothing but the best for my girlfriends.'

'Would you go on with you and your girlfriends. I bet I'm the first who's ever said yes.'

'You'll go then. Seven o'clock, Saturday? I'll pick you up at the mall, not here. Don't want herself getting in touch with your parents just yet.'

'Goodnight,' she said, in mock exasperation at a boy who thought he might keel over in pure delight. I stayed until the door closed and then ran down the street. Retrieving my bike, I cycled as if I was representing Ireland in the Olympics, speeding past fields, whooping at cows that might have lazily raised their heads too late to see my ghost of a cap pass by.

Saturday couldn't come quick enough. I hadn't seen Sadie for two days, but it may as well have been a year. Arriving at the mall good and early, I waited, leaning up against my vehicle with as much panache as any farmer from Meath with a pushbike could manage. My stomach did somersaults as I paced up and down the path, hopping from kerb to road, anything to distract myself, until eventually I saw her. And as she approached me in a white dress with red roses, it began to dawn on me that I was about to make this picture of beauty sit up on a cold, uncomfortable crossbar for the two-mile journey out the road. By the time she reached me I was sure she could smell the panic.

'Well, what do you think, do I scrub up well?' she asked.

'I can tell you now that I'm the envy of every man on the street.'

'So is this my carriage? Well, it'll do, I suppose.'

I swallowed hard and felt my armpits go damp, again.

'This, I'll have you know, is also the envy of every man around.'

'Well, let's go show off, so.'

I took off my jacket and laid it down on the cold crossbar. And up she hopped, not a hesitation. White dress and white high-heeled shoes. All I needed was the chain to come off. I said a quick prayer in my head as we pushed away from the kerb. Normally, with Jenny or May, who never got the jacket treatment, there would be an initial wobble but not with Sadie. We glided down Patrick Street and off out the road heading for Rainsford like a pair of professional ballroom dancers. We took the breeze with us, pulling it along to our advantage. I had honestly never laughed and smiled so much as on that journey. She spent half the time with my cap on her head, grabbing it off me when we passed the Duncashel Arms. I couldn't get enough of that deviousness in her eye that made me wonder what she might get up to next. I am happy to report that we skidded to a halt outside the dance hall with not an oil stain in sight.

I kissed her on the cheek later, when we took some air on the wall behind the dance hall. After, I reached for her hand and she caressed my thumb with hers as the summer evening heat still managed to warm us. It wasn't for another week before the real kiss came. Have you the stomach for all of this, son? Tune out now, if you want, I'll tell you when it's over.

I will never forget it. It felt as if someone had lit a fire in my belly when her lips touched mine. I'd planned for nothing more than a repeat of that first peck on the cheek and had reached down to do just that as we stood at her door, Mrs Durkin being out at bingo, but her head turned and her lips found mine. Sweet divine, I was transported, to heaven. My urge, of course, was to continue and, I'll be honest, to do much more. But I refused the temptation to pull her back when she moved her head away. She looked up and smiled.

'Where did a wee innocent girl from Annamoe in Donegal learn to kiss like that?' I asked.

'That would be telling, wouldn't it.'

There were more of those encounters over the coming weeks, each one lasting a little longer and becoming a little deeper. But I always pulled away, not tempting myself and maybe her too, beyond a point of no return; it wouldn't have been right no matter how much I wanted it. Nowadays, of course, it's all different. I'm not sure I'd have had it any other way, though; the waiting and the longing built up a good thirst in me by the time we said our vows.

It was three months later that the official invite came to meet her parents. Nervous was too weak a word to describe the torture I felt at the very prospect of meeting the father. My own father was forever berating my poor sisters about the men who he found 'sniffing' around. I wouldn't mind, but these poor lads were no more dangerous than me;

'sniffing' involved nothing other than the neighbouring farmers' sons raising their caps as they passed down the lane or on the road that ran outside our house. If that was all they were guilty of then Mr McDonagh would surely have me arrested as soon as I crossed the Donegal border.

'Are you sure it's the right time, Sadie? Might we leave it for a month or two? Sure I've very little saved. I've no ring or anything.'

'Is that right? Remember I've seen your bank book, Mr Hannigan.' She had me there, while meagre, my savings were steadily growing. 'And might that be a proposal?'

This woman was a force to be reckoned with.

'Oh, you know what I mean. I don't want your father thinking I'm some Johnny come lately, trying to take advantage.'

'What, of my wealth and status?'

'Well, Sadie, there aren't many women who've a job in the bank and are as beautiful as you.'

'Maurice, you'll be fine. They know all about you. I've told them everything. They know you're upstanding and aren't about to have your wicked way and then run out on me.'

'Sadie!'

'Oh would you stop. I want you to meet Mammy and Daddy and our Noreen, to see who I am and where I come from – to see what you're signing up for, so to speak.'

'But I know all that, nothing will change how I feel about you, even if your family turn out to be a pack of nutcases.'

'That's not funny, Maurice!' she snapped. The weather had suddenly turned.

Now bear in mind that at this point I knew nothing of

Noreen's issues, so I was completely thrown, totally unaware of what I'd just landed my two clodhoppers in. I allowed the silence to settle between us as she manhandled her magazine, violently flapping the pages back and forth.

'He'll not bite, you know. Although, if you go around saying things like that I'm not so sure.'

'Ah Sadie, I didn't mean it. It was just a joke.'

Flick, flick, flap, flap, page after page. I almost felt sorry for the magazine. She refused to look at me while I took terrified peeks at her. Slowly, however, the thaw began to set in, the tempo eased, finally the exhausted magazine came to rest on her lap. My eyes glanced sideways to assess the significance of the alteration. She was staring ahead of her, thinking her thoughts, possibly mulling over the wisdom of having agreed to go on that first date at all. She remained that way for a moment or two as I sweated beside her. In the end she sighed, a beautiful Donegal sigh.

'Ach, Maurice,' she said turning to me, 'I promise, he's a wee dote. He'll just love you, how could he not?'

'I'll go then. To meet this "wee dote".'

She smiled and nodded; and I kissed her, the rest of that journey to Annamoe, you know.

But today has been about trying to make amends for the many times after that great beginning when I stole that smile from your mother's beautiful face; for all the things I never did or half did and for the many promises I made and broke.

Like the honeymoon suite for instance, where I'll lay these exhausted bones down tonight. Remember how I promised to take her there on your wedding night but never did? Or how about the dinner in The Estuary restaurant today? Oh yes, I dined like a King. Stood at the 'please wait to be seated' sign of Duncashel's award-winning restaurant, bold as you like, pressing down my wispy white hair, looking at the white-linened tables, the shining knives and forks, three deep, the lilies tall and erect, sniffing out the interloper, until Felix arrived, whisking me away from my demons and my guilt to the exact table I'd asked for over the phone when I'd made the reservation – the one your mother always said she wanted to sit at, when we passed in the car and she looked in.

And then there is the matter of the tea.

I don't need to tell you about my reluctance to buy a cup of tea when dining out. Why waste the money when there's a perfectly good kettle at home? In all our years of Sunday carveries, Sadie went along with me on that one. I'd have even gone so far as to say she wholeheartedly supported my approach. But on reflection, perhaps she chose her battles wisely. After all she'd managed to bring about one of the biggest coups in our house back in the nineties. Can't even remember exactly when she said those fatal words: 'I'm done with roasts.' But I didn't buck, despite the shock. Just knew to pay the money of a Sunday and say nothing. But not long before she died she fairly told me what she really thought of my tea policy.

We were sat over in Murtagh's, our empty plates in front of us. I had just leaned over to get my coat from the seat beside Sadie when her hand arrived to stop me with a strength I never knew she had. I stared at the puzzle of her fingers: arthritic worn joints bent at the top – she couldn't get her rings off by the time she died, did you know that? Her wedding finger was permanently strangled by our love. Now that I think of it, those rings were the only jewellery I ever bought her. Instead, I handed her money when birthdays and Christmases came round. She could buy what she wanted then. Everyone won that way.

'Tea,' she said to me that Sunday, loud and clear, staring straight ahead of her. 'Earl Grey.'

Always Earl Grey. Not that she was born into it, mind; the McDonaghs were Lyons people like the rest of us. 'You can blame Dublin for that one,' she had told me years before. She'd been given it by accident in a tearoom on Grafton Street. I can't remember the name of the place now. It'll come to me. 'It was like a tingle on my tongue,' she said, 'I was an Earl Grey convert from then on.' There was always a box of Earl Grey to be found in our house, do you remember? At first it was leaves and then, as time went on and the wheels of industry turned, it became bags. Being the more expensive, she only ever had it for her elevenses. The rest of the day she slummed it with the rest of us on the bog standard.

'Give me my coat so, woman,' I said, still trying to release it from her hold, 'and we'll go home and get one.'

'And I'd like it here, no matter what it costs, no matter how long we have to wait. I want it here, served by someone else. And what's more I'm having dessert. Banoffi.'

I looked at her wondering what I was to do with that information. In the edgy silence, I realised she expected me to go off and find the waitress. I rose, knowing full well it would be impossible to waylay a girl in Murtagh's at that hour when all and sundry were out for the carvery after twelve Mass, and so queued again at the counter, dragging my annoyance, pace by pace, until I stood in front of the dessert fridge.

'I'll have that yoke,' I said, pointing my finger at the plate of banoffi behind the glass.

'Anything else with that, sir? Ice cream?' the young lad asked. Sadie loved ice cream. I gave him my best stare, considering his offer.

He followed behind me carrying the tray with her banoffi and her rattling teacup. When we arrived at the table, I placed the dessert in front of her.

'No ice cream, no?' she asked, looking at the plate.

'No,' I said. 'They're out.'

I knew the lad was staring at the back of my head but I didn't flinch as I turned to take the tea things. I didn't give two hoots what he or my poor long-suffering wife thought of me. When I sat, I watched the couple at the next table trying to feed their young toddler a carrot rather than looking at Sadie taking her time eating her pudding. Out of the corner of my eye I could see her measure every spoonful with equal amounts of cream and caramel and banana. Savouring it in her mouth like she was sucking a mint. After each swallow she reached for her teacup. Holding it like a chalice. Nestling in, all snug on the couch, looking around at the other diners. Not caring for one second that the Sunday game would be about to start on the telly at home with Mícheál Ó Muircheartaigh's commentary keeping pace with the speed of those young bucks. But I refused to be riled and continued to watch the couple next door, locked in battle, with his nibs.

'Just a little bite, Markie, and then you can have the jelly.'

'Our Kevin would be at that too,' Sadie said, putting

her cup down on its saucer. Her elbow rested on the table now, her head at a tilt, leaning on her hand, watching the woman's pitiful attempts at getting some goodness into her son.

'You should try mushing up the veg so he can't see it.'

The mother gave a tight-lipped smile.

'I even used to mix it up in his custard. Kevin loved custard.'

A carrot already cut in two was halved again and waved in front of Markie's mouth, then nudged at the gripped lips.

'Just this tiny bit, pet.'

'You could blitz it in a blender.'

Markie was by now sticking his fingers into his jelly and licking them enthusiastically while his mother sat back practically in tears.

''Course Kevin is at that himself now, trying to con the greens into his own. What goes around comes around, I told him.'

'Jesus,' I muttered under my breath. But she refused to look my way. 'I'll be in the car. I'll see you there when you've finished with your parenting tips,' I added, rising and leaving her to it.

She didn't take to the bedroom when we got home like I'd expected. But she never spoke a word to me. Flitted about the place like I wasn't there. In and out of the sitting room the whole day. I couldn't tell you what she was at. But what I do know is that when I sat to the kitchen table later for tea, no cup and saucer sat at my place. I watched her pour her own and let the pot rest back down on the coaster. She didn't lift her head once. In the end, I got my own cup and found my very own pot after about ten minutes of searching. We finished our meal in total silence, refilling our cups from pots that sat like two canons pointing at each other across the divide.

This afternoon, after I'd finished the first four courses of my meal – sorbet they gave me, not for the dessert, right after the starter – I waved Felix down.

'Earl Grey,' I said to him. 'Give me a pot of Earl Grey.'

When I took the first sip, the liquid scalded the top of my mouth. It felt like she was sitting in the room, glaring at me as I drank, reminding me that it was far too late to make recompense for my sins now.

Casey's, that was the place in Dublin.

Ours was always a difficult relationship when it came to our wealth. Individually our views were clear: I loved it, she despised it. For the sake of our marriage, therefore, it rarely got discussed. I felt bad tainting her with it. She never knew what we had in the bank or how much land we really owned. And when she did happen across some revealing paperwork, she just handed it straight to me like it was a dirty sock I'd dropped on the carpet.

On a Friday at tea, I'd leave the weekly amount for all the shopping and whatever else she needed against the teapot. I'd never even see her take it. I'd look up at some stage and it'd be gone, into her apron pocket. But here's the funniest thing, when I began to clear away some of her bits after she died – well, when I say 'clear' I more rummaged through them, reluctant as I was to part with even a thread – I kept finding money. She must never have spent all I gave. Never bothered sticking it in the bank or the credit union account. Trusted it instead to the pockets of old cardigans and dressing gowns and an old box that held your childhood drawings. Rainy day, I suppose. I must've found seven thousand in all. Don't ask me, son, I've no idea.

In all our years I never stopped wanting her. Never. Not for one moment. Not for one second. I watched her skin survive the years, softly, folding upon itself. I touched it often, still hopelessly loving every bit of her, every line that claimed her, every new mark that stamped its permanency. We had our tough times like everyone else, but through it all I never looked at anyone else. Never desired another.

My hands begin to shake when I think over it all, son. Can I, hand on heart, say that I did my best for her?

'Moanie Maurice,' she used to call me in the latter years. But the awful truth of it is I would have been a thousand times worse without her. I could almost feel it as I walked through the door, the armour slipping away as she took my coat or kissed me on the cheek or put her hand to my back as she laid my dinner down. Jesus, son, I should have told her every feckin' day what a marvel she was.

I've stopped sleeping, have I told you? Two hours, three if I'm lucky now and then I'm awake. Staring at the ceiling, going over it again, this bloody decision, because although I know it's time to go, son, it's still hard. Even now, there's a little part of me that wonders am I doing the right thing at all. There was a woman in her eighties somewhere in England, so desperately lonely that she sat at her kitchen table and put an empty bag of frozen spinach over her head and suffocated herself. I mean, when I heard that I just thought, is that me, is that what it's really come to?

*

I get off the stool and shove these quaking wrinkled hands deep down in my pockets. I need to move. I need to shake this off me.

'Wait there,' I say to my refilled glass as I take to the corridor again. Head down, I count: twenty-seven flowers in the carpet, six pairs of passing shoes, one fallen abandoned napkin. Swishing skirts and high-pitched voices filled with the night's excitement pass me but make no impression. This place could be on fire and I wouldn't give a damn now.

My piss is unreliable as usual. Of late it's become erratic, threatening to flood its banks one minute and refusing to squeeze a drop the next. I stand at the urinal waiting for it to make its mind up.

'Get out to fuck,' I order. And for once in its life it obeys, flows like the Shannon, in a flash flood. A good omen, I think.

After, I stare down at the Armitage Shanks sink, letting the water flow for far too long, not wanting to look in the mirror just yet. But when I eventually lift my white fluffy mane, it is my father that greets me. It's not the first time. As the years have gone on I've noticed him creep into my face more and more. Sunken cheeks and high forehead. But it's mostly in the eyes. Grey marble beads of wisdom. I stand as tall as I can and smile. And then I reach my hand to touch the cold glass.

'You've done mighty, son,' he says, 'mighty.'

It takes me by surprise, so much so my eyes sting, and I know if I'm not careful tears will force themselves out, making a spectacle of me. Enough of that now, I think, as I shake my head and make for the door.

On my way back up the corridor to the foyer, I wonder what would happen if I shouted out my intentions to the world. At the double doors I dance a shuffle as I manoeuvre my way through the couple coming in the opposite direction. Still got the moves. What would happen, do you think, if I leaned in to whisper in their ear to tell them of my plans, would they believe me? Would they whip out their phones and ring 999? Or would they simply smile and walk away from the drunk old raving fool?

On I go, overshooting my turning for the bar, my feet bringing me to stand once more at the picture of Hugh Dollard, in the foyer. He still looks nothing like the man I remember. What might he say were he to know that tonight I'll sleep in the room that was once his? And that everything that was ever dear to him is now mine. I sway back and forth, my hands still in my pockets, thinking of my victories all over again.

'Did you know Great-uncle Timothy?' A voice asks me, interrupting my simple pleasures. I look around and see a face that I've not seen in years.

'Hilary?' I say, 'Hilary Dollard?'

'Dollard was never my surname, not even before I married Jason. It's Bruton, please.' She gives me a tight-lipped smile that suggests friendliness, but you can never be too careful. She's got her daughter's eyes, though, or Emily has got hers, whichever way round it might be. Soft brown. The generations washing away the Dollard sharpness. Oh, but all the Dollard ghosts: Amelia, Rachel, Hugh, Thomas, are there in hints, around the mouth and her cheekbones, diluted down into something . . . kinder. Thin, vulnerable, grey hair surrounds her face.

'Mr Hannigan. I don't think we've ever formally met.'

She gives me her hand. Unlike when I refused her husband's, I take hers now and hold it. When she finally pulls it away she sits on the couch and watches the suited and booted men pass by. She bends her head to those who say hello like she is the Queen of Rainsford, which I suppose in a way, she is.

'I thought I'd come and see the place in full swing, as they say.' She gives me a smile that, again, seems genuine and pats the seat beside her.

I move towards it, but stay standing, so she must look up at me.

'I will not bite, Mr Hannigan.'

'I stopped being afraid of you Dollards a long time ago.'

'Is that so?' she says with a laugh. 'I rather hoped we haunted your dreams.'

I look at her and can't help but smile, I can imagine why Jason Bruton fell for her.

'I'd take a nightmare any day, if it meant I could sleep. I haven't been doing much of that lately,' I say, finally sitting beside her.

She glances over to me and smiles the smile of a fellow sufferer before looking down at her hands, her face becoming serious.

'Since the day Jason died I don't think I've slept one full night unaided. In the beginning I would bolt awake thinking it must have been something I did that caused him to get so ill.'

I look at her but she doesn't turn to me. We sit in the awkwardness of our silence for a moment, while all around us the place bustles. A man carrying a keyboard comes through the front doors and makes his way to the back corridor. I think of rising to assist him with the double doors but know my knees would not let me get there in time and so I watch him put his back to them and push his way through, nearly knocking over a young one coming from the other side with an unlit cigarette. They laugh at their near collision and she skips past him, smiling broadly as he and his keyboard squash back against the door. I see him delay his exit and watch in appreciation of the girl's departing figure.

'Pretty aren't they?' Hilary says. 'Girls these days. They seem prettier than in our day. Taller. Definitely taller.'

I laugh at the compliment of her thinking we are the same age. I must be at least twenty years her senior.

'You said "Timothy",' I say.

'Pardon?'

'Timothy, you said "Great-uncle Timothy". Your man there in the picture. Emily told me it was Hugh Dollard, Thomas's father.' My mouth feels dry and I think of my whiskey sitting waiting for me on the bar. At least I hope it's still there and Svetlana hasn't cleared it by now.

'No, that man there was Hugh's younger brother, Timothy. I never met him myself. I simply wondered as you were looking at him for so long if you knew him from all those years ago before he left?'

She looks up at him wistfully for a moment, while I look at her trying to understand what it is she's actually saying.

'But hang on,' I say, 'Emily's actual words were – "That's Thomas's father." But now you're saying it's Timothy Dollard?'

'Exactly,' she replies, her hands shuffling in her lap. 'You have it all now, Mr Hannigan: our land, our hotel, our shame. Hugh Dollard, my grandfather was *not* Thomas's actual father. My grandmother had an affair with her husband's younger brother, no less.'

Well, she has me there. I had not expected that. I blow out a gust of air from my lips and shake my head.

'Thomas never knew that Hugh wasn't his father,' she continues after a bit, following my eye to him. 'He went to his grave believing his father hated him. When the reality was he never knew him at all. My grandmother started her affair with Timothy before she married Hugh. They met the day she came to Rainsford for the formal engagement. Fell for him instantly, apparently. Well, he is handsome isn't he?'

The handsomeness of men has never been my strong point so I don't reply.

'Unfortunately he was a terribly confused young man. Gay, but didn't fully know it at that point. They continued their dalliance well into the early weeks of the marriage until one day Timothy wrote Amelia a note saying he was leaving for London, off to finally become the man he was. Hugh came home to find his wife passed out on the bed drunk with the letter in her hand. She admitted everything, including the pregnancy. You see, the thing was, the marriage had not yet been consummated. Grandfather had put his new wife's reluctance to have relations in that way down to a shyness that he hoped would quickly pass. When he realised the truth of it all, he left to track Timothy down. Beat him to a pulp, and told him never to darken Rainsford's door again. When Thomas was born, Grandfather couldn't stand the sight of him. Treated him like he was an idiot, his entire life. Grandfather blamed him for every damn thing that went wrong in this God forsaken family. Poor Thomas. No child, Mr Hannigan, no child deserves that.'

I let the applause from the presentations down the corridor distract me from having to feel any pity. But her story is like the wind under the front door, whistling its way through the crevices, getting through the cracks in my skin.

'The years didn't make it any better,' she continues. 'This house was filled with hatred. Mother was only conceived because grandfather got drunk and, well . . .' She looks about the foyer and winces before raising her hand to her mouth. 'Mother hated living here. Only she and father were penniless she would never have come back. They drank themselves to death, literally. Jason saved me from it all, Mr Hannigan.'

I close my eyes against her words. Blocking out the sorrow of others, refusing them permission to stack on top of my own enormous pile. The weight is exhausting and I feel the need to be gone. And yet I sense, there is more to know, as I watch her watching me.

'I'm not meaning to be rude,' I say, curious now, 'but I'm . . . I suppose, I'm wondering why you're telling me all of this? Is there a purpose in me knowing?' Quite right, I think, well said. Let's get to the point.

She thinks about this for a moment and then says:

'To explain, I suppose. I know it was you who took the coin.'

'Look, I've been through this with Emily and I—'

'No, Mr Hannigan. Look, I'm not here to accuse you of

anything. I suppose what I'm trying to do in this roundabout way is to right some wrongs, to end the awful loneliness of this place and all it has done to those who have passed through it, including you, Mr Hannigan.'

She gives me a small embarrassed smile. I don't know what to do, where to look or what to say. So I look at my hands instead.

'Bricks and mortar can no longer fill the void Jason has left for me here now. I've deluded myself for far too long. And since Thomas died, I've realised it's time to leave the awful tragedy of this family behind. It's time for someone else to take up the mantle.'

Loneliness, that fecker again, wreaking his havoc on us mortals. It's worse than any disease, gnawing away at our bones as we sleep, plaguing our minds when awake.

'What is it, Mr Hannigan?' she asks, watching it written all over my face, the utter hopelessness of it all. She knows. She knows it like I do, its touch, its taste, its smell. It is then she lays her hand on mine. I stare at it, and am surprised at my instinct to want to place my other on top. But it will not move.

'How have you coped?' I say, instead. 'With him dying, leaving you, how have you managed to keep going?'

'Ah. That. Does one really? That's more the question. Does one really cope? If I'm anything to go by, then the answer is one doesn't. Your wife died not too long ago, am I right?'

'Sadie, yes.'

'Well, you know then, it's a living hell. You either choose to live with the pain of it or you get the hell out. I decided to drug myself to the eyeballs and imagine him at every corner and in every room of this place. Fat lot of good that did me or Emily for that matter.' I feel her hand press harder on mine. 'And you, you're still with us so I take it you've chosen the former also?'

From the corner of my eye I find her face and watch her lips.

'You've never thought of giving up?' I ask, so quietly I wonder has she managed to hear my words. I wait to watch her mouth form the answer.

'Too weak willed,' she replies, with a smile that transforms her face into something beautiful, 'it would take a stronger woman than me to bow out of this world.' She pauses and turns to me, 'But you didn't answer my question. What is your secret?'

'Whiskey.'

She laughs out long and loud. I haven't a clue why. I never meant it to be funny. I meant it to be true. But still her lips broaden and it's infectious. My own begin to do the same. Soon my insides are vomiting up the laughter. And we laugh together. Laugh our desperation into the foyer, around the youngsters coming and going. Laugh until it's robbed our breath. Laugh so we must pinch the tears back from our eyes. Laugh so we must keep hold of the couch as if we're in danger of falling off. When it starts to subside, we slouch against the velvet back and quieten down, letting our serious heads return.

'The thing I miss most about Jason is not what he said or did,' she says, her hand long gone from mine, lying flat against her chest now, 'it was his very breath, beside me in the room or the next room or somewhere in this place, I didn't care. It was simply knowing he was there, that meant the world to me. I didn't need him to do anything other than just be alive. Is it the same for you?'

I look at her and cannot release the words for fear of the tears that might insist on flowing. So I nod my answer. Nod like a mad demented dog. Nod to my knees, to my drumming fingers, down into my very soul. Closing my eyes, I hold back the tsunami and nod.

We are quiet now. And an image of Sadie comes to me. Her kneeling down out the back of the house at her rockery. Her pride and joy it was. And she is trying to get up. Her knees were bad, you see, arthritis, just like mine. She reaches her hand to a large stone and tries to pull herself up but she can't. She waits a minute then tries again. She looks back to the house but she can't see me standing at the kitchen window. I wave to her to wait. I wave to say, hold on, I'm coming. But before I leave the window, she has tried again and this time, succeeded.

'Emily has never breathed a word about your arrangement over the hotel, you know,' Hilary says, 'she wouldn't, she's a good girl. But I've known since the very beginning, the night you offered her the money to save this place. I overheard it all in the office.'

She leans into me with a grin and looks for all the world like a little girl who is at last getting to reveal a secret she has kept sacred for far too long. I can't speak and even if my throat and mouth allowed the words through, I don't know what they'd say.

'Do you know the truth is, I let you save me,' she says, whispering it to me, grinning. 'Isn't that wonderful, Mr Hannigan? *You* saved *me* – a Dollard – as you like to call me,' she laughs, lifts her head to the ceiling, then back down to her hands. 'I couldn't leave here after he died. Well, when I say couldn't leave *here* I mean, him, of course – Jason. He was my world. He seeps out of every inch of these walls. He loved this rack-and-ruined place. Nothing and no one could dissuade him from the idea of it being a hotel, especially not me.'

She smiles sadly and looks about.

'She would have sold it, you see – Emily, when she came home, when Jason was dying. I knew she was thinking that way and I couldn't have everything he had worked for taken away from me. And then you came along on your white steed. Ironic, don't you think? You might finally have been rid of us Dollards, instead you ensured we stayed.'

Her smile widens.

'I could have laughed. You don't think I'd forgotten, do you? You don't think I'd forgotten how you'd treated Jason that night he stood at your door begging for money for us. He never lived it down. Never.'

Her head, serious now, shakes from side to side, her compassion for me gone.

'You brought a good man low, Mr Hannigan. A good, decent man. My man. It was you who condemned her here, do you know that? My poor daughter. Condemned to this life of servitude, to me, to them,' she says, her outstretched hand indicating those passing, on the way to smoke their cigarettes. She swallows hard and adds: 'And I let you.'

She begins to shake and snivel. Christ, I can't be doing with more tears now. She quivers away beside me while I shift in my seat, looking around to see who's watching. But everyone seems too caught up in the clatter of the night.

'I'm done with the Dollard beatings a long time ago, Hilary. I'm not taking any more now.'

'But no, you misunderstand me. It is me who is to blame. What kind of parent lets her daughter sacrifice her life like that?' she asks, crying now, like I might have the answer. Me, the parenting expert!

My hand begins to rummage in my full pocket. And with difficulty I free my handkerchief that surrounds my little bag of pills, pull it out and place it in her hand.

'Here,' I say quietly, looking away from her, giving her as much privacy as I can.

Hilary blows her nose then considers me for a minute.

'I need you to do something for me, Mr Hannigan,' she finally says, her urgency worrying me, 'buy this place. Buy it. Force Emily to sell to you or to anyone, I don't care. Be the ruthless man you are and force her out. This place has done us enough damage.' She moves closer to me, right in towards my face, searching me out, her hand back on mine. I look closely at her wrinkles that fan out from her pleading mouth, merging with those tumbling down from her eyes. She is so close that I can feel her breath and hear its pace quicken. 'Please, Mr Hannigan, set her free.'

I want to move away. I want to drink my whiskey that's sitting all alone on the bar. I want my peace and quiet. What I don't want is someone else's problems to solve. My scar itches. I need to rub it but she's still too close. I have no choice but to stand, as rude as it may seem. I let her hands drop back to her lap. I rub hard at my skin, smelling the earth of my fingers and watch the rest of the band, or at least they must be, given they're all dressed in black suits with white dickie bows and cowboy hats, pass by me, all amps and equipment and elbows. I step back a little out of their way. And when they are through the double doors, I say:

'You want me to be the bad guy, is that it?'

I look down at her expectant face.

'If that's how you wish to put it, then, yes, I want you to be the bad guy,' she says, rising proudly and taking my hand, 'please, Mr Hannigan, please. Just this one last time for us Dollards.'

I have no answer for her. It is all too much, trying to understand their convoluted history. All I can do is take her hand and hold it there for a moment in the foyer. I have nothing more to give to anyone. I look into those sad eyes of hers one last time, and leave.

I go back to the bar. It's beginning to fill up again with those who don't seem to be fans of the band.

'You're still here,' Emily says, as she comes through from the kitchen. 'Sorry I couldn't make it down before now. It was mad up there. Still, all over now. Well, I mean the speeches and all that. The band is on, now. So far so good I have to say. But I tell you, my cheeks are actually sore from all that smiling for the photographs.'

She sits up on the stool beside me. She looks tired but still she manages to give me a tiny grin.

'So go on, why *are* you still here?'

God but she is beautiful.

'Here,' I say to Svetlana, 'there's a bottle of champagne behind there with this lady's name on it. Will you open it and give her a glass and put another Midleton in that?'

I shove my glass in her direction.

'Champagne?' Emily asks, watching me like I've gone mad.

'Robert tells me it's your favourite.'

Svetlana pops the cork and we watch her pour the bubbles. It looks magnificent, but I know it tastes like pure shite.

'Are we celebrating something, Mr Hannigan?'

'In a way. We are toasting my wife. Who two years ago today decided it was time to leave me.' I smile at her and watch her bright eyes dip a little. 'She was a great gardener, you know,' I say trying to lighten the mood, 'pinks and purples and yellows and oranges everywhere. Especially out the back in a little rockery. Irises, petunias, begonias, nasturtiums, the lot. Couldn't tell one from the other, me. But I loved the smell in the yard when I'd arrive home. Hitting me in the nose as soon as I got out of the car. It was her, the smell was her, not honey, not jasmine. Essence of Sadie. Haven't smelt that in two years. Weeds, that's all there is now, choking the life out of what's survived.'

Emily has the look of a woman who at any minute might reach over and hug me. I lift my glass to hers to ward off any of that.

'To Sadie,' I say.

'To Sadie.'

Our glasses clink, high pitched and clear.

'I was talking to your mother just now,' I say quietly, when the moment's silence begins to stretch uncomfortably. More and more people are arriving, escaping the band maybe, much to my annoyance. Oh, for the quiet hours just past.

'My mother? My mother!'

'Yes, your mother.' I look around to see who might be within earshot.

'You must have that one wrong. Mother never comes out of hiding. Especially not on a night like this. GAA's not her thing.'

'My mistake, so,' I say, not having the energy to argue the point with her. I can imagine her slitted eyes turned on me as I stare ahead.

'What did she want?'

'Oh, you believe me now.' My eyes dart in her general direction. 'She didn't say much. Other than telling me Thomas' father wasn't Hugh Dollard and that she knows all about me and this place.'

I take another sip of my drink, imagining her panic.

'She knows? What do you mean, she knows?'

'What I said. She told me she's known all along.'

'But that . . . but she's never . . .' She breaks off and stares at her bubbles for a bit.

'Tell me something,' I say, when I've given her long enough to digest it all, 'would you have sold this place if I hadn't offered to invest all those years back?' My hand attempts a passing wave of the room but gives up mid-way. She raises her hand to her forehead, looking at me, totally confused. And I feel sorry for having asked the question.

'I . . . eh . . . I've no idea.'

'Would you sell now?'

'What, do you want to buy it?' she laughs sarcastically, 'I thought you didn't give a damn about this place.'

'Just answer.'

But she doesn't, simply stares back at me, trying to figure me out.

'Ah, it doesn't matter. Nothing fecking matters now anyway,' I say, rubbing the stubble on my chin, considering my razor shipped off to Dublin, regretting having sent it now. Then I laugh at the stupidity. No need for a razor where you're going, Sonny Jim.

'If I could go back would I change it all, not take your money, is that what you're asking?' She looks at me, then back at the counter, wondering at the answer. 'I don't know,' she says finally. 'It's made me who I am, I suppose. I was a girl when I started here. And now look at me, a woman who can run the best sports awards in Ireland. Actually, I think I've done myself and my father and yes, Mr Hannigan, even those dastardly Dollards, proud.'

I look at her and smile.

'That you have, Emily. That you have.'

I feel as if I could sleep for a thousand years. My eyes close with the weight of all that has passed this night and all that has yet to come.

'Are you alright, Mr Hannigan?' she asks, those slitted eyes returning. 'I bumped into Robert earlier, you know. He says he's worried about you. Wouldn't tell me why. But he told me to keep an eye on you.'

Fecking Robert. She takes out her phone, threatening me with it. Sets it down beside her drink. I raise my hand to her, waving it in some kind of ridiculous reassurance that all is well.

'The drink, girl. It's the drink. Don't be worrying about me, I'm absolutely fine.'

I look away from her, over to Svetlana who is happy now: the Queen of the bar. Showing off her mastery in front of the boss as she serves the escapees. Emily sips from her glass and I wonder have I done enough to distract her.

'She's good isn't she? That little one. A great worker,' I say, attempting another diversion, pointing my drink in Svetlana's direction.

'Never mind Svetlana. What did Mother say about the hotel and your "involvement"?'

Feck.

'She's proud of you, you know. Proud of what you've achieved, of how you've saved this place. Turned it around.'

'Really? I mean, she's never said anything. Never shows one bit of interest in this place or what I'm up to with it.'

'Parents are feckers that way. I speak from experience. But mark my words. She knows, she sees it and what's more, she appreciates it.' I move my hand to hers and pat it as it sits around the base of her glass.

'So, she's not mad, then?'

'Well, she's had a hell of a long time to get over it if she was,' I laugh, 'but no she's not mad, certainly not at you, anyway. Be proud my girl. Be proud of how you've stood those Dollards tall again. Listen, my best advice is to talk to her. Talking's good, apparently.'

'And she told you about Thomas and his father?'

'Aye.'

'Awful, isn't it?'

I take another sip of Midleton and then ask:

'Do you think if I'd given back the coin on the day he dropped it from the window, would it have made any difference to his life at all?'

She looks ahead of her, her eyebrows raised and her lips pouting as she gives my question due consideration.

'Now,' she says after a bit, 'there was a Dollard that no one, bar the man he called father, could have saved. Not even you, Mr Hannigan, even if you'd felt inclined.'

And she is so right – fathers have a lot to answer for.

I'll admit I'm tired now, son. It's been far too long a day. I'm ready now. Ready to get this over with. So I pat her hand one more time but she grasps mine. Holds it tight and squeezes it like it matters to her. I look at it and then her face. And there I see the bravery of her one last time. And then I do something that surprises even me, I reach across and kiss her on the cheek. Reluctantly, I let her hand go to take hold of the bar to ease myself down. On terra firma, I hold my near-empty glass and raise it one last time in her direction.

'To killing the weeds,' I say and swallow the last drop down before passing behind her and patting her shoulder as I go. 'Goodnight, Emily, it's been a pleasure.' I head out towards the foyer and I know she's there at my back with that bloody phone in her hand.

'But, Mr Hannigan, wait. Maurice,' she calls, far too concerned for my liking. 'Are you sure you're OK? You're not driving are you? Let me get you a taxi at least.'

'And why would I be in need of a taxi when I have this?'

I take the key of the honeymoon suite from my pocket and turn to hold it up to her.

It takes her a second to recognise exactly what it is.

'*You're* the VIP?'

'I am,' I say, a little bit of pride creeping into my voice, 'but before I go up I think I'll take the good Meath air.'

I leave her there with her mouth still open. Her concern bores into my back. She might ring Robert yet, I know, but it's a risk I'll have to take. I make my way to the door, tipping my cap to himself in the picture. I turn to see Emily one last time and point at it:

'Uncle Timothy,' I say, and then give her a smile and a wink before making my way to the open door.

Isn't it funny how Tony and Molly visit me all of the time but your mother doesn't. That one's a bit of a mystery. Maybe she visits you instead. Maybe you talk to her, son. I'd like to think you do, as you go about your day, discussing what you might write next, asking her opinion. God, she'd just love that.

It's raining now, one of those heavy July downpours. You know the kind that makes you think the roof of the shed might finally give up. I needn't worry myself about those things. They're someone else's concern, now. Of all the things to make me sad tonight I hadn't counted on it being the ricketiness of the shed. Rivers will rise and livestock will scare tonight, that's for sure.

A woman in high heels, holding a handbag over her head and squealing, skids in under the awning beside me. I shimmy up to make room. Not that there's any need, I'm the only one out here – the smokers have flicked their fags and taken refuge back inside long ago.

'I'm soaked,' she says, panting like she's just swum the Liffey. She looks at her bare arms and legs and feels her hair. 'Fuck sake.'

I look over at her sparkly toes and smile.

'Aye. Looks like someone's angry about something, alright,' I say, looking back out at the town, hoping it's not my good lady wife.

'Well, I'd like to wring his bloody neck whoever the hell he is,' she says, passing by me, going in through the hotel door and shaking off the rain, like Gearstick used to do. Wouldn't that be an easier way to go? Someone's hands 'round my neck so I need do nothing. It wasn't me your honour, I can say to Saint Peter at the gate. It was your one with the soaking wet hair and streaking tan.

A flash lights up the sky beyond the town. I count in my head until God moves his furniture. A big fucking wardrobe. The roar of it. Six, I get to six before the crack of thunder explodes above me.

Out, I step. My eyes close and I lift my head into its howl. The rain soaks through me and it feels feckin' marvellous, washing away my worries and doubts. Like an electric current it gives me a bolt of energy and I dance. Not a word of a lie, my feet slap, slap in the rain and I kick like I'm in a chorus line. There's no one here now to see me make a fool of myself as my knees jerk high and my legs shoot out. 'Course, they could be watching from the windows, but I don't give them a second thought as I attempt a heel kick but no more leave the ground than an old cow in my field. But in my head I've done it, clicked those heels as sprightly as Gene Kelly. Around I spin and spin. Letting every drop soak into me. Deep down, drenching my very bones. Then gravity takes me and I lunge against the wall. Panting and laughing. Trying to catch my breath. My body bends, as my hands clutch my knees.

The rain quietens, and stops abruptly, like it was one big mistake and it has moved on to the place it was meant to attack all along. A moment of silence hangs over me, the silence that comes with snow. I stand tall, one hand splayed against the wall. I close my eyes so I can let it surround me. Breathing in its calm. Letting it slip down into my jittering bones and fidgeting muscles. It irons me out and I become still. Ahead of me in the street, voices trickle out from other drinking holes. Goodnights are called and engines start. The town comes alive again after its scourging; waking up to the divilment of a Saturday night. Car horns blare and arms wave into the balmy night.

There you have it now – my work here is done. My life boxed away, neatly wrapped, sorted and labelled. My night of celebration is complete. Feck me though, when I set my mind to something, there's no stopping me.

The band is giving it all they've got down the corridor. I can hear their muffled efforts even from here. The tunes mean nothing to me, but I hum along anyway to notes and words I make up in my head: *Eleven o'clock and all is well. Time to go, so much to tell.* I smile at my talent. Then doors open and out they come: the weaklings who ran from a drop of rain. I move upstream, weaving my way through them, back inside. Reaching reception, I stop for a minute, hands in pockets, eyeing the door to my left to the rooms that I must go through.

'Ah, I find you, Mr Hannigan,' Svetlana calls, coming up alongside me, taking me by surprise. 'I thought you leave. I look everywhere. You forget this.'

I look at the bottle of Jefferson's she holds in her hands.

'Well, aren't you the clever girl.'

'I not want Emily to see. I don't want to get sack. Not for you, anyway.'

I laugh and take the bottle.

253

'Where you go now, the dance?' she asks, with a cheeky smile.

'No, that's me done. Me and this boy here have a date with destiny,' I say, looking at the bottle.

'You right. The band,' she says, coming close to me now and leaning to my ear, 'they called the "Rhythm Kings". I don't know why? They have no rhythm. They play only hilly-billy music. I hate hilly-billy music.'

The back of her throat has a way of dealing with h's, taking its time over them then spitting them out, that tickles my ear. I laugh one last time for her and move on, but before I push open the door, I call back:

'Svetlana. Thank you.' I raise the bottle.

She smiles: 'Next time just Guinness, by the neck, yes?'

'By the neck. Now you have it,' I say, pushing my shoulder against the door. At the other side, I stop and listen to it swing shut. And then turn to look back through the glass to watch her disappear into the bar.

I don't use lifts so I find my way to the stairs and begin the climb.

'You and lifts,' Sadie used to say to me, dismissing my distrust.

'Before you start, it's nothing to do with the *Towering Inferno*,' I'd reply, looking at her lips puckering away, 'it hasn't woman. There was a man in Mulhuddart—'

'Ah, the man from Mulhuddart,' she'd say, pressing the button like she was playing some game in an arcade.

'Yes! A man in Mulhuddart who suffered untold and lifelong damage to his legs because of one of those yokes falling and him in it,' I'd protest to her profile that refused to acknowledge me or the poor man from Mulhuddart.

'And pressing the hell out of it doesn't make it come any quicker,' I'd say, my voice raised so she'd be sure to hear me as I began my ascent, step by step, muttering at the injustice with every lift of my foot.

The man from fucking Mulhuddart!

How many times did we argue about a man we never knew? You know, I miss those stupid arguments as much as anything.

My legs feel heavy with my rain-soaked clothes. Slower than I'd hoped, I keep going. So near, and yet, so bloody far. I lean against the top of the bannisters after I've scaled each flight and consider falling asleep right there, standing up. But my brain taps its knobbly internal finger at my skull.

'Not yet,' it says. 'Not yet.'

Chapter Seven

Tonight I will die. There. I've said it. Now you know. But I don't like to hear the words, let alone think them. Not because I don't want to do it but because I feel the guilt for those I leave behind. For you, Kevin. You, who have deserved so much more from me.

I stand outside the bedroom and take in the door. It's grand and deserving of the attention. When I say grand, it's in the magnificent sense of the word, not the Irish one that's robbed it of its majesty. Mahogany. Wide and solid. My hand runs along its smooth varnish and I pat it with respect. The key too, that has knocked against my father's pipe the whole night, is large and important. None of those card jobs. You'd never lose this beauty, I can tell you.

I turn it and open the door to catch the smell of freshly cleaned sheets. I close my eyes and concentrate, stuck half in, half out, wanting to hold on to it for as long as I can, knowing it will fade in a matter of seconds. And when it does, I step in fully and look around at this room's perfection.

White linens, not a crease in sight, on a four-poster bed. Curtains hang around it matching those of the window: deep purple folds that fall to the floor with the weight of the money they must have cost. Cream pillows, with purple flowers, sit three rows deep. A mahogany wardrobe stands at the end of the bed. To its left near the window is a writing desk with a bottle of water and a glass. When I switch on the lamplight I can see the furniture is old but cared for, polished to a shine. A chair with its back to me is pushed in under the arch of the desk, its green leather secured to the frame with brass tacks. And an armchair, to the right, with a high back and generous armrests, sits in the corner like it's been waiting for me all this time – eighty-four years.

My hand bangs the whiskey bottle down on the bedside locker. I didn't mean to do it. I misjudged the distance and I jump at the sound.

'Ssh,' I say, 'they could be coming. Robert might be running up the stairs right now to save the day and wrestle you from me. Quiet now.'

I take off my sopping jacket and throw it on the bed. I look around and try to locate my faded memories, the shadows of your wedding night. Can you remember it like it was yesterday or is it half rubbed out in your head too? Was the room as mighty, as plush and posh as this? I walk around the bed, over to the window, feeling my feet sink into the deep carpet. Not the easiest of dance surfaces, but nevertheless, I take my stance and waltz her. Feeling her back arch under my guidance as I move us through the steps.

'Goodnight, Sadie. Goodnight, Sadie, I'll see you in my dreams,' my tired voice sings.

'Irene,' I imagine her protests, 'it's Irene, not Sadie.'

But I don't listen and off we go again, waltzing through our lives. Humming my way through my one, two, threes, when the words escape me. Dancing her through our highs and lows and all of those bits in the middle that've made up this life of ours. Grinning like the happy fool I am. Faster and faster I spin, brushing by curtains, dicing with corners, colliding with chairs, racing through those moments on my memory reel. Swirling, swirling, until at last I land on the soft down of the bedcovers. Panting, exhausted, the ceiling spinning above me. My eyes shut tight against it all. The soft silkiness of the covers holds me, refusing to let go. Its folds are far too tempting and soon I feel myself drift away.

But my brain taps away at my skull. I moan in protest. My conscience doesn't give a damn and guilts me into moving. I roll on my front and drool down on to the whiteness. My arms push me up. I feel like a heifer, the weight of me.

I unpack my remains. From my jacket, the pictures: Tony and me, Sadie and you. My father's pipe that I run my hand over to feel its smooth comfort one last time. Sadie's hair-clip purse that I hold to my nose for a minute before laying it down with my glasses and my phone.

I search my trouser pocket, for the handkerchief. Where is it? Where the fuck is it? My hand rummages, but it's gone. Did I drop it? Where? Sitting at the bar? In the toilet? My hand pats at my clothing, at my jacket, as my brain goes over the memories of the evening. And I remember giving it to Hilary. My fingers recognise the plastic bag now, in its hidey-hole, scurrying about under my touch.

Thirty little pills. I scoop it out, dig my fingers into the plastic and let the contents spill on to the bed: the yellow, blue and pink. I count them. One all the way to thirty. I get up to get a towel from the bathroom and lay it flat on the writing desk, careful to push the bottle and glass in out of the way. I retrieve the pills from the bed and wrap them in the towel. With the water bottle, I begin to pummel them. Each time I press down with my weight, I cry. Tears that surprise me stream down my face, my neck, reaching my chest. Flow for as far you can go. I'll not stop you now. And when I'm sure my job is done, I shake the contents of the towel on to the table, my hand corralling all that falls, pushing the multicoloured mess to the edge, tipping it over, into the glass. Tears, pills, everything falling down-wards. Tinkle, tinkle. I sit and stare at it, my love-heart mixture. Still crying, for me. I am as reluctant as I am eager to leave this world behind me now.

I got them in Dublin, the pills. Tried to con the Doc into giving me some. But he was having none of it. A counsellor, that's what he wanted to give me. A fecking counsellor.

Didn't take me as long as I'd thought to find Gizzo up in Dublin. Tall as a giraffe and a Jimi Hendrix tattoo on his left hand. Not that young David ever knew why I questioned him so much about his misguided youth. Walked into the Galley Bar and there he was, sat in the corner booth. I wore an old, moth-eaten coat, long enough to cover my shotgun strapped to my belt. All I was short of was a Stetson and a horse.

'I hear you supply all sorts,' I said to him. Another lad sat beside him, Deco or Eamo maybe. We didn't exactly introduce ourselves. Gizzo had me up out of the place fairly lively. His hand jammed right into my armpit, pushing me through the doors.

'What the fuck, man? You can't be at that in there. You'll get me barred,' he said, hoisting me down a lane behind the pub. My blood was pumping. What was the worst he could do, I kept saying over and over in my head, shoot me? Wouldn't that've been a good one?

'I'm a friend of David's. David Flynn,' was all I could think of babbling, God forgive me, I hope the kid never finds out.

'David? Fuck me, man. Haven't heard from him in years. Heard the Da died.'

Polite young man, I have to say.

'You can get anything you want, old-timer,' he told me when I'd explained my predicament, 'once you're willing to pay through the nose.' How he laughed at that one. 'Course, I didn't know what I wanted, I just knew what the end result needed to be. I waited a half hour or so in the lane with the rubbish and the used condoms until he came back like he said he would.

'Amiods, Digs and Zeps man. Just crush 'em and mix 'em. Wash 'em down with a bit of booze. And bam. Gone. Adios Amigo.' I took the little bag he offered and left. Had there been a follow-up survey, he'd have gotten five stars.

I shake those crushed pills about in the glass, still fascinated by them, by this, by me.

There'll be no letter, Kevin. That'd take a whole evening in itself. Instead I want you to hear my voice, so you know for sure this is what I want. My voice. Did I ever tell you it was my voice your mother fell in love with?

'So deep and smooth,' she said, not long after we were

married, 'I could've closed my eyes and listened to it all day, the first time we met.' Imagine.

From the bed, I take your picture, my phone and glasses and bring them to the writing desk. The towel, I fold and push towards the end. Jefferson's, pills, phone and picture – all before me. I put on my glasses. Ready at last.

I tip the red button and my voice tumbles out, exhausted but steady:

'Son, it's me – Dad. By now, I'll be, em . . . gone. I'm not one for letters, as you know. How many of those have you gotten from me over the years, what? No, that was more you and your mother. You were good with the words, the two of you. You got it from her, of course.

'I want you to know, son, I'm sorry. Not for dying, not for going, although I . . . I know it won't be easy. But no, I mean, sorry for the father I've been. I know, really I do, that I could've been better. That I could've listened more, that I could've accepted you and all you've become with a little more grace. I'm in awe of you, is the truth of it. The man you are, the goodness you possess, your brightness, your cleverness. I feel a lesser man standing beside you, having watched you grow into this big strapping man of letters.

'I want you to know I've read your articles, every one. It took me a while, I'll admit but in the last two years I've read every one. Even did a bit of your mother on it and looked it all up, and you, yes, I *googled* you. And there you were. The amount of stuff on you, I couldn't believe it. Sure you're everywhere. I even googled myself and there I was missing. So in my own way, I did find you. I met you there in print and on the screen. I'm sorry it's taken me until now to tell you I see it – I see your brilliance and your kindness. I see it all and I love it – I love you.

'There are things I regret, Kevin, like how I never shook your hand for working beside me every Saturday when you were younger, hating every moment of it but doing it anyway. And how I shut you out when your mother died. That was . . . that was wrong.

'God almighty, I had hoped I could spare you the tears but there you go . . . Achmm, achmm . . . Sorry now.

'I drank your Jefferson's tonight. She's a beauty. I raised a glass in your honour. I had a toast for your mother and Auntie No-no and little Molly and your Uncle Tony too.

'I want you to know I've gone on my own terms, Kevin. This life has been good to me. This is no tragedy. You know I'm not one for illness or nursing homes; I couldn't have done that, Kevin, because the way I saw it, that's where we were headed. Be honest, it's better this way.

'I remember Rosaleen holding your hand the day of your mother's funeral. She's a good woman, Rosaleen. I know I've not given her the credit she's deserved over the years. Tell her I've asked that she hold your hand again now.

'To my Adam and Caitríona, I send my deepest, deepest love. I know I must've played the part of crotchety grandfather well for them over their young years. Give them a kiss for me and tell them Granny and Grandad will be watching over them.

'The will is sorted. Robert has that for you. Everything is taken care of. The land and home is sold and every business interest I've ever had has also been taken care of. You'll find that all the proceeds are yours, sitting in several bank accounts, except of course for the one in Adam and

Catríona's names. I wanted to leave no headache for you. All is ready for you to live your life.

'There is, of course, the issue of the hotel, this hotel. I own half. It's a long story and one I'm sure Emily will tell you. You'll remember Emily from your wedding, nice lady. I want her to have it, Kevin, the hotel; I'm giving it back, although her mother may have something to say on that. She can do what she wants with it then. It's best that way. I'll let her fill you in on it all, no need to bore you with the detail now. But one other thing, you know that brother of Rosaleen's, your man who was one of your grooms-men, can't remember his name, but you might introduce him to Emily someday, I've a feeling they might hit it off. And there's a few bob there for a lad called David as well. Robert'll tell you about him.

'I'm ready for your mother now. Ready for her by my side again. It's a risk, I know. Perhaps there is no heaven. Perhaps she won't be there with open arms. But anything, anything has to be better than this life without her. These past two years have been rotten. I've felt the ache of her going in my very bones. Every morning, every hour of every day I've dragged her loss around with me. The worst thing has been the fear that I'll wake one morning and she'll be gone from my memory forever, and that, son, that, I just can't do. I'm not half the man I was without her. I'm ready, ready to have her hand in mine for real again, not imagined any more.

'Well, my boy, I think that's me. The good and the bad of me. Have a good life, son, keep ploughing on and you'll be doing mighty. Mighty. And thank you, Kevin, thank you for all the years of letting me be me.

'And know this – if ever you need me I am beside you listening, always. I love you, Kevin. Take her hand, my boy. Bye for now.'

The silence surrounds me as my finger presses 'done'. Your picture, I turn over and put on top of my phone with a message I wrote on the back earlier: *For Kevin – Press Play*. And then it's time for sleep. Me and my pills and your whiskey make it to the bed and on to these sheets that are way too good for me.

Whiskey first.

I unscrew the bottle as my glass, unsteadied by the ripples I've caused in the bed, leans into my thigh. I sigh; one last chance to bolt for the door, one final chance to flush these beauties down the toilet.

No?

My hand finds the glass and I raise it and start to gulp them down. Then drink again. And gulp and drink and gulp and drink. I pour and swallow. And then I lie back, my glass at last empty.

My eyes close one final time and I call to her:

'Sadie, are you there? Are you ready? It's me – Maurice. Can I come home?'

Acknowledgements

To friends and family who have shared stories that have helped in creating this book – Tom Byrne, Mary Daly, Gerry Heary, Marése Bell, Séamus Ó Drisceoil, Brian McGovern, Michael Walsh, Anthony Lowry Senior, Joe Brady, Donal Heaney and in particular my parents James and Brigid Griffin. To Brigid, Patrick and Jean for their continued support of my writing, in particular at the final stages of this novel. To two dogs called Dinky, one from Westmeath, the other from Wexford, who inspired the lives of both dogs in this book. To Rosie Bissett and all at the Dyslexia Association of Ireland – the inspirational stories of those who use its services have greatly influenced the life of Maurice Hannigan. To all in Loreto College Mullingar, for affording me the time during the editing process. To the students and teachers of the Creative Writing Programme in University College Dublin 2015-2016 who gave invaluable feedback at various stages of this novel's existence – Joe Crotty, Finnbar Howell, Laura-Blaise McDowell, Lorna McMahon, Aedamar Kirrane, Lorcan Byrne, Rory Kiberd, Disharee Bose, Colm McDermott, Eamon McGuinness, Phil Kearney Byrne, James Ryan, Éilís Ní Dhuibhne, Frank McGuinness, Lia Mills, Anne Enright and Paul Perry. To Alison Walsh and Billy Doran who gave of their time and wisdom in helping me get this book published.

To Louise Buckley whose belief in this book has changed my world.

To all in Hachette Ireland, in particular Elaine Egan, Jim Binchy, Breda Purdue, Siobhán Tierney and Ruth Shern.

To Hope Deilon and Sally Richardson at St Martin's Press USA, who acquired and championed the book. To Stephen Power and Samantha Zukergood at Thomas Dunne Books, who have supported this book's development and not least, given me a great title.

To all in Hodder and Stoughton's Sceptre team in the UK who read and fell in love with Maurice giving him a home I am proud of. To name only a few that have worked so hard on my behalf: Louise Court, Fleur Clarke and Lily Cooper. In particular my deepest gratitude goes to Emma Herdman who first found Maurice and whose talent and eye as an editor has helped make this book shine.

To John Boyne, the man who first encouraged me to write and who has incessantly supported my journey ever since – I am in your debt.

Finally, to James and Adam – for picking me up and brushing me down when I stumble, and for the hands I will always hold.